Zigzagging to the sounds of gunfire, Nova sprinted to the helicopter, leaped into the pilot's seat and shoved the key into the ignition. Blades began to churn.

Leaning out the window, she yelled, "Now, Joe."

He stood, and then twisted and fell, his right leg collapsing under him. She couldn't tell how badly he was hit, but he needed help. She opened the door, but before she could jump out, the three remaining thugs charged toward Joe.

The moment seemed to stretch out forever as she realized she must either take off without Joe, or all of them could be taken captive again.

He looked back at her. "Go!" he yelled.

I can't leave you! she mouthed back.

"Go!" he yelled again.

Discipline took over—fear for the people in her care. She slammed the door and lifted the bird to get it out of the line of fire as fast as possible. All the while thinking, *They'll kill Joe. And I can't imagine the world without him.*

Dear Reader,

To be able to write and share with you this series of Nova Blair books has been a lifelong dream come true. For that, I'm grateful to Silhouette.

As a child I adored Wonder Woman—I wanted so much to be her. As an adult, I've created Nova, a modern-day Wonder Woman of beauty and courage. I've loved getting into Nova's skin as she lays it all on the line to right wrongs and save good folks from evildoers. I've loved imagining that I've got her looks and talent. I've loved living her romance with her hero. I hope you find this latest adventure as exciting and fun as I did when writing it.

And as always, I'd love to have you visit my Web site, www.jhand.com, and find out about my other books and perhaps even send me an e-mail.

Cheers,

Judith

Judith Leon

CAPTIVE DOVE

Published by Silhouette Books

America's Publisher of Contemporary Romance

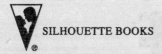

SILHOUETTE BOOKS

ISBN-13: 978-0-373-51425-0
ISBN-10:   0-373-51425-5

CAPTIVE DOVE

Copyright © 2006 by Judith Hand

www.SilhouetteBombshell.com

Printed in U.S.A.

Books by Judith Leon

Silhouette Bombshell

Code Name: Dove #4
Iron Dove #65
Captive Dove #111

*stories featuring CIA agent Nova Blair

JUDITH LEON

has made the transition from left-brained scientist to right-brained novelist. Before she began writing fiction some twelve years ago, she was teaching animal behavior and ornithology in the UCLA biology department.

She is the author of several novels and two screenplays. Her epic of the Minoan civilization, *Voice of the Goddess,* published under her married name, Judith Hand, has won numerous awards. Her second epic historical, *The Amazon and the Warrior,* is based on the life of Penthesilea, an Amazon who fought the warrior Achilles in the Trojan War. In all of her stories she writes of strong, bold women; women who are doers and leaders.

An avid camper, classical music fan and birdwatcher, she currently lives in Rancho Bernardo, California. For more information about the author and her books, see her Web site at www.jhand.com.

Acknowledgments

I am deeply indebted to my friends and writing colleagues who read all or part of this story and whose comments and criticisms were vital to making me work to write the best story I could. I extend to all of them my grateful thanks: Chet Cunningham, Arline Curtiss, Barry Friedman, Donna Erickson, Pete Johnson, Al Kramer, Peggy Lang, Judith Levine, Bev Miller, Ellen Perkins and Tom Utts.

Special thanks go to two others as well. My agent Richard Curtis has been both friend and guide to the world of publishing. And gratitude goes as well to my talented Silhouette editor Julie Barrett. Without Julie's appreciation for my work and her championing of it, none of my Nova Blair and Joe Cardone adventures would ever have seen the light of publishing day.
I will always be profoundly grateful.

Chapter 1

Nova Blair drew in a breath of Colorado Rocky Mountain air, savoring its cold, pristine edge, wishing she could stop time. She was thirty-four. Staying thirty-four forever in beautiful Steamboat Springs could be fun.

But tomorrow, after six days of skiing, hot mulled wine, fabulous dinners, dancing, and good sex, she and David, who was skiing next to her, had to leave. Time did not stand still. In fact, only eight shopping days stood between her and Christmas and she still hadn't found perfect gifts for the loved ones on her remarkably short list.

Dead ahead, the Storm Peak chairlift would drop the two of them at almost 10,400 feet at the top of this last run of their Steamboat Springs getaway. Every tree hunkered under the weight of glittering white crystals, soon to turn pink in the sun's fading glow. Nothing here, at least in this moment, hinted at the dark side of human existence. How perfect it would be to remain in this moment, never doing a lick of work for the CIA again. Maybe the next time Smitty called, she would say no to him.

But go back to San Diego she must, to a tight schedule that would delay gift shopping still longer before flying out the next morning to New York to make an appearance at the latest showing of her photographs.

She took another deep breath as they neared the mountain's crest, soaking up snow-capped peaks and the azure-blue sky. *Life can be good.* She felt complete freedom. Was this joy? Had she ever felt true joy? Yes. At least once. Making love with Joe.

Joe Cardone. Her partner for two missions. Just thinking his name planted an iron fist of pain in the center of her chest.

The lift chairs arrived at the summit. She pushed out of her seat, David beside her, and dropped onto the hardpack. Their skis hissed on the snow as they glided to the side of the slope to avoid skiers coming up behind them.

For a quiet moment they shared the spectacular view, the trails heading down the mountain filled with skiers and snowboarders wearing the pastel "in" colors of the season: pale yellows, greens, blues, pinks and violets. The rainbow of color against the white snow reminded her of spinnakers against a cloudy sky on a windy day in San Diego's Mission Bay.

She wore a fuchsia jumpsuit. She looked good in cool, winter colors, and fuchsia especially complemented her black hair—French-braided at the back of her head at the moment. David, a skiing hot dog and oblivious to fashion, wore neon red.

As owner of David Lake Travel, a company with a dozen branches in resort cities, he spent significant time exploring exciting resort escapes. They shared a love of travel and adventure, one of the reasons she'd been attracted to him after breaking up with Joe six long months ago.

"Okay," she said, forcing a smile. "Let's make this a race."

"Straight down to Christie Base and the Sheraton," he said. "Triangle, Cyclone, Drop Out and then the easy cool-off on Right-O-Way."

All black-diamond runs, except at the bottom.

"You got it."

They shoved off. She hit her rhythm, right, left, right, reading the slope, reading the snow. Adrenaline pumping, heart racing. Freedom!

The Sheraton Hotel snuggled in the snow, right at the base of the mountain—ski in, ski out—with luxury accommodations to match the convenience. David waited for her, his ski poles planted in the snow, his goggles raised, his gloves hung over the tops of his poles. She side-slipped to a stop alongside him, out of breath and thighs burning.

"Outstanding," she said, knowing she was grinning like she'd won a million bucks.

He slid her goggles onto the top of her forehead over her bangs and gave her a peck on the lips. "I love you," he announced, grinning. "You are the most exciting woman I've ever met."

She felt her smile freeze and she blinked, not sure what to say in return. Love? *Love* was a word they had agreed never to use.

Three hours later, showered, rested and dressed in the emerald-green, turtle neck cashmere sweater, a match for her eyes and her favorite, Nova looked into the bathroom mirror. She snatched the hairclip loose and her hair plummeted in a silky cascade to her shoulder blades. David loved to see her hair down, and, she reminded herself, it was David, not Joe, for whom she was dressing. She ran a comb through it as David stepped behind her. He moved her hair aside and kissed the back of her neck.

"We could skip dinner," he said.

She let the comment pass. Instead, she turned and gave him a slow smile. Already wearing his topcoat, David helped her into her black, ankle-length faux shearling cloak, then followed her into the brightly lit and thickly carpeted hallway. The uniformed Sheraton doorman opened the outer door and they stepped from comforting warmth into the exhilaration of Mother Nature's cold, thin breath. At the entrance stood a sleigh, complete with bell-bedecked horse and driver. David led her to it.

Joy suffused the child in her who had feasted on Russian fairy tales, read to her by a loving, handsome and doting father. "What a wonderful surprise, David," she said, grinning.

He helped her aboard, tucked a red-and-green plaid woolen wrap over her lap and joined her. "Maddie Silk's, right?" said their sleigh master, a man with rosy cheeks and nose and all bundled up in a black parka.

"Right," David said. They set off surrounded by the music of silver bells in the cold, black velvet, perfect night.

The ride was as lovely as any fairy tale. He poured her a mug of wine, but before he let her drink, he kissed her. He smelled deliciously of spice himself. For a moment she wished with a familiar pang that she could love him, marry him and settle down into a normal life. She took a sip of wine and pushed the pointless longing for normalcy away. She could love a man—she already did love one—Joe— but thoughts of normalcy were a ridiculous indulgence in fantasy. She was with David, could be comfortable with him, because he agreed that their relationship was special but that it wasn't ever going to be what most of his friends, and hers, thought of as normal.

The elegant dinner setting was a perfect ending for their week. For the first time they talked music. David loved Mozart, too.

"He's my favorite," she said. "When I die, I want them to play Mozart. His music is so radiant it seems wrong he wasn't cherished all of his life and buried with great honor instead of in an unmarked pauper's grave." She stared at the bloodred of the wine in her glass and a deep sigh slipped out. "But then, life is often unjust."

David put his hand over hers, his gaze gentle and understanding. "I'm sorry, sweetheart, for your sadness."

She smiled and shook her head, regretting that she'd let some sliver of the past tarnish the beautiful evening for even a moment. "I'm not sad. Truly."

David knew a lot about her now. Obviously the superficial realities: that she was a professional adventure travel guide and that her hobby—if you could call something she worked that hard at, a hobby—was nature and portrait photography. He had also met her sister, Star, on one occasion, and on their fifth date he'd confided to Nova that he'd paid someone to look into Nova's history. It wasn't personal, he explained. Because of his wealth, whenever a woman really captivated him, he initiated an investigation.

And so he knew about her diplomat father's death when she was twelve and about her mother's marriage to a wealthy Argentinean, Candido Branco. David knew that when she was sixteen, she'd killed the man to keep him from molesting Star. He knew she'd been incarcerated for five years. David knew all that, he said, and it didn't affect how he felt about her.

What he didn't know was that she took her first contract job for the CIA when she was twenty-two, and in the ~~intervening~~ through the intervening years she had already killed six men, as well as a villainously insane woman and a misguided teenage Muslim boy-terrorist bent on killing hundreds of thousands, if not millions, of people. Her sadness didn't come from killing Candido. That had given her nothing but release. Her sadness came from all the others she'd killed and all the evil she'd seen.

She was a contract agent for the Company, not an employee. She never took Company assignments that served the government, such as planting false information or stealing plans for troop maneuvers or for development of weapons. They knew to call her only if the lives of innocents were at stake. She had saved many people. That was true. Still, she often relived the up-close killings in bad dreams, and memories of them had a way of slithering into even the happiest moments.

Like now. But her smile and words seemed to have convinced David. He looked away and gestured for the check. Their feast was over. Time for another magic sleigh ride.

The moment they were back on the snow he slid his gloved hand under their wrap and took hers. He squeezed. She squeezed back. "I know we said no falling in love, no marriage," he said, "but I want, I need, to change the rules of the game."

The unnerving shock of his words caused her to gasp, a cold breath. *Oh, David. Please, please don't. You told me—we agreed.*

He hurried on. "We are so good together, Nova." He leaned closer and wrapped her gloved hand in both of his. "I desperately care for you."

She pulled her hand free. She didn't love him. Maybe she didn't even love Joe since when he'd said the word *marriage*, she'd frozen, her feelings spinning, much like she felt right now. Joe was the only man in her life that she might…just might…love. But even for Joe, she hadn't been able to wrap her emotions around giving up her dearly won freedom. She'd never do so for David.

She clasped her hands together in her lap. "I told you up front that I'm a difficult person with a difficult life and that love and marriage were to be off-limits. We need to keep it that way."

"But you aren't difficult, Nova. And your life, while it involves lots of travel and pressure, isn't all that different from mine."

Oh, she thought, how wrong you are.

"Please, David."

He shook his head and thrust himself heavily back into the seat. She could feel his hurt coming off him like body heat. If she stayed in the relationship, she was going to hurt David terribly. She had thought, wrongly, that she could set up parameters to keep it all safe.

Her spirit, soaring for hours, deflated: a gay balloon slashed by a serrated Ka-Bar, a knife with which she was all too familiar. Sometimes life was good, but too often those times didn't last long.

"Okay," he said. "We stay with our original agreement."

No. That isn't possible now. You care too much.

Later, when he snuggled up beside her in bed after they'd made love, her heart aching with every kiss, guilty, sad, knowing that she was saying goodbye but unwilling to utterly destroy their last night together, she closed her eyes and sighed, dreading what she had to say to him tomorrow.

Chapter 2

The Amazon—Ten Miles Downriver from
Manaus, Brazil, near the Meeting of the Waters

A birding tour group of ten Americans intending to cruise the great Amazon River for fifteen glorious days, stopping each night at a different site, had rented a two-decker, forty-foot boat. This afternoon they had anchored at a wide spot on the Amazon's north shore. Half a mile down lay the Meeting of the Waters, the point where the black Rio Negro and the reddish-brown Rio Solimões joined to become the mighty Amazon. A little like pouring molasses and water together, the two feeder rivers didn't mix right away. For many kilometers they ran side by side, black and red, although eventually the red color would win. That marvelous natural phenomenon thrilled and fascinated them all.

But in the darkness, shortly before eight, their trip took

a turn into nightmare. Fifteen heavily armed men boarded their boat.

One of the men, Carlito Gomez, had until now never been much farther than fifty kilometers from his own home in southern Brazil. He stood, bloody machete in hand, over the corpse of the man he'd just killed. The dead man, identified to Carlito and the others by a photo they had brought with them, lay face down on the floor of the cruise boat's main cabin surrounded by the nine other terrified *Americanos*, also sprawled on their bellies. They had stopped screaming, but most of the women were crying.

The dead man's arms were both pinned beneath him. Carlito reached down and pulled the left arm free.

"No, no!" his boss, Felipe Martinez, yelled. "The Eagle says it must be his right hand."

Quick to obey, Carlito pulled the right arm free and used the machete to finish the job. The other passengers began screaming again. A woman, probably the dead man's wife, shrieked, "Ellis!" so loudly it hurt Carlito's ears.

Using his body as a screen, Carlito snatched up what looked like a real gold watch from the dead man's wrist. Felipe didn't notice. Felipe's big concern was the black boy, and he had turned his attention to securing the boy's hands. The Eagle's other men were also occupied with binding and gagging their prisoners. Carlito felt a quick flush of greed rev his already adrenaline-fueled pulse. It looked like he could get away with keeping and then selling the watch for himself. He stuffed it into his pocket.

The other teenaged boy, the pretty blond one, attempted to be Mr. Macho and tried to stand. Felipe bashed him in the head with the butt end of his Beretta. The kid collapsed onto the deck, blood running down his forehead and dripping off the tip of his nose.

"Get it up to the iced package," Felipe commanded. "Now!"

Carlito dropped the machete and gingerly plucked up the severed hand. He scrambled across the cabin, clumsily kicking the machete, and climbed the short flight of steps to the upper deck, which was covered but open on the sides. From the roof over his head came the heavy splatting of Amazon basin rain. He stepped around the boat captain, who was still out cold on the deck and now bound.

Carlito opened the white, insulated box. Felipe had brought it with them, already prepared to deliver this message from Manaus, Brazil, to the office of the vice president of the United States of America. The package, delivered by an untraceable courier, should arrive in Washington no later than tomorrow afternoon.

Carlito slipped the hand into a plastic bag and then took care, using a pair of gloves brought for the purpose, to arrange the dried ice around it before replacing the interior insulation. Finished, he taped the package shut. An address and postage were already on the top.

Felipe emerged from the cabin followed by the other men, shoving hostages. One by one, the men walked the captives on a makeshift plank across the black water onto their own riverboat, stolen earlier in the day for this purpose.

Carlito was now suffering a nagging worry about getting away. There were no roads between here and Manaus. In fact, there were no roads at all going south into Brazil from Manaus. The single road out went north to Venezuela. Plane fare being expensive, common folk left by riverboat, a trip to the coast taking four or five days.

But with their prisoners, they would cruise ten miles

back upriver, running under cover of darkness to the small port of Ceasá. From there, a lorry would drive them to Manaus's international airport, where a plane chartered by the Eagle, using a false name, would return them home. There would be no record of their arrival to or departure from here. Felipe had made it clear, when Carlito had asked about it, that money could buy anything in Brazil.

It would likely be some time, maybe not until midday tomorrow or even later, before anyone cruising the river became curious enough to stop at the boat. They would find the bound and gagged boat captain and notify the authorities, who would be pissed to learn they had a huge international mess on their hands: one dead American and nine missing tourists.

Soaked to the skin but still warm in the tropical night, Carlito watched the heavy drops of rain pour from the boat's roof to batter the gangplank and shore and pock the surface of the water. Once the Eagle's other men had all the hostages aboard, Felipe quickly cast them off, heading them back to Ceasá.

Their passage was slow, guided by three men at the front manning strong searchlights. The package would be on its way right on time out of Manaus, but, given the heavy rain, Carlito wondered as he wiped himself down with a dry rag if the visibility would be good enough for them to make their planned quick exit by air.

Chapter 3

Still sweating from a twenty-minute jog and anxious to find out if there were any last-minute disasters for the New York show, Nova made a final check of her answering machine. No new messages.

This latest show of her award-winning photos of the world's most beautiful coastal drives seemed to be progressing without serious glitches. Putting on this show was costing a bundle and although her agent, Deirdre, was enthusiastic about the photos—she always was—Deirdre was worried for the first time that they might not be able to sell enough to cover costs, let alone make a profit. It had been a long time since Nova had had to take a loss in order to get her work into circulation. This time she was going to have to do more than just show up. She would need to put on the razzle and dazzle needed to sell.

In her kitchen, she rinsed and dried her favorite

Florentine cappuccino mug and returned it to its hook, satisfied that she could leave knowing that the condo was in order. If she never returned—in her life, always a possibility—she could still hold her head up in heaven. She'd not left a mess behind.

A small, rueful smile touched her lips. Star had said more than once, "I think your problem with men is that you're too damn neat. What man can relax and scratch his balls in comfort in such a neatnik home?"

Although they never discussed it, she and Star both understood just why Nova had such a "thing" about control. For four hellish years, their stepfather, Candido Branco, had controlled Nova's existence while secretly molesting her. When Candido turned his attention to Star, Nova had instinctively reacted and threatened Candido with a knife. During their struggle, she had killed him. She'd not planned it, but she also hadn't regretted it. And since she could not prove the molestation, a jury had convicted her of manslaughter. She'd served five years, from age sixteen to twenty-one. And in prison she'd been unable to decide things as simple as when to turn out her light at night. Between Nova and Star, Nova's passion to be always in command required no discussion or explanation—or excuse. But it did have consequences. For Nova, living the rest of her life unmarried might just be one of them.

A sigh slipped out as she closed the blinds that let in generous swaths of western light and a stunning view of the Pacific Ocean. Last night in Steamboat Springs she'd said nothing to David, not wanting to spoil the end of their trip, but when he'd dropped her off at the condo early this morning, she'd told him it was over.

He'd been so surprised. She felt another rush of sadness mixed with guilt. Breaking up right before Christmas and

New Year's had seemed especially unkind. On the flip side, maybe at some big holiday party David would meet someone new. Someone to make his life complete.

She leaned over the couch to pick up Divinity, her white Angora cat, a treasure with one green and one blue eye. She scratched gently behind one of Diva's ears. "Time to visit Penny, sweet thing."

She left the condo's door ajar and strolled along her balcony to Penny's door. Their two condos took up the three-story building's top floor.

Today's gorgeous blue-skied weather in San Diego could not be bettered any place in the world she'd been to, and from working for the Company and Cosmos Adventure Travel, she felt like she'd visited an impressively large selection of the planet's offerings. Sunny, clear, a pleasant eighty-two degrees.

To her left, the Pacific Ocean beckoned, framed by four palm trees. A pleasant December day in exclusive and beautiful La Jolla, named "The Jewel" for its beauty and perched on the coved edge of the sea. Seven days before Christmas.

Reginald Pennypacker, her closest friend, was an African-American with delicate, Ethiopian bone structure and large, dark eyes. Penny owned La Jolla's most exclusive beauty salon and, bless him, he took care of her plants and Diva upon request, no advance notice—something that happened rather often.

Today, Nova didn't even need to knock. She'd told him weeks ago about the New York trip. Apparently hearing her steps, he flung open his door and stood there, regally dressed in a gold jogging suit with black trim.

"Come to me, precious one," he commanded, lifting Diva from her arms.

"Back in three days," she said.

"Right. And if not, you'll call."

He smiled and studied her face to see if she had further suggestions or requests.

She hugged him and offered her half of their ritual parting. "Don't do anything I wouldn't do."

"I intend to do a bunch of things you'd never do," came back his reply.

She turned and saw the Airport Shuttle service pull up. Now it was off to New York and sell, sell, sell.

Chapter 4

CIA field agent Joseph Cardone unbuckled his seatbelt. He should have been tired but instead he felt "fired up and raring to go," one of his father's expressions. Within the hour he'd be driving on a summer evening through moon-washed Texas sagebrush, soaking up vistas from a child-hood that had been damn near perfect. He'd grown up in a loving family on a Texas ranch, where he'd ridden horses, milked cows, mended fences, driven a tractor, and baled hay. He was almost home.

The man next to him in first class, an oil exec also re-turning from Baghdad to Houston, had the aisle seat. They stood, and the man opened the overhead bin and pulled out his briefcase. Like Joe, the exec had traveled casual: chinos and a short-sleeved shirt, white for the exec and a light blue for Joe.

"It's been damn pleasant sharing the hours with you,"

the exec said. He stuck out his hand and Joe shook it. "You decide to come into town for some fun during your stay, give me a call. Or if IBM ever sends you to Houston on a troubleshoot. I'd love to show you around."

IBM troubleshooter was Joe's cover identity, and he would never take the likable guy up on his offer of hospitality. CIA business was Joe's real life, one that occupied virtually all of his time. He had no idea where the Company would send him next, although it sure wouldn't be Houston. "Like I say, I'm just here for a few days for my brother's wedding. Family stuff. It's not likely I'll get away from my folks' ranch or into any town other than Placita. That's where the church is."

At the door leading from first class into the Boeing 737's exit, the flight attendant on this leg out of Baghdad pressed her business card into Joe's hand. She said, "I don't fly out again for four days." He flipped the card over and checked the back. Sure enough, there was her phone number.

He smiled and used his forefinger to touch the tip of her chin. "I don't know my schedule right now. But thanks for great service."

He pocketed her card and strode down the gangway.

There had to be sixty or seventy people waiting for arrivals, but drawn by the unerring pull of maternal love, the first face that registered was his mother's. Rosalinda Cardone. She stood next to his brother, Manuelito, and seemed to glow from within, her smile identical to the one for which Joe was legendary among CIA colleagues of both sexes: brilliant white teeth, sensual lips.

He dropped his overnighter as she embraced him, plump arms hugging his waist, her head pressed hard against him. Standing on tiptoes, her head came to his midchest.

He closed his eyes and let a warm sensation spread up his neck to his face. He was flushing with happiness. And something else. Some powerful feeling. *This is absolutely the only place in the world where I am safe.*

His mother pulled back enough to look up at him. His eyes were dark brown with some gold flecks, like his father's. Hers were deep pools of velvet black from her Spanish heritage. "Your muscles are firm enough, but you are too skinny, Joseph," she said.

He laughed and kissed her on the forehead. "You are my home."

"Been too damn long," Manuelito said, grabbing Joe into a bone-crushing hug.

"And how's Dad?" Joe asked.

His mother took his hand. "He's fine, he just didn't want to wrestle the wheelchair through the airport. He's waiting for us at the ranch." His bullock of a father had finally been broken by a car accident that had robbed him of the use of his legs.

Joe checked out Manuelito, head to toe. Levis. Red shirt. Black, well-worn cowboy boots. He'd let his hair grow long and wore it pulled back in a ponytail, Antonio Banderas style. It looked good. When they were young they were often mistaken for each other. Same dark brown wavy hair, light brown skin, brown eyes, and quarterback physique.

Joe at thirty still had rock-hard abs. He patted his twenty-eight-year-old brother's midsection, softer-looking than the last time they'd been together. "Well, Manuelito, looks like you're ready for marriage, all right."

"You bet. Time for the really good life." His brother picked up Joe's overnighter.

"I can get it," Joe said.

* * *

The ride Joe had been imagining took place in the cab of a beat-up Chevy truck, Manuelito driving, Joe riding shotgun and their mother in the middle. Life could sometimes be so damn good.

Chapter 5

Paraguay. A landlocked country in the heart of the South American continent.

In area, slightly smaller than California.

A country that in the east had grassy plains and wooded hills; in the west, low dry forest and thorny scrub in the vast, sparsely inhabited emptiness of the Gran Chaco; and that in the extreme east, possessed a magnificent strip of tropical rain forest where Paraguay shared a border with Brazil and Argentina.

In Paraguay, Tomas Morinigo Escurra—born in Manaus on the Rio Negro in northern Brazil—found refuge at the age of fifteen, after he killed his first man.

According to the *CIA World Factbook* on Paraguay:

Population—95% Mestizo.

Languages—Spanish and Guarani.

Capital—Asuncion.

Religion—97% Roman Catholic.

Government—constitutional republic.

Economy—poor economic performance attributed to political uncertainty, corruption, lack of structural reform, internal and external debt and deficient infrastructure.

International Disputes—an unruly region at the convergence of the Argentina-Brazil-Paraguay borders that is a locus of money laundering, smuggling, arms and drug trafficking, and fund-raising for extremist organizations; a major illicit producer of *cannabis*; a base for transshipment of Andean (Colombian) cocaine headed for Brazil, other Southern markets, Europe, and the U.S.; and a center for corruption and terrorist money-laundering activity, especially in the tri-border area.

In the years that followed his arrival from Manaus, Tomas Escurra hacked out success and imposing wealth in his adopted country, working as a hired hand, then a small rancher, and finally he married a rich man's daughter and became a legitimate cotton grower. Later, he moved into more lucrative endeavors, ones more challenging and exciting—his specialty: drug smuggling. In his younger years he had also gained fame as a champion practitioner of capoeira, the distinctive martial art of Brazil, a combination of music, dance and fighting. But that time of young glory now lay thirty years in the past.

Six days before he would celebrate the birth of Christ by throwing one hell of a huge party for local honchos from hundreds of miles in every direction, Escurra was hosting a dogfight at ten o'clock in the evening for his soldiers. He'd built this fighting pit on the grounds of his massive Rancho Magnifico, half a million acres hacked out of the jungle on the Brazilian side of the tri-border area.

He sat in his place of honor surrounded by shouting,

swearing, cheering, unwashed men watching a German mastiff and a German shepherd tearing each other to death. And days hence, on Christmas Eve, while the local VIPs wined, dined and danced at his home, his less savory business partners would enjoy an even more exciting blood sport. Naturally, he had cocks and dogs lined up, but a pair of human fighters would be selected too, the final choice made only the day before the event.

The smell of beer and marijuana was enough to get high without even taking a hit. He'd put his money on the mastiff. The German shepherd lay whining and writhing on the ground in a messy pool of its own blood mixed with arena dirt. Escurra leaned forward. Finish it! he thought, his pulse pounding warmly at his throat, his passion with the mastiff. Escurra would win his bet. He usually did.

This rough fighting complex was comprised of wooden pens for dogs, cocks and even men—for special, highly secret events, such as those on Christmas Eve—plus a viewing stand. The viewing stand was part of an arena his men could enlarge for the bigger contests or make smaller for the cockfights.

The fight was over; the dogs were being hauled away. Escurra checked his watch. He'd not heard from Felipe, not one word about the Manaus operation. The operation had been planned down to the finest detail, but experience had long ago taught him that it was impossible to control everything, hence his anxiety.

Rodrigo, the man seated beside him, was Felipe's brother and Escurra's cattle manager. Rodrigo said, "He will call, *jefe*. Felipe is smart. Don't worry."

Rodrigo knew everything about raising prize beef, as well as the ins and outs of Escurra's many illegitimate projects. "Felipe's smart, Rodrigo, but it's a different kind of cargo we're dealing with this time."

The Casa Grande, where Escurra lived with his wife and youngest daughter, lay only minutes away by private road or by golf cart across perfectly manicured lawns. He really ought to go, now, to say good night to them. Early tomorrow, both women would leave for the States to visit his wife's family in Washington, D.C., for Christmas and New Year's. They went every year. They much preferred the sophistication of Washington, plus holiday shopping in the expensive boutiques in New York, to the rough people and countryside celebrations of this isolated island of jungle in Brazil.

Convention required that he say good night and pretend that he would miss them. He wouldn't. He'd learned young that he was different from other people. Stronger. He didn't need anyone. He wouldn't miss anyone. He cared for no one—but himself.

Such lack of feeling had to be cleverly disguised, though, in order to be successful, because if it weren't, you couldn't get people to trust you. You could achieve greater success if you used fear, or as he liked to think of it, respect and trust, in dealing with others. Whichever worked best in the circumstance. He knew how to work people, had been fucking brilliant at creating a benevolent, honest facade as local benefactor and charitable giver.

He stood, saying to Rodrigo, "I need to go say goodbye to the women."

To reach Casa Grande he would drive past tennis courts, three guest *rancheritas*, a pool and spa, the helicopter pad, and various other buildings for workers or supplies. He seated himself in the golf cart and his cell phone vibrated, the one with the direct and secure line to Red Dog, his main business contact in the States. Quite a number of U.S. covert operations were funded by drug money. Ordinarily, Felipe made all contacts and arrangements with Red Dog, the code name of this extremely highly placed man in the U.S. military whose actual identity remained a secret, even from Escurra.

For over five years, Red Dog had provided cover for Escurra's drug smuggling into the U.S., always taking a big cut. Escurra had never discovered how Red Dog had found out about the drug smuggling, but Red Dog had made an offer that Escurra could not refuse: cooperate and share profits or Red Dog would expose his operation to Brazilian authorities. Then a month ago, he had approached Felipe about this crazy operation involving kidnapping and blackmail.

Escurra would have opted out if he could have. Smuggling drugs he knew from every angle, but kidnapping and smuggling people was new; doing something new entailed major risks and invited disaster. Triply so because so many well-connected Americans would be involved.

Red Dog, however, refused to accept his no. Furthermore, the American implied that he might find some other middleman who was more cooperative. Fuck all. So much of Escurra's business now depended upon this contact. How could he refuse the operation? Even Red Dog's sweetening the pot with the promise of two million dollars didn't make the deal sit any better in Escurra's gut.

He fished the cell phone from his pocket. "The Eagle," he said in English.

In his capoeira fighting days, his insignia had been a harpy eagle in flight clutching a dead colobus monkey in its talons. The harpy eagle—biggest eagle in the world. All who knew and feared Escurra still used the nickname behind his back. He had found it amusing to use it himself with the American.

"I was told I'd get a call by nine o'clock your time." The low, tense voice was that of Red Dog. Escurra had personally talked only three times with the main man. Never before had Red Dog sounded agitated, angry or even tense. He'd always impressed Escurra as one very fucking cold Americano.

Escurra said, "I haven't heard from my operative yet."

"Has something gone wrong?"

"How can I know? I told you, I haven't heard from him yet."

"I don't like it."

"I can't help that. I sent my best people, led by the man you usually talk to. When I hear from him, I'll call."

A long silence stretched to the point where Escurra said, "You still there?"

"I'll be waiting."

The connection went dead.

Escurra sat thinking about that strained sound in Red Dog's voice. Maybe Red Dog was the top man in Washington. Maybe not. Maybe he reported to someone with even more power. Escurra would have to do a lot more thinking about that. But one thing for certain, Red Dog wanted those hostages much more than he had ever wanted profit from drugs. Somehow, for some reason, Red Dog was vulnerable. If all went well, Escurra would demand more money.

Just as he reached the main house his other phone vibrated. He answered.

Felipe said, "Your packages have been picked up and are on their way. Anything new for me?"

"No. Just get your ass back here."

Chapter 6

The priest was explaining to Joe's brother, Manuelito, and his bride-to-be, Susa, exactly where to stand and what to say tomorrow during the actual wedding. Joe, along with the rest of the wedding party, stood in places lined up near the altar.

Joe's youngest brother, Diego, and two other friends of Manuelito's who would serve as ushers, stood on one side of Joe. On the other side of the bride-to-be, the bridesmaids were whispering among themselves, but the priest, Susa and Manuelito seemed not to notice. Joe stood facing the entry.

For a moment, as he looked down the rows of pews toward the door, he imagined the seats filled with people, the bride's processional music playing and Nova dressed in a white gown and veil walking down the aisle toward him. He chuckled to himself. Actually, in his mother's worldview, white would be entirely the wrong color for

Nova. No virgin there. Light-years from being a virgin. Maybe Nova, the seductress, should be wearing red. Or maybe even black. Nova had eliminated bad guys, and more than once.

Then a different image replaced the wedding scene, a memory of sitting across the table from her in a funky little restaurant smelling of cinnamon. Their last weekend together. She'd picked a bed-and-breakfast in a tiny mountain hamlet called Julian, northeast of San Diego, a place famous for apple pie and the orchards that produced them. A place where the two of them could be assured of anonymity. He was holding her hand across the table.

He had presented her with an engagement ring, fully expecting her gorgeous green eyes to light up with joy. Instead they had dimmed as though a gray cloud had suddenly covered his sun. Nothing he'd said could change her mind. She'd quickly grown angry, saying he'd agreed they would be lovers. But no big commitment like marriage. He'd grown angry in response. They had locked in a test of wills. He'd finally said, "Either marry me, or I'm outta here."

Her reply, as she'd pulled her hand out of his, her tone both sad and final had been, "Then, I guess it's over."

Now, clenching his fist, Joe swallowed down a golf-ball-sized lump and forced his attention to the priest. A dumb phrase popped into his head—"Real men don't cry."

He had actually found and loved a woman like no other. He would never love another woman because in his eyes, none would ever compare to Nova in beauty, intelligence or courage. So why the hell had he insisted on marriage? Why the hell had he let her push him away? And just when the hell was he going to swallow his pride and call her?

Chapter 7

Nova's photo agent, Deirdre LeDoux—her name matched her flamboyant looks—stepped onto the squat platform at the Franke Gallery of Fine Photography. She'd piled her blond hair up in dramatic swirls and wore a purple, floor-length Dolce & Gabbana that would also be smashing on her look-alike, Charlize Theron. The string quartet had just finished playing Vivaldi's "Spring" Concerto and fell silent. Deirdre said huskily into the microphone, "May I have your attention, please."

The one hundred invited guests cruising the gallery floor, most of them dressed in black tie or a gown equal to Deirdre's, turned toward Deirdre and wound down their chitchat. A last sip of champagne. A final bite of foie gras or Russian caviar.

Deirdre had explained that half the guests were already Nova Blair collectors, eager to meet the photographer and perhaps buy something new from Nova's collection of *Scenic Ocean Drives of the World*—at prices ranging from one thousand to fifty thousand dollars. Nova always felt squeamish about the prices Deirdre insisted upon. Taking the pictures was its own payoff in the pleasure she derived from it, even when capturing the image involved danger or hardship. Especially then. But, as Deirdre relished repeating, when hazard and beauty were brilliantly combined they merited very special recognition. Such works always brought the highest prices, and Deirdre, from the beginning of their seven-year friendship, had put Nova in that elite class.

"I see you are all enjoying yourselves," Deirdre said. "I've interrupted just briefly because I want to share with you, and with Nova, the announcement that her photo of *A Boy and Butterflies* has just been awarded The Nature Conservancy's photo of the year. Their top prize."

All gazes switched to Nova, and enthusiastic applause showered her. She felt the warming glow of a blush of pleasure and surprise.

Deirdre finished. "Now please, do continue to enjoy your evening." She stepped down and slipped her arm around Nova's waist. Deirdre's perfume, Llang Llang Myrrh, enveloped them. The quartet resumed its mood-setting, *Canon* by Pachelbel.

"Nice surprise, huh?" Deirdre enthused. "Come, I want to introduce you to the mayor's assistant. She loves photography and her husband is a nature freak. He's always off on wilderness trips. Do what you can to sell her a photo and maybe you can sell her hubby a tour as an added bonus."

They were halfway across the room, the two of them smiling, shaking hands and kissing cheeks as they walked, when Deirdre's assistant, Donnie, approached. He said, "There's a call for you, Ms. Blair. He says to tell you it's Smitty."

The pleasurable fizzing of her spirit flattened immediately into alarm. She grabbed at a straw of hope. *Maybe it's nothing serious.*

But of course it was serious. The CIA never called her when there was "nothing serious." To her surprise, she also felt a quick burn of excitement. Over five months had passed since her last Company assignment, and her subconscious was apparently eager for action.

"Where can I have a little privacy?"

Donnie led the way. Over the phone and sounding tense, Smith said they needed her as quickly as was convenient this evening. He gave her the name of the hotel and the room number where he would be waiting. "How long do you think you'll be?"

"I can finish up here in thirty minutes. I'll see you within the hour."

She left hearing good news. "I've sold three photos," Deirdre said, looking relieved. "We'll for sure make expenses, and probably then some."

"There were nine tourists and a guide," Leland Smith said. "The boat captain was knocked out and tied up."

Smith lounged in a green wingback chair opposite Nova, a hotel table between them, a Scotch and soda in his hand. He wore a plain brown suit and white shirt, tieless and open at the neck. Plain brown shoes. Plain brown hair. She had met in person with "Smitty" twice before, and each time she had had a hard time afterward remembering exactly what his face looked like. The perfect CIA field agent or controller.

Smith's assistant, Marvin King, sat propped up in the queen-size bed with his back against the headboard. Marvin, a light-skinned black man who wore elegant gold-rimmed glasses, would never be nearly so invisible.

Smith continued. "The note that came with the severed hand says that the hand belongs—belonged—to Ellis Stone, Colette Stone's husband, and that he's dead."

"*The* Colette Stone?"

"Exactly. So what the bastards have is nine tourists and the guide, ten hostages in all, one of them the rather famous niece of the U.S. vice president."

"You know, I think I will have that drink," Nova said to Marvin. He rose. She detested the vice president, who had never seen a forest he didn't feel needed harvesting or an oil field that didn't beg to be drained. She added, "Is the hand Stone's?"

"Yes. Confirmed by fingerprints and DNA."

"Who received the package?"

"Came by express mail to the secretary of defense with instructions to forward it to the office of the vice president. We might not be able to pin down the actual origin."

"Fifty million is a lot of dollars." She took the Scotch and soda from Marvin and sipped. Chilled. A nice burn. Marvin returned to his perch on the bed.

Smith said, "They hold major bargaining chips. In addition to Colette Stone—well—" He reached into a leather briefcase on the table beside his chair, extracted a sheet of paper from a folder and handed her a list of names. She read them, sipping the drink, as he continued. "You see Colette's and Ellis's names at the top. Kimball Kiff is the birding tour's leader. Kiff's the curator of birds at the Los Angeles County Museum of Natural History and has taken other clients on the same trip three times before.

"Redmond Obst, it seems, is what they call a world-class birder. He keeps a list of all the species he's seen, a world list, because he's been to so many places. He's a personal friend of the leader, Kiff. Ronnie Obst is his sixteen-year-old son and is also considered a serious birder. Alex Hailey Hill is the grandson of our Supreme Court Justice, Suleema Johnson. He likes the outdoors but isn't an especially big fan of birding. He and the Obst boy are best buddies."

"I like Justice Johnson. This will certainly be frightening for her."

Seeing the next two names, she caught her breath. Nancy and Otis Benning were among the most enthusiastic collectors of her work. Smith saw her reaction. He said, "You know the Bennings?"

Nova had first met the famous Washington, D.C. socialite, Nancy Benning, about six years ago at a party at the French Embassy. Nova had been undercover as a cocktail girl, tailing the wife of a Saudi diplomat newly arrived from Saudi Arabia and due to return to her home within the week, Nova still on her tail. Nancy Benning had spilled a Bloody Mary on her dress and Nova had helped with a cleanup in the ladies room.

Their second meeting, the one Benning would remember, happened at Nova's second D.C. photo showing. Nancy Benning had purchased a scene of thousands of pink and white flamingos lifting off from a remote, unnamed lake in Kenya. "I've met Mrs. Benning. She loves birds. She's purchased at least one of my photos."

"Well then you may know that her husband, Otis, owns Benning Corp. Big into plastics. Rolling in dough, the both of them."

"Fifty million dollars is suddenly sounding like peanuts.

Or like the kidnappers don't really know the identity of all the fish they've caught. Something's strange. Have they not contacted anyone else, just the vice president?"

"Maybe it's still too early. But to answer your question, the only ransom demand so far is the one centered on Colette Stone."

Nova looked at the remaining names. "Who are Linda Stokes and Annette Coulson?"

"Stokes is a librarian from San Diego. Coulson is a dance teacher, also from San Diego. They're friends and enthusiastic bird watchers. Dennis Chu, the last on the list, is an entomologist from NMNH, the National Museum of Natural History. Apparently pretty famous in his own world."

Seeing her frown of puzzlement, Smith added, "Insect expert. According to the NMNH people in Washington, he took the trip because he wanted to collect bugs in the Amazon. He has no real interest in birds."

"Clearly they're holding some pretty important people, but what do you want with me? If you pay the money, you'll probably get them back." In truth she was skeptical of that last statement and knew that Smith would discount any such hope as well.

Smith leaned forward, eager to reach her with his argument. So far, only one man was dead. This wasn't the kind of op Nova normally considered working and Smith knew it. In every case that she had worked, multiple innocent people had already been killed or the threat posed was the kind that could result in the deaths of many people. In her last case, in Amalfi, thousands if not million of lives had been on the line, justifying, in a way, the dirty work that Company jobs too often entailed.

"The State Department has already put together an FBI team," he said. "They are on their way to Manaus and will officially work with the Brazilian authorities. But these hostages are high profile. The vice president wants us to do more, much more, than that. Christ, Nova, they have his niece! We have orders to send down a crack undercover team. At least undercover in terms of being U.S. government. We want someone who can go down there saying they are looking to find a relative, one of the hostages, and be convincing. We want you."

She said nothing, just took another sip.

"No one in this government is going to depend on the Brazilians to get our people out. And no one is going to sit around hoping that when the money is paid, the bastards will keep their word and let everyone go. The plan is to locate the hostages and then send in a special operations team to extract them. You know Brazil. Even better, you know Manaus and the Rio Negro. You've been there, how many times?"

"Seven trips to Brazil, four of them included stops in or around Manaus."

"You speak Spanish fluently, and some Portuguese, right?"

"No real Portuguese."

"And then there is your main advantage, always your strongest asset. You're a woman, who can put on a great act of being helpless and nonthreatening."

She smiled, feeling a bit devilish and wanting to tweak Smith a bit. "Well, there's something else to consider. I detest vice president Ransome. I have no desire to do anything to help that SOB."

Chapter 8

Sixty-three-year-old U.S. Supreme Court Justice Suleema Johnson stooped slowly to the sofa. She picked up and cradled her calico cat, Hypatia, and headed for her bedroom. "I'm tired, my dear. It's been a long one," she said, bone-weary but smiling. Hypatia was named for the famous mathematician who had lived in ancient Alexandria and was stoned to death by a mob led by the Catholic priest, Cyril. She was Suleema's closest confidante, privy to Suleema's most private thoughts and desires. Suleema considered Hypatia to be as wise as the woman for whom she'd been named.

After an especially tedious, work-filled day, Suleema had decided to retire early. Tomorrow she would hear arguments in the case of Wade v. Lemonn—very technical stuff on the patent rights of biopharmaceutical companies. Although it was barely eight o'clock, the arthritis in her hips and lower back cried out for her to lie flat.

Fortunately, this house suited her aging body perfectly, since the previous owners had redesigned it to place the master bedroom on the first floor. She'd purchased the house a little over a year ago, just before her swearing in as the first black woman to serve on her country's highest court. The location was ideal for getting to and from her office at the court and was only an hour and a half's drive from her daughter's lovely home right on the Chesapeake Bay.

Suleema had calculated that on occasion, Regina and Clevon might want to stay in Washington for an evening at Lincoln Center for a fancy dinner or show, so in her home, they had an upstairs bedroom to themselves. But sixteen-year-old Alex was getting too old to visit Grandma anymore.

She flicked off the living room floor lamp and eased down the hallway. Alex was, at this very moment, off someplace in the Amazon birding with his buddy, Ronnie Obst. Suleema had met the young Obst once, at Regina's house. She had liked him, and thought him a good friend for Alex. Alex, so exceptionally bright and mature for his age, was too serious. Ronnie was outgoing and adventurous and had traveled all over the world with his rather famous father. Ronnie encouraged Alex, who had been more devoted to his computer than to nature before their friendship, to get out and explore life.

She used the wall switch to light her nightstand lamp. Another night of sleeping alone. Her gaze was drawn to her favorite photograph of Raymond, gone from a heart attack for just over five years. He'd not lived to see her elevated from the Ninth Circuit Court, but he'd always believed she had a good chance to be "the one."

Hypatia wiggled, and Suleema let her drop onto the quilt.

"I know it'll happen," Raymond had said. "You're the smartest woman, the smartest person, I've ever known, Sulee. You're a natural for the Supremes."

He'd been right. He was a building contractor, the practical one, she the one who lived a life of the mind. They'd been a great match. The place in her chest where her heart had been ripped away by his death still throbbed with longing and loss.

It took no more than ten minutes to undress, snuggle into a cotton nightgown and down under the covers. Hypatia curled up at her hip. She'd never had trouble sleeping, and quickly drifted into the state of fractured thoughts that came just before full unconsciousness. Then she heard a sound.

What was it?

Silence. She let her mind drift again.

Another sound, a definite click. She stiffened in the bed, eyes open, peering at the dark ceiling, ears straining.

Hypatia lifted her head from her paws and looked toward the bedroom door. Suleema sat up halfway on one elbow, peering into shadows formed behind moonlight flooding through the bay window, and then a shadow, dark as a cave, blocked off the pale glow. A gloved hand grabbed her throat and shoved her back down into the bed.

The man, it had to be a man, knelt so that he forced one leg between hers, right through the covers. He grabbed Hypatia by the scruff and lifted the calico into the air.

Suleema clawed at the gloved hand, unable to suck in even a tiny breath. She raked her fingers down his sleeve. He leaned on her, his weight that of a man at least as tall as Raymond's six feet.

"If you don't want me to kill your cat," the dark shadow said, "lay still."

Lie still! Shouldn't she fight for her life?

Could she even fight for her life? She was sixty-three years old! His hand felt huge, his body enormous. He was probably going to rape and kill her, and there wasn't a damn thing she could do about it.

She tried to say, "Can't breathe," but no words would come out.

"You gonna lay still?" he said. He spoke softly, an ominous near-whisper, but clearly and with authority. He moved so that some light fell on him and she saw that his head was bald and he wore only one gold earring.

He wasn't masked, not hiding his identity. Yes, he was going to kill her.

He let up enough on her throat for her to drag in a choked breath, then another.

He sat Hypatia on her chest. "I could kill this cat right now. I could kill you right now. Right?"

She nodded. Clever Hypatia leaped off the bed and headed for a safer place.

"I got in here, I can get to you anywhere. I have a message for you. You listening?"

Again she nodded. That seemed to be all he wanted from her so far. To listen. Her mind was going lickety-split, thinking what a woman was supposed to do. *Try and talk to him.*

"The Supreme Court's decision in the case of Sharansky versus the United States Government is due in eight days. On the twenty-seventh of December. I'm telling you that you are to vote against Sharansky."

This is insane. It doesn't make any sense. What the hell is he saying?

"You hear me? In Sharansky versus the U.S. Government, you are to vote against Sharansky. And if you don't, your grandson, Alex Hailey Hill, will be killed."

She got it. He was here to make her vote for the U.S. Government in this bitterly fought case brought by New

Hampshire's lieutenant governor and the lieutenant governors of seven other states. The court was split. Their deliberations were secret, but it was widely assumed that the decision would be up to the new justice, Suleema Johnson, the swing vote, the tiebreaker. And this assumption was, in fact, correct. And someone choking off her breath claimed to be able to kill Alex unless she voted against her conscience and her judgment.

But Alex wasn't even in the country. The threat seemed preposterous.

"Now here's the way it's going to be," he said. He leaned his knee hard into her groin. "You will not tell anyone—and I mean anyone—what I've just told you. You will vote for the government. That is why I'm here. To make sure you do. If you tell anyone, the boy will be killed. You understand?"

She nodded, wondering who she could safely tell. Someone would have to be told.

"I know that when I leave, you'll want to call your daughter to check whether the boy is safe or not. Don't. She won't know yet that we have him. Your calling would tip her off you know something you shouldn't, and we will be listening."

The very mention of Regina from this thug sent Suleema's mind bounding off in a rabbitlike panic.

"You just wait a day. Watch the news. Maybe give your daughter a call tomorrow. She's in for a nasty surprise."

"Get off me!" she managed to hiss out.

With his free hand, he pulled something from his pocket. A knife. The blade—short and thick and serrated along the top—gleamed silver in the moonlight.

One quick stroke toward her chest. She felt nothing at first, then a stinging sensation and then liquid trickling warmly across her skin.

"That's just a little taste," he said, his voice still that ominous whisper, "of what could happen to the boy. And to you."

He released her, stood, turned and strode out of the bedroom.

Suleema lay still, afraid to even move enough to touch her chest. How badly had he cut her? Maybe he was still in the house.

No. He'd want to get out.

She forced her hand to move, touched the cut beneath the cotton, and felt a surge of relief that it was sticky but superficial.

She should get up. Call 9-1-1. Call the federal marshal's office.

But what if he, or whoever had sent him, did have Alex? How could that possibly be? Maybe Alex hadn't gone on the trip. Maybe they had taken him from school. Kidnapping was FBI responsibility. She must call the FBI, of course, not 9-1-1.

But the FBI could only help if Alex was in the States. Wasn't that so? What if Alex wasn't? She crossed her hands as if lying in a casket and hugged herself, still terrified to get out of the bed, nightmare images and thoughts scrambling through her head. How could they know how much Alex meant to her? The man had been so confident that he wasn't even wearing a mask.

What if she didn't call the FBI at once, if she waited until tomorrow to call Regina to find out if the threat was real? If she called the federal marshals, they would insist on putting a bodyguard on her, even when she was away from the court. Except occasionally at high-profile speaking engagements she had never felt the need for a bodyguard, provided when requested to Supreme Court judges by the marshal's office. Until now. Having her driver, Sam, with her had been reassurance enough. Asking for protection now would wave a red flag.

Someone was trying to influence the vote of a justice of the United States Supreme Court. Surely duty required her to call in the authorities at once.

But at the risk of Alex's life?

Chapter 9

Smith's raised eyebrows indicated genuine surprise. "Come on, Nova," he said. "You don't expect me to take your dislike of VP Ransome seriously. When has politics ever affected the Dove's decision to take on a job for Langley?"

She allowed herself a soft laugh. "Dove" was her Company code name. "I do seriously dislike the vice president's politics."

Smith grinned and lifted his glass as if in a toast of agreement and then continued, all business again. "Surely I needn't point out that these poor people are all innocents. And Colette Stone certainly can't be blamed for her uncle's bad political judgment. In fact, the word is that Ms. Stone and the VP don't get along. And she loves birds. She's a bird painter, Nova. They all love birds. Shit, it was a goddamn birding trip!"

She smiled at his urgent attempt at persuasion. But it

was true that it did tick her off that people who simply took a trip to the jungle to soak up some of the Earth's beauty were being brutally mistreated. And she knew the Bennings. They were real to her, names and faces and voices. She could not say no and live with herself. She gave Smith an exaggerated smile. "Oh, well then, that decides it."

He grinned and leaned back. "Just jerking me off, right?"

"Right."

Smith set his glass on the table and clasped his hands together as if warming them over a fire, ready to get down to business. "Okay, then. Your cover will be that you are the sister of one of the San Diego women, Linda Stokes, and you're looking for her on your own dollar. You don't trust the government, and so on. I have people setting up your cover as her sister as we speak. Another reason you're ideal for the op is that you already know San Diego, which will save the preparation time we'd otherwise have to spend with someone else."

"It does look like saving time would be a good idea," she said in understatement.

"Absolutely. Today is the nineteenth of December. The kidnappers have given us two days, until midday Washington time on the twenty-first, to wire-transfer the fifty million to an offshore account in the Bahamas before they start killing a hostage a day."

"Will the government or her family pay the ransom?"

"I don't know. The negotiators are taking a position initially that they won't pay any ransom and will not negotiate with terrorists. To stall for time, they eventually will start negotiating. But no one is actually counting on the bastards releasing the hostages whether a ransom is paid or not."

Smith took another shot of his drink. "They claim they'll save the VP's niece until last, but no one's counting on that either. The State Department has been assured complete cooperation by the Brazilian authorities. At least four FBI men are on their way to Manaus. The Company has only one man on station there. Until now there's been no big action we needed to watch; one pair of eyes has been sufficient."

"I want to do a quick stop with whoever is in charge in Brazil to get their stats on Brazilian terrorists or other illegal operations. I presume that person is not in Manaus."

"That would be Leila Munoz, head of station in Rio."

Nova felt mental gears hitching up, her pulse increasing. "If I'm to stay completely undercover, I'll have to avoid being honest with the FBI guys or anyone official. So who will you get to cover my back and worry if I don't check in?"

"Your backup is in the works. Joe Cardone again. You two already know each other, always a plus when you're undercover and in a rush, as we are. No time wasted getting familiar with your partner's habits and MO. We've already contacted him."

Smith said it casually, but she thought he was studying her. She kept a straight face, but her pupils had likely done a quick dilation from an extra-sudden squirt of adrenaline. Smith was a trained observer. Did the Company know about her affair with Joe after their last op together? Was Smith expecting her to be pleased? Or did they also know that her budding romance with Joe had ended in a head-on collision of wills?

Neither she nor Joe had made any special effort to hide their intimacy from the Company, or anyone else. But they hadn't volunteered information on the subject, either.

God, sitting right in this hotel she suddenly smelled cinnamon and apple pie, felt again the panic tightening her chest. She was back in Julian on that last day. Joe had said, "Marry me or it's over," or words to that effect. To marry meant loss of freedom. Compromise. Always compromise. So many things could go wrong if they tied the knot that bound their lives together, presumably until "death do us part."

Joe had said, "You can't always control everything."

She'd fired back, "I can't control the creeps of the world, but I do control my private life. And giving that up scares me."

"You're saying no because you're scared? I don't buy it. You aren't afraid of anything."

That's what he'd said. And he'd taken off angry and hurt because he'd believed that and thought she didn't love him. He'd been wrong.

"Cardone," she said to Smith in what she hoped was a sufficiently neutral tone.

"Right. It also works out well because we can get him there quickly. He's currently in Texas, not on the other side of the globe. But this time we want the two of you to use separate identities. Make no public contact. Joe will be doing a freelance article on terrorism and money laundering. His cover name will be Joseph de los Santos. He speaks Spanish and Portuguese fluently."

She couldn't sit still, not while thinking about seeing Joe again. Hell, working with him again. She stood and went to the makeshift bar Marvin had set up and added two ice cubes and fresh Scotch to her drink. To protest would look strange and unprofessional. Joe was a top agent. She should be relieved to have him back her up.

Piss all.

She sat again. Both Smith and Marvin were waiting for her reaction, no doubt about it. For years she'd felt that someone at the Company kept close tabs on her private life. Joe had more than once claimed that Claiton Pryce, the deputy director of operations, had the hots for her. Maybe so. Or maybe this was all just her imagination and no one from the Company had any idea how much she loved Joe.

She stirred her drink with the tip of her finger, making a concentrated effort to do it oh so casually as Smith added, "We'll have him on his way ASAP directly to Manaus." To Marvin, Smith said, "Let's see the map."

Marvin rose and flipped open a laptop sitting on the table, already booted up. One click and a screen showed a map of South America. Smith pulled his chair around so he could also see the map. Her eyes went first to one of her favorite places, Iguazu Falls, located on the spot where the northern border of Argentina, the eastern border of tiny Paraguay and the western border of Brazil met, halfway down the continent, right below the bulge—the tri-border area, famous for rampant crime. Her first trip to South America had been to Iguazu Falls, so she tended to use it as her South American orientation point.

Her gaze quickly moved north, though, to the equator, to the Amazon River, which lay just below the equator and ran parallel to it. Smith pointed to Manaus, a rundown city that hugged the north shore of the Rio Negro seventeen miles up from the Amazon.

"You ever been to Manaus?" she said, looking first at Smith and then Marvin.

Marvin shook his head. Smith said, "God, no. It's in the middle of nowhere."

"It's a surreal experience. Here you are, dead in the heart of the world's biggest jungle in a city that has beautiful black and white inlaid stone sidewalks, elegant old mansions and a central market with wrought ironwork that looks like something designed in Paris. But everything's gone totally to seed. Rubber built Manaus, and when someone smuggled out some rubber tree seedlings to Southeast Asia, the boom busted. And the place is always hot as Hades with a miserable ninety-five percent humidity."

"So you won't need much luggage," Smith said, smiling. "Only light clothing." He set his glass down, earnest again. "The kidnap took place on the Amazon River, not far below something called the Meeting of the Waters, a few miles downstream from the last little town that has a road into Manaus."

"Ceasá," she said.

"Correct. So tell me what you'll need."

"This is an isolated area." She turned ideas over in her mind a moment. "I need to anticipate whatever might come up. There'll be no getting anything special quickly."

"I'll have Operations working on it tonight. You'll have everything you want before you fly out tomorrow."

"A Glock, broken down. Thin jungle camouflage top and pants and light-weight pull-on boots and socks for climbing or hiking. A BlackBerry. And could you send some quinine to me tonight? I might not have a mosquito problem in the city, but I'd be better off having some malaria protection if things go native."

"Why don't you have your own BlackBerry?" Smith groused, frowning. "I always have to leave phone messages."

"I don't want to be that connected to the world unless I'm working for the Company. Could you also please have the techs put onto it whatever they think I might be able to use?" She continued compiling her mental list out loud. "Pen recorder and the smallest video/still camera that's resistant to water. A GPS in a locket I can wear and one built into the kit. It's all got to be able to fit without detection into a woven, not flashy but still fashionable, shoulder bag, between the cover and a thick, quilted inner lining."

"You'll have it."

She could feel excitement bubbling strongly now. She was going on a hunt once again.

"You going to have any problems getting away?" Smith asked.

"I'll tell my agent I've decided I can't take the time to stay and shop in New York after all. She won't ask any questions I can't answer."

"Good, then," he said and rose.

She stood. Marvin handed her a packet with the necessary papers and tickets. Smith had the last words. "Marvin will pick you up at your hotel in the morning. You'll be met in Rio by the head of station, Leila Munoz." That was it.

She walked toward the elevator with mixed feelings about seeing Joe. How would that go? For a moment, she'd had a refusal on the tip of her tongue; maybe he would refuse the job.

She jabbed the elevator button three times. She wasn't ready to see him again. She should have said no to Smith.

She turned, looked back toward the room, but her feet stayed planted. For all the reasons Smith had laid out, she probably *was* the best person to find Colette Stone and the others before anyone else got killed.

But I have to find some way to get Langley to stop throwing Joe and me together.

The elevator door opened, she turned and stepped inside, hit the first floor button as though she'd like to punch it clean out. *I hate it, I absolutely hate it, but the truth is, I can hardly wait to see him.*

Chapter 10

After enduring an interminable morning of oral arguments, and having already doffed her judicial black robe, Suleema hurried down the marbled corridor toward the private entry to her office suite. She entered a room shared by her three senior law clerks. Seeing her, Patrick Hagan, fair skin, red hair and freckles, rose with a manila folder in his hand and stepped toward her.

"Absolutely not now," Suleema snapped at him as she forged ahead, her temper frayed by her desperate need to call her daughter, a need she'd put off for over fourteen hours since that abominable creature had cut her with his knife.

Patrick braked to a startled halt. Her two other clerks looked up in amazement as she brushed past them and into her office. She closed the door behind her.

Mistake, mistake, her mind cautioned, in a panic. She ought not do anything to draw suspicion. Certainly she should not begin to show an uncharacteristic ill temper.

Her swivel chair creaked as she threw herself into it. She placed her hand on the phone receiver. She would not use a cell phone, of course. Cell phone talk wasn't secure. But it was quite natural for her to call Regina. No need to hide the fact of making a call to her daughter.

The answering voice on the other end was Clevon's. "Hello, hello," he said, almost shouting. A cold chill ran up Suleema's spine. Clevon home in the middle of the day?

Suleema had not called the FBI. And no matter what Clevon told her now, no matter what the details were, she knew the man with the knife had not been lying.

"Is Regina there, Clevon?"

"Let me have the phone," Suleema heard Regina say, her voice shrill. "Mama, I have to tell you something," Regina said. The terror in Regina's voice pierced right into Suleema's heart. "Mama, the people that Alex went with on the trip to South America have all been kidnapped. Alex has been kidnapped, Mama. I'm terrified."

Remember, act like you know nothing. "How do you know he's been kidnapped?"

Through sobs Regina said, "The feds came here about half an hour ago. Colette Stone's husband, Ellis, is dead. They've killed him."

"Who, Regina? Does the FBI know who's responsible?"

With a clarity that shook her even worse than she'd been shaken last night, Suleema knew that if anything happened to Alex, it would utterly break her spirit. She could not endure the loss of this boy, her legacy. The phone receiver grew slick in her hands.

"It's Secret Service, Mama, not the FBI. And they don't know who. They were kidnapped somewhere around Manaus. That's in Brazil. And the monsters sent Ellis

Stone's hand to Vice President Ransome with a demand for fifty million dollars." Regina giggled nervously, a grotesque sound. "Ransome being asked for a ransom."

For a moment Suleema's mind stuck, baffled by a money demand being sent to "Wild Bill" Ransome when what the man had said last night was that the kidnappers wanted Suleema to vote for the government in the Sharansky versus U.S. government case. It only took a flash, though, and she realized there was no reason for the terrorists not to demand money for all their captives as well.

"Alex will be okay, Regina. You have to believe that. He's so smart. Even street-smart, for his age."

"But I don't know if they let him take his medicine with him. Do they even know or will they care that he's diabetic?"

"Maybe the Secret Service can find that out from them." Suleema suddenly remembered that Otis and Nancy Benning were also in the birding party. And likely there might be others whose lives would be valuable. Blackmailing a Supreme Court justice was unusual but not contradictory to a ransom demand. What it implied, however, was that someone in the United States, not some terrorist in Brazil, was the driving force behind the plot. Money they might want—but sewing up her vote, due to be officially announced in seven days, surely topped their agenda.

Big money, military power, and in no stretch of the imagination, ultimately world domination, was at stake in Sharansky. Congress had passed a law authorizing the deployment of lasers on space-based, orbiting platforms. These offensive weapons, touted as being deployed for defensive purposes only, could, of course, also be used to suppress virtually any opposition to American positions in any global conflict over anything, anywhere. The international consternation caused by this U.S. policy was significant, affecting U.S. allies as well as the country's opponents.

Citizen groups in a number of states were also violently protesting this expansion of human warfare off the planet, and so unless they were stopped by law, men would do what men so love to do—weaponize yet another sphere. They would take their violence right out into space and off to other worlds.

Sharansky, who was the lieutenant governor of New Hampshire, and the lieutenant governors of seven other states had filed suit against the U.S. government on constitutional grounds. Sharansky and the other lieutenant governors argued that the space above the atmosphere over their states was part of the commons and that the federal government could not appropriate the use of space for any purpose, military or otherwise, without the consent of the citizens of those states. Maybe her vote might only slow the process down; Suleema had at least prayed for that. But if she voted against Sharansky, there would be laser weapons in space within her short remaining lifetime, she was sure of it. If the lieutenant governors won their case, numerous powerful interests would be thwarted. Any one of them would want to make sure Judge Suleema Johnson voted their way.

"I'll come right now, Regina. I'll be there are soon as I can."

Suleema hung up. She rubbed her sweating palms against her skirt and then, feeling the urge to throw up, stood and rushed to her small private toilet and knelt over the john. She retched once, but nothing came up. She'd been unable to eat anything for breakfast. Heat flushed over her in waves, and under her arms, perspiration soaked her blouse.

She knelt there for a full minute, then, shaking, she

pushed to her feet. She had to make up her mind right now if she was going to call the FBI or the Secret Service or anyone official. "Please, dear God, help me decide."

Nova sees that there are other people in the small, flying-school plane with her, and every last one is calmly putting on a parachute, getting ready for the drop. But the straps of her harness are crossed, seemingly hopelessly so. And she's running out of time. Any minute now she'll have to jump. The jump master keeps demanding that she hurry. She twists the straps one way, then another. Her heart is beating like crazy. Her fingers seem too thick and awkward. She can't grip the straps correctly, let alone get them untwisted.

But the jump master won't listen to her protests. The man puts the parachute harness onto Nova and clips it shut. "The straps aren't done right," Nova says, her panic now threatening to explode her heart.

He turns around, Nova thinking it's to help another student, but then a buzzer sounds. The jump door opens, and the other students all rush toward it, shoving Nova along in their hurry, and all of a sudden she's in the air and falling. Plummeting toward the dark earth she can't see but knows is below.

She fumbles to find the pull for the ripcord…but…but she doesn't have one. And if she hits the ground, she will die.

It's the dream, *she says to herself.* Wake yourself up! It's the dream.

She finds the ripcord pull and yanks.

And nothing happens. Her parachute has failed.

It's the dream! *part of her mind protests again.*

She's going to die if she doesn't wake up.

Breathing hard, her heart racing, Nova pulled herself into consciousness.

She was gripping the armrests of her Varig business class seat so tightly she imagined she might bend them. God.

"Are you all right?" This from the gray-haired woman beside her who had disappeared into a Nora Roberts novel the moment the plane had lifted off from JFK.

"Yes. Fine. I just dozed off."

This was the single recurring dream of her life, one she'd had so many times when she was in prison that she couldn't count them. She'd had it less often in her early twenties. In fact, other than once or twice after Ramon Villalobos had loved and left her and right after she'd broken up with Joe, she had been free of the dream.

What had brought it on now? She couldn't imagine. She didn't even know why she had had it so often when she was in prison for killing Candido, other than the very obvious fact that in the dream she was in a blind panic. She'd spent many of her days in that monstrous prison cage in a panic.

She had slept very little last night, and the monotonous droning of the Varig's four big jet engines had caused her to drop off. Whatever the meaning of this terror-inducing, recurring dream, she just wasn't going to let the damn thing freak her out.

Nova smiled grimly and fetched the BlackBerry from the beautifully designed shoulder bag Marvin had brought this morning. Woven into its dark brown fiber was a pattern of green leaves and vines. The Company knew that she often wore emerald-green, the color of her eyes, and perhaps someone had taken note of that when planning how to design her kit to be tasteful and not stand out.

She'd also purchased two pairs of khaki pants, dark brown sandals, three capped-sleeve tops and a lightweight emerald-green pantsuit should she need something more formal. Woven from fine hemp, the pantsuit would breathe and also wick away the sweat she knew was going to plague her the minute she hit Manaus.

For now, most of the items she'd requested from Smith rested in the bag's two spacious inner pockets, looking quite innocent. A camera that looked like a pen. A recorder built into her lipstick. The BlackBerry itself. And so on. The brown and dark green camouflage suit and collapsible boots were hidden inside the specially designed lining, along with the broken down Glock, its nonmetallic composition and un-gunlike components assuring that the bag would sail right through any metal or X-ray detectors.

She powered up the BlackBerry and opened up the directory for the files some tech from the Company had downloaded into it. Brazilian terrorists. Brazilian drug runners. Other Brazilian criminal organizations. Kidnap victim profiles.

She had spent most of the night reading about the woman who was supposedly her sister, Linda Stokes, and Linda's friend, the dance teacher, Annette Coulson. She'd memorized enough details to make her cover story sound convincing to anyone who didn't know Linda or Annette personally. Now she clicked open the victim folder.

There they all were. The birding guide, Kimball Kiff from the Los Angeles County Museum of Natural History. The world-class birder, Redmond Obst, who Smith had said was a personal friend of Kiff. Next came Obst's son, Ronnie, and his son's friend, Alex Hailey Hill. The boys, being the youngest, would probably have the shortest bios. She'd save them for last. Then there were Otis and Nancy Benning. She already knew a lot about both of the

Bennings. They could also wait. Last came the bug expert,
Dennis Chu.

She decided to start with the primary victim and clicked
open the file on the vice president's niece, Colette Stone,
a woman who may well have watched as her husband was
killed and then hacked up. Nova went through all the files,
noting ages, professions and possible worth in terms of
ransom. She also looked at photos, flashing the pictures
on and off numerous times. She needed to recognize these
people on sight.

For dinner she chose the vegetarian lasagna with braised
mixed vegetables. Varig clearly didn't stint on their
business class food: the pasta, with its hint of basil, was
perfectly al dente, and the ricotta cheese on the vegetables
melted in her mouth.

Her seatmate, Mrs. Remington, was traveling to visit
her daughter, who was pregnant with her first child and
married to a Brazilian who'd made a fortune selling
gems. Their dinner conversation rotated around gems and
kids, Nova thinking wistfully of Star's children, Maggie,
Blake and Bryan, as the closest she was ever going to
come to having children. After dinner, for the remaining
two hours to Rio, she turned her attention to files on the
Brazilian terrorists.

Once off the plane and through customs in Rio, a
woman waiting in the receiving area just outside Immigra-
tion and Customs held a Cosmos Adventure Travel sign
that said, Nora Smith, Nova's cover name for the op.
Cosmos ran a lot of legitimate adventure trips in Brazil. It
was also her CIA cover operation.

The contact was a forty-plus stunner, a woman who Nova
immediately imagined could still flaunt her body on Ipanema

Beach in a topless swimsuit and win the admiration of every man or woman she passed. They'd all say "Ahh!"

"Ms. Smith," the Brazilian beauty said through a radiant, white smile. "I'm Leila Munoz."

Chapter 11

Leila Munoz matched Nova's height of five feet, eight inches, but where Nova had well-toned muscles honed for bringing down men fifty pounds heavier with a single aikido move, Leila was all soft curves in the right places. Her honey-colored skin and wavy black hair were typical of the racial mix of black, Hispanic and Indian heritage of Brazil.

Leila took charge of Nova's rolling suitcase. "I can manage it," Nova offered.

"No problem. Part of the service. Love your earrings."

Nova laughed at the unexpected appraisal concerning her jewelry. The earrings were the silver doves with emerald eyes that Joe had given her. Among friends and within the Company, Nova was the Imelda Marcos of earrings; she never felt quite complete without them. Out of fear of embarrassment, she'd never counted how many pairs and half pairs she owned.

"And I love your dress," she countered. Leila had wrapped her luscious curves in a lemon-yellow dress cut above the knees and decorated with butterflies in all colors of the rainbow. No one would ever suspect her of being CIA, and station head at that. For cover, Leila held a position as a translator at the U.S. Embassy.

Outside the terminal building, a balmy Rio December evening greeted them. A Ford SUV with the Cosmos Adventure Travel logo on its doors idled curbside. Leila tossed Nova's bag into the SUV's backseat and said, "Do you want to go to a hotel? I've reserved a room for you. Or would you like to stay at my place? Not so cold and impersonal. I have the files you wanted with me, so either place works."

Leila's slight accent was quite lyrical. Nova said, "Your place would be much appreciated. I get sick of hotel rooms."

As they moved toward town, Nova caught a glimpse of the massive, lit statue of Christ on top of Corcovado Hill. Leila obviously intended to put their travel time to good use. "Our one regular agent in Manaus is Oscar Chavez," she began. "He knows everything that goes on. All the major players. He'll contact you in the bar of the hotel where I've rented you a room. The Gioconda. It's modest, discreet, clean. Right in the center of Manaus. If you think it would bolster your cover as a rich American, you can show disgust and move in a day or so to something more fancy."

"What's his cover?"

"Government surveyor. It allows him to be out and about pretty much wherever he needs to go."

They were now skimming beside a row of towering hotels that stretched along the beach south of Sugarloaf Mountain. "Copacabana," Leila said. "You'll have to come back and visit me sometime." Leila gave Nova a long appraisal and then a big smile before turning her attention back to the street. "I like your looks, Ms. Smith. And I'm a great judge of character. Maybe you could come in February for Carnival."

"I'd like that."

They soon pulled up to a guarded gate leading into the underground garage of a high-rise condo building. Leila pulled a card from her purse and inserted it into the slot of a reader, the gate rolled upward and Leila waved to the guard in his little stand as she drove inside. "Lots and lots of crime in charming Rio," she said. "You do know, don't you, that it is quite unsafe to go out at night."

Another security guard sat beside two elevator doors reading a comic book. He beamed at Leila, who was now lugging a hefty lawyer's briefcase while Nova toted her overnighter. When he looked at Nova, the guard kissed the back of his hand.

Inside Leila's condo, the view of Rio from the tenth floor at night, with the chains of lights stretching along the beach and the huge lit-up Christ and the dark patches that Nova knew were the favelas—dangerous slums housing abject poverty—was nothing short of spectacular.

But what took her breath away were all the butterflies. Butterfly lamps, butterfly pictures, butterfly images on rugs, coffee mugs and telephone notepads. "Go ahead," Leila said, "ask about the butterflies. Everyone does."

"I do get the feeling the condo might lift off any moment, but you don't need to explain. I've got my own fetish."

Leila smiled. "Good. I said I was a great judge of character."

While Leila showed Nova the guest bedroom, she explained that Manaus was now crawling with Brazilian authorities, not only from Manaus but down from La Paz as well. "Ten very high-profile Americans kidnapped on Brazilian soil, one for certain killed. Big scandal. Bad news all around and a political hot potato, as the English slang puts it."

"I will appear to be working alone, pretending to be the rich sister of one of the victims."

"You're alone!" Leila said, her eyebrows lifting elegantly.

"No, no. Of course I have a backup, but he stays deep. Seeming to be alone works well for me. I've done most of my ops that way." The German and Italian missions, when she'd worked as a photographic team with Joe as her assistant had been exceptional…in a lot of ways. Soon she would see him. She licked suddenly dry lips. What if he was still angry? What if he was cold to her?

She pushed her fears away. "The bad guys tend to underestimate me. And because I'm a woman who comes off as rather gentle—"

Leila laughed. "Yeah, I make you for gentle. I was a bit surprised when you said you were Ms. Smith. Not at all what I expected."

"Well, I can safely say I don't live up to that image. But it serves me well because people tend to trust me and often divulge secrets they ordinarily wouldn't."

Leila chuckled again. "I guess I fit in that category with everyone else. I rarely bring an agent to my digs." She put her arm around Nova's shoulder. "Want something to eat or drink?"

"If you have a diet drink or iced tea or just ice water, I'll be happy. I need to start to work on the Brazilian files in that big black briefcase of yours. See what you guys have on terrorists and gangs that we don't. Any action in the Amazon, in particular."

Leila set Nova up at the small dining-room table and

then said, "I'm off to bed. It's after ten and I like my eight hours of sleep. Do you think you'll be up long?"

"I don't need much sleep. Three or four hours is my regular dose."

"Really!"

"Reading these files will also be good for me. I don't read or speak Portuguese all too well. This will jump-start me into speaking and thinking in the local language."

"Well then, I'll see you early tomorrow. We need to get up about six to make it to the airport in time."

"*Obrigada,*" Nova said.

"My pleasure," her hostess replied, strolling down the hall.

Nova's fully-booked flight to Manaus took off thirty minutes late. For the first ten minutes of waiting, she fantasized about Joe, who, if he had accepted the mission and was on schedule, was already there, waiting for her. Only two, two-and-a-half hours at the most, and she'd see him.

Surely he wouldn't have agreed to come if he were still angry. She imagined the strong muscles in his arms and shoulders. She knew every part of that body. The first time she'd seen him naked, on Capri, was after their visit to Rome's central jail. She'd delivered a message to a terrorist from the man's son. In Amalfi, she'd caught the terrorist behind the unleashing of a killer virus that, ironically in the end, had killed the bastard's own son.

On Capri she and Joe had made passionate, hot love for virtually all of their two-day rest and recreation, if you counted sweet talk and petting part of making love. Even eating had been a sort of devouring of food while devouring each other with their eyes. They ate every meal in her room, stark naked.

When she got to Manaus she would look first for his dark brown wavy hair and then those big, dark, chocolate-colored eyes. He virtually always had a deep tan.

This bloody longing she had for Joe felt as if something was burning slowly under her skin. The hours between them would not go fast enough.

She questioned again her decision to refuse to marry him. Had that been a truly stupid mistake? When Star had said Nova was crazy to let a great man get away, actually drive him away, Nova had countered with, "I've created a life I'm comfortable with, Star. I don't know who I'd be if I married anyone, not just Joe. I need to be me. Not Mrs. Someone Else. I didn't want to split up. He just wouldn't settle for anything less than marriage."

Star had snipped back with, "You're just afraid to give up even a teeny bit of control."

The businessman seated next to her finished skimming the paper he'd brought along. He folded it, stuffed it in the pocket in front of him, stroked his mustache and interrupted her gloomy thoughts, asking in Portuguese, "Have you been to Manaus before?"

"No. And I fear I don't speak Portuguese very well."

"Then let us speak English," he said without missing a beat.

In this case it was perfectly true that her Portuguese was lame, but even when she was using one of the nine languages in which she was fluent, when she engaged the public on an operation she usually pretended language ignorance, another often effective way to trick people into divulging things they shouldn't.

He continued. "Business or pleasure?"

"Quite honestly, I'm here to find my sister. She's been kidnapped."

He jerked in surprise and stared at her. "I've been following it in the paper and on the television. I'm so sorry."

"I told her not to come. I told her Brazil was dangerous."

"I can understand your distress, but this is quite exceptional." He stroked his mustache again, a quick, nervous gesture. "We do have a lot of crime, especially in Rio and São Paulo. But certainly nothing in Manaus like an attack on so many foreigners."

"My husband was a policeman. And I'll admit, I'm the suspicious type. I wanted to see for myself what they're doing to find her."

He sighed. "I'm sure the Brazilian authorities are doing everything they can to help."

The flight attendant, a petite, pouty-lipped woman with the same honey-colored skin as Leila, stopped at their seat. Handing out juices and sweet rolls, she had undoubtedly overheard Nova's cover story.

Nova pointed to an orange juice on the attendant's tray, and as the attendant handed it to her, the attendant said, "The men four rows back, in the tan linen suits, are American FBI. You might want to talk to them."

Nova smiled. "I sure will."

For a while her seatmate chatted about business. He was trying to make a success out of coffee but grown in the shade of trees. That method, he assured her, was less environmentally harmful than just tearing out the trees and planting fields of coffee plants. "It's a bit more expensive, but coffee grown in shade is of superior quality."

She already knew that Brazil grew some of the finest coffee in the world.

As they were landing, she made a mental note to ask for shade-grown coffee at Starbucks in the future and accepted his help with her overnighter.

The second they left the plane's air-conditioned enclosure and she strode down the loading ramp, the heat and humidity slapped her like a hot, wet rag. Once again inside the air-conditioned terminal she felt better, but that little walk had been a reminder. This was summer in the tropics; the temperature here yesterday had been one hundred and four degrees Fahrenheit, the humidity was the customary ninety-five percent, and this was a poor city where air conditioning was a luxury.

The Manaus terminal, although small, resembled international terminals around the world. The hamburger concession was a McDonald's knockoff. She caught up to the four men the stewardess had fingered as FBI. "May I talk to you a moment?" she said.

All four looked her over, crown to sole. Although there was nothing particularly sexy about her khaki slacks and red cotton top, short of wearing granny clothes or a burka there was no way to hide the nice curves of her hips and breasts.

"My name is Nora Smith and I'm Linda Stokes's sister. The flight attendant said you're FBI. You must be here because of Linda."

Maybe it was just her imagination, but she felt emotional and mental barriers go up with a solid bang. "We really can't talk about the investigation," said the one with the least, and grayest, hair.

"I intend to find my sister. I do not intend to leave here without her."

Two of them shifted their briefcases to their other hand, clearly put out that she was taking up their valuable time. Still, all of them except the senior man were smiling in that way men did when sizing up female flesh.

The balding guy with gray hair said, "I wish you well. I think you'll find it very difficult here, trying to deal with authorities in a foreign country. In a foreign language. I assure you that we will be doing absolutely everything we can to find your sister."

And that was it. As one, like a tiny school of tan fish, they shifted away from her and headed toward the nearest exit.

Smiling inside, she followed.

Leila had reserved a hotel room, but Nova didn't scan first for a taxi. She looked for a tall man, broad shoulders and brown wavy hair.

Ankles and arms crossed, Joe was leaning against a nondescript, white four-door Toyota parked in a public parking lot on the other side of two feeder lanes of traffic. He was scanning everyone coming out of the terminal.

Her breath stopped as he caught sight of her. Neither of them moved. For Nova it seemed like the longest time before she took another breath.

What will he say? She would soon see him in the hotel.

The rest of the world fell away—no heat, no traffic, no taxis, no people.

She swallowed hard, amazed that she had the ridiculous urge to cry. Forcing her eyes to the line of waiting taxis, she marched toward the one at the front.

Chapter 12

"The Gioconda," Nova said to the taxi driver who had hopped right out of his cab to help her put her overnighter in the trunk. She clutched her beautiful, specially crafted woven bag like it held her most valuable possessions, which, for the purposes of this op, it did.

In Portuguese, she added, "Downtown Manaus."

The humidity already hung on her like a wet wool suit. Perspiration trickled down her temples. She'd braided her hair into a French twist and pinned it up in back, but she knew the back of her neck had to be drenched anyway.

The trip into the city usually took about twenty minutes along a mostly four-lane highway. She turned around once to check for the white Toyota. Joe was well behind them but definitely following.

From leading several trips to or through Manaus, she knew its checkered history by heart. Around 1890 it had boomed into the richest city in the world. Macintosh had made the first raincoat, and someone had found out that latex erased pencil marks. Goodyear had found a way to keep latex soft and pliable in cold weather, and when Henry Ford needed tires for those cars he was building, the boom was on. Rubber, extracted from rubber trees by slave labor, was king, and rubber was shipped out of Manaus.

The city's elite had even built an opera house to rival any in Europe. Everything in the building that wasn't made of exquisite Brazilian wood had been laboriously shipped from Europe and brought upriver: French roof tiles, staircases from England, stages and the enormous painted curtain from Paris, chandeliers and porcelains from Italy. *La Gioconda* had been its premier performance, and Enrico Caruso had once been scheduled to appear. To everyone's disappointment, he didn't make it because a cholera epidemic raged through the city at the time and the troupe refused to get off the ship.

The old town proper looked as seedy as she remembered: uncollected trash, broken pavement and curbs, graffiti-marked buildings alongside shops and businesses you might see in any third world country. No honking of horns, though, a welcome blessing.

On earlier trips, she'd stayed at two very different accommodations. One trip had been strictly jungle oriented and their hotel modest and on the edge of Manaus because they'd spent one night's sleep there. The next day they'd moved on into the jungle with a local guide and had slept in hammocks—whether it rained or not. It had rained two nights out of three for the entire two weeks, but they had been rewarded with two jaguar sightings, an anaconda, sloths, parrots, army ants on a rampage and, her favorite memory, a howler monkey nursing her baby.

On two other trips, her group spent nights in the five-star, luxury Tropical Hotel forty minutes outside of town. It lay on a bank of the Rio Negro, just past a neighborhood of mansions for the big shots in Manaus: the heads of the Brazilian military's jungle warfare unit and owners of the city's bigger businesses.

The Gioconda turned out to be located only two blocks from the Opera House and seven blocks from the central market and long wharves that were the city's beating heart and lifeblood. Her room, probably the best in the place, looked out from a postage-stamp second floor balcony onto the luxuriant green lawn of a plaza with pigeons and a few scattered wooden benches with wrought-iron legs and armrests. A gazebo dominated the plaza's center. Nova imagined concerts played there in the evenings. Stores sold everything imaginable: shoes, clocks, bread, bridal gowns, photo equipment, cheap kitchen appliances, colorful pet tropical fish; and there was an Internet café.

She knew she should be thinking of how and when Oscar Chavez would contact her. Her instructions, relayed by Leila, were to go to the bar downstairs and wait. But maybe five percent of her thoughts were on Oscar and the op. God help her, ninety-five percent of her thoughts were on Joe. On seeing him and hearing him and touching him.

No! Not touching him. Touching him must be avoided at all costs.

She checked her makeup in the mirror over a dresser that looked old enough to have been brought over from France a century ago, and then headed downstairs.

The bar was no more than a small room with a few tiny tables, most but not all of them occupied. Behind a counter at the rear stood a skinny man with thinning, black hair. He was leaning on his elbows, chatting softly with a

pretty blonde of middle age who was sipping a tall beer.
She wore a cheap dress with a pretty floral print and black
pumps. No tennis shoes. None of the women in Brazil, not
even the hot, teenage chicks with tight jeans and tank tops,
wore tennis shoes. Flip-flops, wedgies, even heels were de
rigueur. The woman's beer was likely the coolest thing in
the stifling, hot room.

Both sexes and all ages occupied the tables. The hum
in the room gave off a pleasant sense. All eyes studied the
unfamiliar *gringa* who had just walked in, but, with curi-
osity satisfied, they went back to their own affairs.

Booze of all kinds weighed down the shelves behind the
counter along with what looked to be the fixings for caipirinha—a refreshing drink with sugar, lime and cachaça
liquor. "A caipirinha," she said, her voice trailing upward
into a question.

The man gave her a gapped-tooth smile, nodded and set
to work. Nova sat at the only remaining free table, her back
to the wall so she could see the room. Joe walked in.

He wore jeans, brown jungle boots and a dark brown
short-sleeved shirt. With his dark skin, hair and eyes, he
blended in, although no one would be surprised to discover
he was an American freelance journalist. He sauntered up
to the counter and ordered. The bartender placed a tall
brown beer bottle in front of him.

Bottle in hand, Joe turned around and leaned his back
against the counter and surveyed the room, oh so casually.
His eyes passed over her like he'd never seen her before in
his life. The bartender and woman took up chatting again.

A scruffily dressed little girl with walnut-colored skin,
bright, black eyes and pink flip-flops bounded into the
room, looked around and walked directly to Nova. She
carried a piece of paper, holding it like a strange but

valuable object. She said nothing, just held it out to Nova with a captivating smile.

"*Obrigada,*" Nova said.

The child curtsied, grinned like she'd never done a curtsey to anyone before but had always wanted to and then scampered out the door.

The note had been folded twice and sealed with Scotch tape. It was from Oscar. It directed her to sit on the park bench on the southwest corner of the plaza in front of her hotel within twenty minutes and start reading something. The international edition of *The Wall Street Journal* in her bag, something she'd read on the plane, would do just fine.

She stuffed the note into the bag as well and was gathering herself to stand when two men walked through the door and swaggered toward the counter. The sullen looks on their faces raised the hair on the back of her neck. The room froze. All chatter ceased.

One of the men spoke to the bartender in Portuguese, too softly for Nova to hear. The bartender, suddenly shrunken two sizes, shook his head and said he didn't have it.

Nova's immediate thought—they were gang members shaking the man down for protection money.

The blond woman straightened and in a loud voice told them, in Portuguese, to, "Get out."

The gangster closest to her slapped her.

Joe, who had been amiably drinking his beer as if he had all the leisure time in the world, grabbed Mr. Ready-to-Slap-Women and, with his face now hooded and his eyes gone dead cold with anger, he slapped the bastard. In fluent Portuguese Joe repeated the woman's demand for the men to get out and added, "I don't like to mix beer with shit."

The first guy turned on Joe, pulled back his arm to deliver what he probably assumed would be an easy, terrifying punch to this civilian in the Western jeans and nice, clean shirt. He didn't even see the fist that caught him in the jaw and knocked him to the floor.

Joe's sudden violence surprised Nova almost as much as it surprised everyone else in the bar. Except, of course, she knew him. With her, with women especially, and with men he liked, Joe was a charming daredevil with a wicked sense of humor. But rile him and another side, a dark side with a fierce sense of fairness and justice, took over, and he had all the necessary skills to enforce his feelings.

Mr. Slapper picked his buddy off the floor, and the man who'd been hit drew a gun.

In a nanosecond, he got his arm twisted up behind his back so hard he howled as Joe took the gun and shoved him toward the door. The bullies made a quick retreat.

Joe's gaze caught hers. They both knew the disadvantage of an elevated profile for anyone undercover. Joe had acted out of instinct—but now everyone stared at him. To the bartender he said, "Sorry about that." He laid the gun on the bar and made for the door. There would be no questions about or discussion of what had happened.

She gave him time to disappear into a doorway or shop, then rose and left. Dodging traffic, she zigzagged across the street to the plaza, walked to the southwest corner and sat on the bench. A man already occupied the other end. Middle-aged, khaki slacks, simple blue cotton shirt, silver-rimmed glasses with modest but noticeable correction and reading a paperback novel—something by Isabella Allende.

Nova sat, opened the paper and once more skimmed the front page headlines.

"I'm Oscar," her contact said.

Chapter 13

"Delighted," Nova said.

"You look just like your picture," Oscar Chavez said in lightly accented English. "No. Far more attractive in person."

She let the compliment pass. Besides, she felt wilted from the heat and knew that her underarms were already showing signs of perspiration, not at all attractive. From the corner of her eye she spotted Joe across the street outside a business. He appeared to be shopping for sunglasses.

Chavez got right to business. "Things are absolutely frantic here. Besides putting virtually all of Manaus's police resources into a hunt for bodies or any trace of where the Americans have been taken, at least thirty Brazilian federal agents are swarming."

"I met four FBI on the plane."

"Two Americans also arrived yesterday. I understand

that the victims are all very important or wealthy people. No resources are being held back."

"Not all are high profile. Two women from San Diego are just ordinary folk who love birds and could afford a rather expensive trip. And two teenage boys aren't famous or wealthy, although it's true they have relatives who are. The father of Ronnie Obst, Redmond Obst, is a famous birder. The man is a surgeon who can afford an expensive hobby."

"Expensive?"

"Birding all over the world in many inaccessible and exotic places takes a lot of money."

"Ah."

"The grandmother of the other boy, Alex Hill, is Suleema Johnson, one of our Supreme Court justices. Certainly famous, but she doesn't have all that much money and neither does the boy's family. The severed hand was sent to the vice president, and that family could cough up a lot of ransom and so could the Bennings."

"I suggest we start by going to the police."

"It's also my thought that going to the police is what a distraught relative would do. But I'll go alone."

"That's dangerous. You need someone to back you up. We can claim that you have paid me to assist you and translate because you don't speak good Spanish or Portuguese."

"No, it's better if I go alone as just Linda Stokes's sister. People—men—will tend to underestimate a woman, and I can better gain trust where I need to."

"Really, I insist that I should come with you."

The look on his face showed genuine concern that seemed to be not only for the sake of the operation. She appreciated his care, but she also knew what would work best.

"No. And I'm in charge of this op. You must trust me. I want you to be available when I need information about local people, places, whatever. But in the background. I have your cell and landline numbers."

"I don't know—"

"If it makes you feel better, I have a backup man. We've worked together before. If I can help it, I will never be out of contact with him. He also has your numbers."

Oscar pursed his lips but nodded. "Okay. I stay deep in the background." He grinned. "But let me assure you that my phone will be with me even in the shower." He grinned.

"Appreciated," she said, and returned the smile.

He gave her directions to the police station and told her the local price the taxi driver should ask. "Don't let him overcharge you," he said, still smiling.

She walked slowly to the street, holding her hand across her breast and on her left shoulder long enough to be certain Joe had seen the signal that she now intended to take a cab. She gave him two minutes to reach his car by studying a display of CDs and DVDs in a bin outside a store, and then she hailed a cab and directed the driver to the police station.

Her watch indicated fifteen minutes to high noon when she stepped from the cab. The police station, although not air conditioned, had thick walls that offered relief from the heat. Doors and windows let in welcome cross ventilation, but there was no palliative for the debilitating humidity. Even the small of her back felt sticky. All sane people who could possibly do so were now heading for home and siesta.

She explained in halting Portuguese that she was Nora Smith, sister of one of the kidnap victims. With pleasing speed she was directed into a room vibrating with fifty or sixty men busily generating even more heat with activity and talk.

The man who approached her, lean and short with intense black eyes, spoke only Portuguese. His family name was Sanchero. They had such a hard time that he quickly called over another cop, Cruz, who spoke a little English. Between the three of them, she made some progress.

"I intend to talk to anyone and everyone who might help me find my sister," she said. "I have money. I will pay well for information." She hoped—trusted—that knowledge of her willingness to pay for information would spread quickly.

"I want to know the name of the man who found the tour boat," she said.

"That would be Angelo Santiago," Cruz answered.

"And I want to talk to the boat captain."

"His name is Diego Santiago." Cruz then explained and she understood, at least as best she could understand given all the fractured English and hand waving, that police and feds grilled Diego Santiago for two days and he continued to claim he knew nothing. The kidnappers had knocked him out, tied him up and he never saw or heard anything.

She insisted on the address where he lived or where she could contact him.

Cruz complied, but when he handed her the piece of paper, he said, "You understand. You waste time here?" Both men made quite clear that they thought her being in Manaus was pointless. Of course, she was supposedly the sister of a victim and didn't speak Spanish or Portuguese, so she agreed, hard as it was to keep a straight face and persist with the cover. She left feeling that she had been satisfactorily convincing as the distressed sister.

She took a cab to the docks where the detectives said the captain might be found. There, after a few polite questions and dropping the word that she was willing to pay for useful information, she found the boat, the *Fiesta*, and its captain, Diego Santiago.

Having hosted English-speaking passengers for years, Santiago spoke excellent English. "I am so sorry about your sister. Terribly sorry. You must be in great distress. I wish I could help you, but I can't. They knocked me out and tied me up. I really know nothing. It's obvious they only wanted the Americans."

She watched his eyes, his lips, his shoulders, his breathing. She'd had a lot of training in reading people, and according to Star, she also had a natural talent. She didn't believe him. He was hiding something, but what?

It was nearly 1:00. Sweating like nothing she'd ever experienced anywhere else in the world, she stepped out of another cab in front of her hotel and called Oscar. "Get to your police contacts. Tell them they should haul the captain in again and grill him. He's lying. He knows a lot more than he's telling."

She rang off, went inside and trudged up to her room. She went straight to the bathroom and ran cold water, cooled a cloth and used it on the back of her neck, throat, her forehead.

A quick knock on the door, and Joe stepped in.

Chapter 14

"Hey, Joe."

"Hey, Nova."

Over six months had passed since she'd seen or talked to him, but the electricity that arced between them zapped her as strongly as ever. She couldn't move, wouldn't have been able to drag her gaze from his face if she'd wanted to. "Place is bloody hot as hell, isn't it?" she managed to get out.

"I was just home in Texas. Texas doesn't hold a candle to this jungle paradise for heat." He paused. She waited. "It's the humidity that does it, right?" He broke eye contact first and looked around the room. "Looks really good."

Did he mean the room, or did he mean her? The room was spectacularly less than special. She said what she thought. "You look good."

His gaze locked onto hers again, and to her surprise he barged across the room and pulled her into his arms. With one hand he cradled her head as he kissed her. The familiar, sweet touch of his lips cancelled any resistance. She held back a little—she was the one who had sent him away—but only a little. She savored that special something she'd craved for months without fully knowing it.

Her pulse raced, her heart seemed to expand in her chest and she felt her skin flushing even hotter. He let her go, stepped away and looked around again. "Don't attach anything to that," he said. "I just needed to get it out of my system."

"Sure. Don't worry. I won't."

He strode to the French doors that opened onto the balcony and scanned the plaza across the street: lawn, gazebo, cafés, stores, traffic.

She said, "I didn't know what to say when Smith said they were teaming us again. I wasn't sure you'd come."

"I go where they send me."

Well now, that wasn't strictly true. Joe hadn't been working for the Company all that long. Maybe two years. He had no habitual pattern of doing anything they asked, but he could have found a way out if he'd wanted to badly enough. But he'd come. In spite of her rejection, he'd come.

She said, "I'm glad it's you and not someone else. We work well together."

He shrugged and turned back to face her. "Yep. That we do. We fit super well together."

She saw them in bed, remembered his passion, felt again the taste of his kisses, his skilled touching of her every pleasure point. Just being in the same room with Joe made her feel like she was glowing, but she intended to keep herself from falling into the silken clutches of love—somehow. She simply wasn't going to go through the hell of saying no to him again.

"Look," he said as he took the room's only comfortable chair. "We keep everything business. We do what we can to find and save ten people who deserve saving. I have no problem with that."

"Okay." She sat on the edge of the bed, surprised by disappointment. Maybe she was reading him wrong. Maybe Joe *was* cured of Nova Blair. *I guess I'd deserve that.*

He leaned forward, both arms on his knees. "So tell me, what do you have so far?"

"Your action in the bar, it was risky. You shouldn't have—" She wasn't going to criticize more than that.

He nodded. "I know. Dumb. Pure reflex. No thought."

"You can be very convincing."

"But sometimes not convincing enough."

There it was again. She was certain he wasn't talking about convincing the creeps in the bar to lay off and get out; he was talking about not being able to convince her to say yes to marriage. How could she keep this operation on track if he kept veering off into their private life?

He grinned. "But not to worry. I remember what you said. You can't imagine being Mrs. Anyone. You're comfortable with your life just like it is. You don't want to mess it up with lots of compromises." With a long pause, he made a show of scanning the room. "And I have to agree. This is about as comfortable as it gets."

She laughed as he continued to grin, amusement dancing in his eyes. She didn't deny herself and him another confession. "I've missed your desert-dry sense of humor."

"Good," he said. "So I repeat my question. What do you have so far?"

"The boat captain is lying. I wouldn't be surprised if he was in on it. No. I take that back. That's too strong; his responses when I talked to him didn't suggest guilt. He wasn't part of the planning, but he does know more than he's telling. Fear. Money. Something has his mouth glued shut."

"I've been here a little over twenty-four hours." Joe leaned back in the chair, propped one ankle on his knee, and folded his hands behind his head. Her eyes went to his crotch. Aware of the blunder, and knowing for certain he would have watched the trajectory of her gaze, she felt herself warming and snapped her eyes to his chest.

No help there. Instead of diverting her thoughts from throwing herself into his lap, she was thinking how very much she would like to unbutton the light blue linen shirt and run her hands over his tan skin and sculpted chest muscles. She'd let her fingers wander down his abdomen…and as far as they might want to go. As far as he'd let her go.

He grinned and, quite evidently savoring her embarrassment, did not change his body's position so much as a millimeter. "Even though it sprawls for miles in all directions along the river, Manaus is a tight world. It's like a small town—the authorities pretty much know everything going on. There just aren't a lot of ways kidnappers could hide ten Anglo hostages for long. I think they must have taken them out of here pronto. I'd say out by air."

"That means the airport. I suggest we go there next."

"Fine." He pulled his cell phone from a breast pocket. "Give me your secure numbers."

They exchanged numbers so that they could reach other directly or by text messaging on secure lines. She stood. He uncrossed his legs and also rose.

Her stomach growled. Joe chuckled. "Want to eat around here or at the airport?"

"There are a couple of small cafés on the plaza. Why not here? I'll take the one on the south side. You get something at the one directly across from the hotel."

She found that the Café Hidalgo had a diverse menu posted outside its front door. A man smelling of a spicy cologne stopped beside her, apparently to study the menu. "You look for information about the kidnapped Americans, no?" he said in English. "Please keep looking at the menu."

"Yes."

"I am brother of the boat captain. I have information but I don't want anyone see me give it to you. You will pay?"

"Yes."

"How much?"

"That depends on what you have to say."

"You pay in American dollars?"

"Yes."

"Okay. Meet me at third fish stand inside fish market. Fifteen minutes. You just look like you think to buy some fish."

He turned and sauntered off toward the market.

Nova immediately text-messaged Joe. "Plan change. Have contact. Fish market. Inside entrance. Walking."

Joe would most likely follow her in his rented Toyota.

Chapter 15

The central market of Manaus stretched along the Rio Negro's north shore and could rightly boast about the beauty of the French imported wrought-iron grillwork and stained glass window that arched over its entrance. Even in the heyday of shipping rubber, the docks to the right and left of the market had probably never been busier than now: tour boats, fishing vessels, tankers bringing in supplies and carrying out the exports that kept the town thriving even in this middle of nowhere. Luxury seagoing cruise ships berthed here carried thousands of passengers from Manaus a thousand miles down the Amazon to the Atlantic; from the street, Nova looked up at the white and blue colors of the *Amsterdam Queen* towering over the single-story shops lining the bustling waterfront.

She had not noticed Joe following her although she checked once. She stepped inside, and found herself in the hurly-burly of the fish gallery. The smell of the sea pounced on her, but fresh and clean; no reek of death in spite of all the fishy corpses. Counters bearing a dazzling variety of colorful or silvery forms laid neatly out on ice stretched down both sides of the broad, rectangular building. Behind each counter stood a man or two cutting up and laying out the morning's catch.

Her contact, presumably Angelo Santiago, had said third counter on the left. He wasn't there. She sauntered toward the opposite end of the long hall, wanting to check for a rear exit. Halfway down, a wide entry to the left opened into another, even larger gallery, this one offering vegetables. Reassured of a second way out should one be needed, she strolled back. The single man behind the counter indicated by Santiago smiled at her. Before he could say anything, her contact materialized from the crowd. He said, "Come," and moved far enough away that the owner couldn't listen in. She stood beside him. He spoke quickly and softly. "I have information about the men who took the Americans. You said you pay."

"Who are you?"

"Angelo Santiago. The captain of la *Fiesta* is my brother, I stopped at the boat to see why he hadn't called me for over a day and found him still tied up. You will pay?"

"Yes. I'm desperate to find my sister."

"I need one hundred American dollars."

"I have money. How do I know that what you have is worth one hundred dollars?"

"You went to police. What did they tell you?"

Yes, information in Manaus did travel fast. The brother of the *Fiesta*'s captain already knew she had been to the police. "Not much."

"Correct. They won't tell you anything. But I can tell you who the men were."

She leaned toward him, genuinely surprised. "Who?"

"You pay one hundred dollars American?"

She dug into her woven bag to the little pocket for cash, fingered around to pull out five bills, all twenties. She showed him the greenbacks.

The owner of the stand started their way. She smiled but shook her head and he went back to laying out fish. He probably figured that she and Santiago were dickering over how much she would pay him to be her tour guide for the day.

"Before the police came," Santiago said, "when we were still on the river, I talked to my brother. He told me the kidnappers all spoke Guarani. Not from Manaus. Not from Brazil. They are criminals from Paraguay."

He reached for the money.

"Is that it? Is that all you know?"

"Give me the money. It must be worth a hundred dollars to know that you will not find your sister here. These foreigners are gone by now."

He was right. She handed him the money. He turned to leave. She grabbed his arm.

"Are you certain that's all you know? Did your brother tell you anything else?"

"I only need one hundred dollars."

The way he said he needed only one hundred triggered her sixth sense. Gambling debt? Sick child? Expensive mistress? Whatever. He knew more. She released his arm. "But I can pay you a great deal more money if you have more information."

"I only need one hundred."

"How would you like five hundred?"

His eyebrows went up in surprise. This man's brother,

Diego, had probably told Angelo Santiago everything he knew about the attack and the attackers. Five hundred to learn what Angelo knew would be well worth the price, and to him it would be a mouthwateringly large sum given the exchange rate of dollars for reais.

"I have to be careful," he said, drawing out the words.

"I swear I won't tell anyone who I've talked to. I just want to find my sister."

Santiago looked over one shoulder and then the other. She could almost see calculating circuits in his brain sparking.

He stared at the floor, then shook his head. She cut him off before he could say no again. "A thousand U.S. dollars. I need to know whatever you can tell me."

The fire of greed sprang into his eyes. "There is something that belonged to the kidnappers. A machete. My brother found it on the floor of the main cabin. It has blood on it. I think fresh blood."

Fingerprints! DNA! "Your brother has it? Why didn't he give it to the police?"

Angelo looked away and licked his lips. "Does it matter? I can get the machete, but my brother will not just give it to me. I will have to…to take it without his knowing."

Perhaps the brother had been paid off to keep silent. Or maybe he had simply agreed in exchange for his life that he wouldn't cooperate with the authorities. If so, giving up the machete would put him at risk if whoever was responsible found out he'd turned it over to the police. Whatever the reasons for his silence, she had to have the machete.

"One thousand dollars can buy a lot of things you must need."

"I will have to…to take it without Diego knowing. He would not give it up, not even for twice the money you offer. It is dangerous for him to deal with the police."

"I'm not the police. When can you get it for me?"

"I meet you tonight, then. After dark. I can't take it during the day. I meet you inside the church across from the Opera House. It's public and a church. A safe place. You sit in a back row. Thirty minutes after seven."

Santiago backed away, turned, and quickly disappeared into the crowd on the street. She wasn't exactly sure why he felt he had to steal the machete from his brother. Most likely because he didn't want to have to split one thousand dollars.

In the taxi going to the airport she text-messaged Joe, letting him know she had a hot lead that might yield fingerprints and that she would make contact with Angelo Santiago again at seven thirty in the evening. The thought crossed her mind that Santiago might lose his nerve and not show up. Maybe she'd have to ask Oscar to arrange for the police to search the captain's house. But if the captain had been paid off or was in contact with the bad guys, having his house searched would alert him that he was a suspect. He might in turn alert the kidnappers. Scratch that idea.

After the cab let her off at the airport, she went directly to the manager's office. The middle-aged male receptionist at the counter smiled at her and twirled one side of his heavy mustache. "Hello," he said in English.

She let a worry frown crease her brow and continued in English. "I am here in Manaus looking for my sister, Linda Stokes. She has been kidnapped, and I'm thinking the kidnappers took her out of Manaus by air. I need to speak to the manager."

He frowned. "There is no possibility that a kidnapped person could be flown from Manaus."

"But maybe there is. Could I please speak to the manager?"

He picked up the phone, and spoke in rapid Portuguese.

When he hung up he said, "The manager suggests that you go to the police. I can give you directions."

She smiled, one of her best, most disarming and innocent smiles. "I'm sure I understand. The manager is of course a busy man. I hope it will be okay with you. I will just take a seat and wait until he can see me."

She moved to a row of battered armchairs covered in an icky green plastic, sat and then smiled once more at the flummoxed receptionist. She had been sufficiently pleasant, but she was also sure that he understood that she would wait here in the lobby to see the manager until Manaus froze over.

Twice when other men came in and noticed her and then chatted with the receptionist she heard him mention Linda's name and hers. One of the men even stopped and said in English, "I am so sorry about your sister."

It took an hour of sweating in the minimally air-conditioned office, but finally the mustachioed receptionist said, "The manager can see you now. Five minutes only." She wondered how many people the manager might have contacted about her visit during that hour, especially ones not on the side of the law.

Chapter 16

Nova's chat with the airport manager turned out to be singularly uninformative. He'd already told everything he knew to the local police and to Brazilian federal authorities. No flights out had included passengers that fit the description of the kidnap victims.

She asked about charter flights. All had been accounted for. None carried Americans.

He barely gave her the five mentioned minutes. A large clock on the wall next to the café that looked like a McDonald's said it was now one o'clock. She strode through the cavernous lobby toward the street exit, caught herself and headed for the outside baggage area. It wouldn't hurt to ask more questions and spread further the news that she would pay money for information. She wondered if the FBI guys were having any better luck.

The first two baggage handlers spoke only Portuguese.

She made no obvious progress, although she received genuine smiles. She spotted three more men in similar blue uniforms loitering and smoking a bit farther down the concrete. Halfway to them, a similarly dressed man with gray hair at his temples caught up to her. He took her elbow and pulled her into a doorway where, she supposed, they couldn't be seen.

"You take taxi to big white Assembly of God church on Avenida Constantino Nerv," the man said. "Wait in the Café Maria that faces the church. Bring dollars."

He left her standing in the doorway, just sped away toward the street exit. She noticed that the sky was starting to darken toward the south, and based on previous experience that meant rain might be on the way. Just great, she thought. More humidity.

The boulevard Avenida Constantino Nerv ran from the airport into the town center. The taxi ride to the distinctive Assembly of God church took maybe fifteen minutes. The Café Maria couldn't be missed. At two forty-five, she went inside, purchased coffee and stood to drink it at one of several tall round tables. The man came in, ordered a coffee and then asked in Portuguese loud enough to be overheard if he could share the table with her.

In a much lower voice he quickly said, "You are a very pretty lady. It is dangerous for you to be asking questions."

"You mentioned money. I was hoping you had information about my sister."

"For fifty dollars I can tell you something valuable. But I think…I have come also to warn you. Men involved in illegal things are not happy you asking questions. Not pleased you paying money."

"What kind of illegal things? Drugs? Contraband electronics? Kidnapping?"

"Can you pay me fifty dollars?"

"If you have information, useful information, I will pay."

"A charter plane came to the airport the night of kidnapping. It left the same night. You will find no record. Money has been paid to keep mouths closed."

He pushed his napkin toward her. She fished into her bag and slipped two twenties and a ten under it, which he quickly retrieved. He gave her a last look with a warm, fatherly smile. "You will not find your sister here, and this place is dangerous for you."

He slugged down the last of his coffee, and left. At two forty-five, when she stepped out of the shade of the Café Maria onto the busy traffic artery, the heat slammed her as if someone had dropped a hot iron onto her chest. She felt a slight drizzle from the black sky, indicating that it would rain within minutes.

Her BlackBerry jiggled; it was set high enough that she could feel its signal right through the woven bag. "It's me," Oscar said. "Let's meet as soon as you can. I have some new information."

"Fine. I'm free. Where?"

"Internet café. Not far from your hotel. Three blocks down, at *Rua 24 de Maio.*"

They agreed to meet in twenty minutes. She hailed a taxi. When they made the turn off the Avenida Constantino Nerv to head into downtown, she checked behind for Joe. She didn't see his car, but noticed an ancient, tan Chevy Bronco.

Two blocks later, the Bronco was still there.

"Turn right. Here! Now!" she said firmly to the driver.

"It's not the way."

"Just turn right, please."

The driver took the next right and she looked behind. The tan Bronco followed.

"Go left at the next street."

The driver, puzzled, looked at her in his rearview mirror.

"Just go left, please."

The tan Bronco followed for a block. But then it turned off.

"I can go to the Internet café?" the driver asked.

"Yes," she said. *"Obrigado."*

When they passed her hotel at 3:10, she checked behind once more. Her heart skipped a nervous beat at the sight of the tan Bronco. The drizzle had strengthened into a typical Amazonian rain—big, heavy, warm drops.

When the taxi stopped in front the Internet café, the Bronco kept going. Two men with heavy beards and Western-style cowboy hats kept their eyes straight ahead, but she stamped their faces deep into memory. She also text-messaged Joe: Hope U R on me. Did U C tan Bronco?

She dashed through the door of the Internet café. The young male attending the counter gave her a thorough once-over but said nothing as he gestured for her to help herself to a computer. She spotted Oscar and plunked her bag on the counter next to his booth and took a seat. The booths immediately next to them on either side were unoccupied. She logged on to the Internet to check e-mail.

"I thought you ought to know," Oscar began, "that more ransom demands were sent to the families of the other hostages. All received messages saying their loved ones could be saved by the U.S. government and telling them to contact their senator and the office of the vice president to ask that the ransom be paid."

She had stared so often at the faces of the hostages that for a moment a mental gallery of their photos flashed through her mind: the Bennings, dressed in black tie and holding hands; Kiff and Obst, the two great birders; the insect scientist, searcher for subtle truths about the world—she imagined Dennis Chu in a museum room surrounded by boxes and boxes of preserved and labeled insects; the two teen boys, Ronnie and Alex, at the beginning of lives that held so much promise; and her supposed sister Linda and Linda's friend from grade school, Annette. She knew enough about Linda, a soft-spoken librarian, whose two great loves were birds and helping the elderly by bringing them Meals-on-Wheels, that she did not find it hard to simulate love and concern for Linda. And then there was her fellow artist, Colette Stone, a painter of birds, a lover of nature.

To Oscar she said, "The focus on the vice president almost makes me think it might not be just about money. Maybe there's some political grudge motive as well."

"There is some good news. The first hostage was to be killed today at noon. The negotiators got them to delay a day. But there will be no further delays. Pay up or hostages start dying, the first one tomorrow at noon."

Who would it be? Was there any hope of finding all of them before tomorrow noon? Or would life end too soon for one of them?

She told him about the appointment to pick up the machete. She explained about the kidnappers speaking Guarani and about the unlisted charter in and out. "The hostages are clearly long gone from here." She didn't bother to voice her great fear, that the hostages might have been split up into separate locations.

She heard his computer signing off. He said, "There is another bit of bad news. It seems that one of the teen boys, Alex Hill, is a diabetic. His family is horribly distressed. He is type II. Must watch his food intake and exercise carefully. They say the boy had with him on the *Fiesta* a bag with both insulin and glucagon pills and candy bars and juice and some sugar-testing gizmo. It's a kind of diabetic's travel kit. The police didn't find it. Maybe they let him take it along."

"Damn. He's the grandson of one of our Supreme Court justices. She must be going out of her mind."

"I have a teenage boy. I know how I would feel if this were my son. Words do not describe it." Oscar stood. "You keep in touch, before and after the meet for the machete. Do you want me to arrange to get you out to Rio tonight or tomorrow?"

"Tonight. Time is running out for that next hostage. Make it a flight for two. Me and my backup."

Oscar left. On the computer she'd signed onto she checked her e-mails: Star and Deirdre and even one from Penny assuring her that Diva missed her. God, they all seemed distant by ten thousand miles and a thousand years.

At 3:40 she stepped outside again. The rain, hard but brief, had stopped. The heat of the computers made even the modestly air-conditioned Internet café hot and humid. She imagined that the lifespan of a computer in this climate must be pitiful.

No taxi passed. Besides, her hotel was only a five-minute walk. She took off at a stroll. She had nothing to do until her seven thirty meeting. She text-messaged Joe: Going 2 hotel 2 wait.

Would he come and spend the hours from now until seven thirty with her? Being alone with him in what was essentially a bedroom was dangerous. But that's what she wanted.

Chapter 17

Nova wasn't in her hotel room more than five minutes when Joe called on their secure line. "Did you ever see the tan Bronco?" she asked immediately.

"Yep. Had two raunchy-looking guys wearing cowboy hats, right?"

"That's the one."

"They were definitely following you. I did send their license plate to our local guy, Oscar. He can sic the FBI onto them."

"You'd like Oscar. He's arranging a private flight out for us tonight, as soon as I get the machete. He'll work on the lead. But knowing who these local guys were isn't likely to be useful. They're just thugs hired to keep the lid on any local leaks. This operation was planned and is being driven from elsewhere. No one here is going to know diddly-squat."

She waited for him to ask if he could come up. The

silence stretched out for an uncomfortably long moment. Was he waiting for her to ask him to come up? She wasn't going to do it. Asking him up would send all the wrong messages.

"So, are you going to wait in your room?" he asked.

She paused, then said, "Right."

Another brief—much briefer—pause. "I'll hang out down here. There are plenty of ways I can kill time around this plaza."

She bit her lip, disappointed, and then told him she'd leave for the church at twenty minutes to seven. "It's a ten-minute walk. I'll be at the church in plenty of time."

"I'll be on you," he said. He chuckled. "Oops. Didn't mean that the way it sounded."

"Jeez, Joe."

He hung up.

At two minutes to seven, she walked into a small, dimly lit sanctuary built like most Catholic churches with an altar at the front, small naves along the sides and two banks of wooden benches separated by an aisle down the middle. She inhaled the familiar odor of scented candles and furniture polish. The simple stained glass window showed Mary ascending into Heaven, her smile sweet and forgiving.

Nova took a seat on the aisle in the back-row pew on her left, sliding in far enough that someone could sit beside her without having to cross over her. Two chandeliers with dim lightbulbs provided most of the sanctuary's illumination, but votive candles also flickered here and there in the naves and near the altar.

Only two other people were evident, both black-shawled elderly women, one on the aisle directly in front of Nova but near the room's center and one just four rows in front of Nova but on the other side of the aisle.

She waited. Noting that her breathing was rapid, she sucked in a deep breath to slow it and her heart rate down.

The door behind her creaked, and she heard soft footsteps. She resisted the urge to check behind to see who had come in, and moments later Angelo Santiago took the seat on the aisle. He laid a long, slender object covered in what looked like a red mechanic's rag on the seat between them, his hand solidly holding down his end.

From her bag she pulled out the fifty twenty-dollar bills, wrapped in a napkin from her hotel's bar and held together by a rubber band. She slipped the money down the bench.

"Do you need to count it?" she asked in a whisper.

Before he could answer she heard the creak of the door behind her. This time instinct caused her to turn toward the sound. The two men from the Bronco, now without hats, stepped inside. Both drew guns as they approached what they probably thought was a silly American woman and an unskilled laborer.

Angelo Santiago snatched up the packet of cash.

In one smooth motion, Nova rose into a crouch, shifted the rag-wrapped machete onto the floor under the bench, and knocked Angelo down as a shot rang out. Wood splintered in the back of the bench in front of him. She jumped onto the bench and launched herself toward both thugs, both hands out and her eye on their gun hands. She pushed their gun hands upward as the force of her weight brought all three of them to the floor. The women were screaming.

Nova grabbed onto one man and rolled with him. His buddy leaped to his feet, shouting something in Portuguese and waving his gun at them, trying to get a clean shot at Nova without hitting his partner.

With her left hand, she grabbed the gun hand of the man now below her and with her right, she delivered a breath-crippling blow to the man's windpipe. As he went limp, she quickly rolled him as another shot from the standing man rang out and the man in her grip took the bullet meant for her. It struck him in the back.

A booted kick to her side sent an electric shock of pain to her heart and stopped her breathing. She scrambled to her knees and tackled the legs in front of her. If she didn't get him down, his next act would likely be to send a bullet into her head. She sucked in a breath as he tumbled backward to the floor.

Another pair of legs—Joe in jeans—appeared beside her attacker's head. Joe stepped on the wrist of the man's gun hand. The man howled in pain as Joe ground his foot into the wrist. Joe then stooped and took the man's gun.

"I could have taken him," Nova said, as she pushed to her feet, sucking in another breath that made her side hurt again. The pain didn't seem to be sharp enough to signal a cracked rib, but she was going to have a horrid bruise.

"Of course. But I have to be useful now and then." Joe gave her that big, heart-stopping grin.

She checked the pew and the room. Angelo was long gone.

Joe flipped her attacker onto his belly. "Hands behind your back," he said in Portuguese.

Given that Joe was holding a persuasive Glock, the man readily complied.

They needed to get out and quickly. Joe pulled a plastic security tie from a pocket and knelt to bind their bad guy. The two elderly women, having sufficiently recovered from shock to get their feet into gear, shuffled out the door. A priest was scurrying toward them from the front of the sanctuary.

"Let's get out of here without questions," Joe said.

She snatched the machete from under the pew, and the

two of them rushed outside. Maybe a dozen people hovered, hesitant but also curious.

"This way," Joe said.

She followed him to the rented Toyota.

He turned the ignition. "Where to?"

"Start for the airport. I'll check with Oscar."

When she reached Oscar by cell, she told him the police should pick up a body and a prisoner in the church. He explained that a charter plane was waiting at the airport to take her and her backup to Rio.

"Obrigado, Oscar," she said. "For everything."

"Boa sorte!" he said. "May God help you find your Americans before another one dies."

"We'll need a lot of luck," she replied. "Only fourteen hours until their killing deadline, and I can't imagine that any amount of negotiation will persuade them to cancel this one."

Chapter 18

At nearly one o'clock, Leila unlocked the door to her condominium. Nova followed the CIA head of station inside with Joe following. "I'm perfectly happy to have you both crash here," Leila said, dropping her keys onto a yellow-and-blue-butterfly cloth covering the top of a small cabinet by the entry. A fresh lemony scent lingered in the air. "It's too damn early in the morning for you to be checking into a hotel anyway when I have a guest room and comfortable couch."

They had lost some time coming to the condominium while waiting for a fingerprint expert to come to the CIA's lab and take the machete off their hands. At the airport, Leila had said, "We'll get this to the fingerprint tech first thing tomorrow. Six o'clock. It's pointless to go there tonight. No one will be there to lift any prints until morning."

Six in the morning wasn't much more than six hours

away, but waiting even one extra hour, let alone six, to get the experts working on their best clue had troubled Nova.

"Are you certain it's out of the question to call your main fingerprint guy and ask him to come in now and get started?" she'd asked as tactfully as possible. "They're threatening to kill a hostage at noon tomorrow. Actually, that's today."

After a brief pause, Leila made a call, and when they arrived at the CIA offices, a chubby man with sleepy eyes and a coffee cup in his hand greeted them at the lab door. He would look for prints and, if he found any, digitize them and send them off to the FBI, Interpol, and several other places. He smiled but said little as he took their package.

Now, as Joe sat his overnighter on the floor, Leila said, "I'll fetch some bedding." To Nova she said, "Make yourself comfortable in the same room you had before. I'll lay out towels and stuff in the bathrooms. Nora's room has its own bath, Joe, but there is a small one off the kitchen you can use. It has a shower."

Nova stood way longer than necessary in the hot shower followed by a cool rinse. She'd tossed her khaki slacks, the cotton top and her underwear in a heap on the floor. To be able to hear sounds in the condo, she left the bedroom door slightly ajar. This was surely unnecessary, given who Leila was and the tight security on the building, but years of experience had developed protective habits. It was always better to be as much in contact with your surroundings as possible. The sooner warned, the sooner armed.

She preferred to sleep nude, but she usually brought along something, in this instance a red, spaghetti-strap nightie that folded into something not much larger than a handkerchief. She slipped it on, thinking that if for some reason she would have to get up in the night or if her hostess should for some reason come into the room, she didn't want Leila to be embarrassed to find her guest *au naturel*.

Nova was standing next to the bed when the door opened. She turned, and Joe stepped inside and closed the door. Only a white towel covered the midsection of his tanned and chiseled body. His hair, still wet from a shower, gleamed.

Nova hugged her waist with one arm, her breathing suspended.

He walked to one of the room's windows and looked out at the nighttime view of Rio. The bedroom faced Ipanema Beach and the string of high-rise hotels that lined it. Between the buildings that made up the band of dazzling light lay the deep, velvet blackness of the Atlantic Ocean. "I thought I'd take a look at your view." He turned from the window and looked her over, tip to toe, nice and slow. "The view is superb."

That's when she noticed the condom package in his hand. He was a professional at many things, and one of them was the ability to slip into a condom so fast a woman hardly knew when it happened. "You shouldn't come in here dressed like that."

"Okay." He dropped the towel to the floor.

"Jeez, Joe." She shook her head. "You shouldn't have come in here at all."

Three steps and he had her in his arms. She shivered. He smelled faintly of lemon. He kissed her. Her legs felt shaky. She felt her judgment oozing like a lump of butter spreading on a hot skillet. He used his tongue to part her lips, and she let him inside. Then, after he'd pulled back and played long, lingering, delicious moments with her lips, all sanity fled and she slid her tongue into his mouth.

That was enough of a signal for Joe. He backed her to

the bed, sat her down, knelt in front of her and slowly spread her legs. Low in her body, that amazing fire struck.

She leaned back, knowing what was coming, longing for the pleasure that was coming. Warm hands slid up her outer thighs. He pushed up the nightie and spread her legs still more. As he bent to her, she put her hand on his wet hair. She could smell him strongly now, the scent of lemon soap, clean, fresh.

His fingers slid to the inside of her thighs and she sighed. "Oh, God, Joe. This is not good."

He spread her and his tongue licked.

I shouldn't let him do this.

But it was too late. The ability to reason departed to wherever it went when passion overrode it. She was hot all over, the pleasure starting to swell. "Oohhh. Yes."

The perfect licking continued. "Uh-huh."

He went slower, to make her linger, to build her up.

Then very fast.

She moaned as the world finally disappeared in a burst of throbbing heat that for a moment flashed through and shook her whole body.

"Good," he said.

He climbed onto the bed, lying beside her. With that skill that both amused and amazed her, he ripped open the condom package and had the damn thing on in no more than two heartbeats. "Come here," she said as she pulled him over her.

She watched his face every moment until he climaxed, remembering that she loved him and that it was he who had walked away. Not her.

As he always did afterward, he kissed her forehead and then her lips and finally both of her eyes before he went into the bathroom to get rid of the condom and bring her a warm washcloth.

"I still love you," he said as he lay beside her, his arm across her belly. "But I understand your feelings. Just consider this a bit of fun for old times' sake between good buddies, okay? Nothing to get serious over."

She couldn't think what to say. The man was maddening. She'd refused to marry him. He'd left her with not a goodbye or one further word in over six months. And now he'd made fabulous love to her, before announcing that, of course, they were just friends.

He left soon thereafter.

And she had the dream again. Panic overwhelmed her as she struggled to untangle her parachute lines, struggled to find a ripcord.

The smell of coffee pulled her out of the dream in time to avoid hitting the ground. Leila fed them juice, croissants, fresh guava and coffee. Joe said nothing and gave Nova no special smile or secret signal. Total zip. So it seemed that they were going to pretend last night's exchange of pleasure had never happened.

Since the fingerprint expert, Peete, had the machete, Leila had let them sleep late. Leila had checked with Peete at six and learned that he had found two prints. When they arrived at the CIA headquarters at ten, Peete still had no identification results.

Nova did her best to hide her disappointment and stifle a nagging sense of urgency. Waiting was one of the hardest parts of the work. Since the kidnappers had been speaking Guarani, a language used in Paraguay and second in usage in that country only to Spanish, Nova and Joe settled down with files on Paraguay: what were the main illegal operations going on there, where were they centered, who were the major players?

At twelve thirty, Leila fetched them into a conference

room where she joined them in consuming damn good take-out food: burritos and a fresh salad. Nova didn't enjoy a bite of what she forced down. It was quite possible one of her ten people—she thought of them as hers now—had already been killed.

And in the peculiar way that the subconscious mind works, the meaning of her bad dream had become clear in the middle of working on the Paraguay files. This nightmare she'd had from childhood had an almost ridiculously obvious meaning. It had nothing to do with anxiety about skydiving, something she was actually good at. It represented lack of control, her greatest fear. In the dream, the jump master was in control, setting the pace, forcing her when she wasn't ready. She wasn't in her comfort zone. Living in fear of Candido had been the beginning of the dream. Prison its continuation. And the fear of losing control in a marriage, even to Joe, had triggered it again. The moment she realized the dream's meaning she had thought, *Do we ever really escape from our childhood?*

As she half listened to Leila and Joe discussing soccer, she once again mulled over the dream's meaning. Just because she knew the cause didn't change, probably couldn't change, how she felt. Being married was never going to be an option for her. But maybe, just maybe, she could convince Joe to stay with her on her terms.

Peete strode into the room, his smile encouraging. "We have an identification from the Asuncion police. The prints belong to a low-level Paraguayan thug. Carlito Gomez. He has a long arrest record for petty stuff. He's employed by a man named Felipe Martinez. Martinez owns a big cotton ranch. Cotton is big in Paraguay and of course legal, but the authorities suspect Martinez of smuggling."

Nova felt a spark of hope warm her.

"Excellent, Peete," Leila said.

Peete laid a file on the table showing a photo of Gomez and two sheets of information.

"Anything else?" he asked Leila.

"No. And thanks for coming to work in the middle of the night."

He smiled. "Just get the pigs."

He left. Joe said, "So we're off to Paraguay?"

Leila stood. "I'll get tickets lined up, and by the time your drivers get you to the airport, the tickets will be waiting. Joe in coach, Nova in first class. I'll also arrange for you to meet our man in Asuncion. Separately, of course, at least in public. You are not to be seen in public together. Directions for where to meet him will be in the packets you'll receive at the airport."

As Nova settled into her car's backseat, she thought about the kidnappers' deadline. Twelve noon, tomorrow, they would kill someone. Maybe the negotiators would secure a delay.

She pushed that line of thought away.

No, better not to think she had more time than she really did. Better to keep focused on the thought that they only had twenty-four hours reprieve to find the hostages or lose at least one of them. The pressure was on.

Chapter 19

The winter's first snow had arrived last night and a soft white blanket covered cars, signs and the branches of trees. Suleema's driver braked the black Cadillac sedan to a halt beside a row of cars parked in front of Andre's Salon, three blocks east of the entry to the National Zoo.

From the backseat, Suleema opened her door and stepped out. "I'll call you when I'm ready to be picked up," she said, then closed the door.

Her driver zipped the window on the passenger side down and leaned across the seat toward her. "You want me to pick up your cleaning before I find some place to park?"

Sam was a dear, no doubt about it. "Yes, please, Sam. That's very thoughtful."

She bit her tongue to keep from begging him to stay right in front of the salon and keep an eye out for anyone with a shiny bald head and an earring in one ear. The last three days of hell had crawled passed. Three days of worry about Alex. Three days in which she had not told anyone of the threat to Alex's life or her own.

From moment to moment she swung between panic and dread. Her heart would race. She felt suffocated. She could not escape from feeling guilty. She thought she might explode from holding it all in, from pretending that she knew nothing, but the news about the kidnapping had got only worse. And the more details she and the family learned, the stronger grew her compulsion to protect Alex at all costs.

Whoever these monsters were, they did in fact have her grandson. Half her mind urged her to inform the FBI and the Marshal's Office that she was being blackmailed. The other half said that what little she could tell them wouldn't be useful. The authorities would either find Alex and the others or they wouldn't. But if these manipulative, sadistic criminals kept their word, her vote, to be announced in only five more days, might keep him alive.

If she voted the way they wanted.

She realized, like waking from a dream, that she was still standing motionless on the snow-covered sidewalk. She trudged up the four steps to Andre's entry. The silver bell on the door jingled as she strode inside, where smells of perfume, shampoo, nail polish and coffee assaulted her. As Andre himself hurried toward her, she hung her coat and scarf on the coatrack.

"Well, Sulee," he said, a genuinely warm smile on his tanned face, "come right on in. I'm ready for you."

All of the hairdressers, four women and four men, smiled or waved a comb or curling iron as she moved between the two banks of stations. Doris Madsen, the head of the Children's Zoo, always had her appointment at this same time. Doris smiled and called out, "Don't you just love the season's first snow?"

Suleema forced a smile to her lips and nodded.

"Coffee?" Andre asked.

"Yes, please."

He waved his hand and one of the two hair washers, Suzie, hurried to fetch a cup. Suzie knew that Suleema took it black. As Andre draped Suleema's shoulders with a glitzy gold and silver cape he said, "Just relaxing and a trim. Or shall we consider a bit of a style change?" He ran his fingers over her chin-length hair and lifted its edges.

Suzie handed her the black coffee.

"The usual. Nothing fancy."

The doorbell jingled. Glancing in the mirror toward the entry, she spied a young woman with long, wavy, bright-red hair looking around, searching. The young woman's gaze stopped on Suleema. She approached. Andre turned toward her. "May I help you?"

The young woman held out an envelope to Suleema. "This is for you," she said. "It's an early Christmas present."

Suleema took the plain white envelope, noting that her name had been written in a pleasant script on the front. "Is this from you?"

The young woman smiled. "No. I'm just to give it to you." She smiled at Andre. "Thanks," she said. She turned and headed for the door.

"Wait," Suleema called out. But the redhead left as quickly as she'd come.

"Well," Andre said, propping one hand on his hip. "That's different."

Suleema slipped her middle finger under the flap and tore the envelope open. Inside was a plain white card folded in half. She opened it.

> You Shouldn't Have Opened This Card
> It Could Have Been A Letter Bomb

She snapped the card closed, fearing that Andre might be looking over her shoulder, and slid it back into the envelope, her hands shaking.

"Are you okay, Sulee?"

"Yes, yes, of course. It's from a friend. What a nice gesture."

She could not have described what happened during the remainder of the hour and a half she was in the shop if her life had depended upon it. The minute she stepped outside, before she entered the car, she stood in falling snow and read the full note.

> You Shouldn't Have Opened This Card
> It Could Have Been A Letter Bomb
> I Can Reach You Wherever I Want
> Continue To Keep Your Mouth Closed

The last line chilled her even more than the words Letter Bomb. "Continue to keep your mouth closed," it said. "Continue." She was certain now that someone in the government, someone who wanted the government to prevail in Sharansky and who was sufficiently high up to know whether or not she had informed anyone in authority, was responsible for Alex's kidnapping.

Chapter 20

Joe had been running on adrenaline since arriving in Manaus, so it didn't surprise him when the flight attendant had to wake him up upon their arrival in Asuncion. He'd crashed into a deep sleep the minute the plane reached cruising altitude out of Rio and turned for Paraguay.

Standing by his seat, he stretched, grabbed his overnighter and his laptop, and as he strode out of the plane, he wondered if he'd dreamed about Nova. He thought maybe he had. That also would not be surprising. After he had done the stupid thing of making love to her, he'd gone back into Leila Munoz's living room and kicked himself mentally all over the place. Christ. He wouldn't describe himself as a masochist, but only someone willing to get hurt again would have done something so stupid.

Outside the terminal, he snagged a taxi and directed the driver to the hotel and bar Tropica where he would meet their Asuncion contact. The American ex-pat owned the hottest bar in Asuncion and was also the CIA's man in town. Joe and Nova would both have rooms in the Tropica for the night.

See, there she was in his thoughts again! His mind just wouldn't let up on Nova. He wanted her. Hell, he still loved her, no doubt now at all about that. Six months hadn't begun to cure him.

And the thing was, the way she'd made love seemed to say that she loved him. His raw animal instinct told him that she hadn't been faking. What had passed between them was true passion, not just sex. And before this op was over, if she did love him, he would find out. And if she did, he would also find some way to convince her that he wasn't a threat, that marrying him would not rob her of her independence or freedom.

He stepped out of the taxi and paid the driver a buck—six thousand guarani.

One way or the other, I'm going to convince her to marry me.

The Tropica, a three-story building, occupied the center of a block in downtown Asuncion. Tiny balconies with iron railings hung outside the hotel's rooms on the second and third floors. At five thirty in the afternoon, the place looked dead.

He tried the door, found it unlocked and strode inside. To his left was a reception desk. His objective was the bar. He turned right, through the door that led into a room where alcohol fumes were so strong a man might almost get drunk just whiffing. Chairs sat upended on most of the tables. Like virtually all bars seen in daylight, the room looked used and abused.

The most attractive Guarani girl he'd ever seen stood

on a small stage singing "The Night Was Meant for Lovers" in Spanish to the accompaniment of a single pianist. Her tiny, bright-yellow strapless dress looked to be plastered to her skin.

Four men, the only patrons, lounged at a table watching her. A first-rate voice matched her great body. A stray, bitter thought struck him. Here she was, a young, nubile, talented beauty, probably buried for life in this corruption-riddled, poverty-struck armpit. The thought shifted. Maybe she would find her way out of Paraguay. Or maybe she loved her country and her family and would never dream of leaving.

A muscle-bound stud wearing three heavy gold chains, one bearing a cross the size of a dollar bill, stood, legs apart, behind the bar wiping dry and then aligning glasses in neat rows. *"El jefe?"* Joe said.

Stud pointed toward the occupied table. The girl stopped singing and bent in earnest consultation with the pianist. Joe ambled to the table and delivered in English the words that would identify him to his contact as CIA for this op. "I'm looking for the Tropica's owner. I was told he could help an American in distress."

A rougher bunch of men Joe had never seen. If he didn't know that, in fact, one of them was his CIA contact, he could have walked into the weekly drug traffickers' meeting. Or maybe a confab of the kidnappers for which he was searching. All but one looked to be of Spanish or Guarani descent. Jeans and simple, sleeveless shirts that showed off the tattoos on their arms, perfect identifiers.

All were visibly drunk. Their eyes wavered, their necks held their heads unsteadily. A queasy feeling struck Joe. Unless one of these guys was acting, his contact could turn out to be more trouble than help. How long had it been since Leila Munoz, or anyone else from the Company, had met with their man in Asuncion?

Joe's training kicked in. He noted the most distinguishing tattoo of each. For the tall, thin one it was a triple-headed cobra rearing on his right forearm. The chubby one with the nasty scar on his right cheek had decorated his left bicep with barbed wire along which were strung some kind of flowers. A little guy with a sharp face had covered his entire left arm with shooting stars. And a magnificent wolf's head stared at Joe from the left bicep of the one Anglo in the pack. The Anglo, the Wolf, grinned and said, "What kind of distress can I help you with?" the reply that identified him as Joe's contact.

Cobra said, in a booming base voice, "Take a load off."

Unlike his forbidding appearance, Cobra's voice seemed friendly enough.

"Right. Sit yourself down," his contact, the Wolf, said, his words slurred.

The queasy feeling intensified. Joe deposited his over-nighter on the floor, his laptop on the nearest free table, took a chair down and joined them.

The girl called out something in Guarani. The Wolf shook his head and waved her to come over to the table. He pulled her onto his lap.

The Wolf, Joe noted, was around forty-five. His black hair had gone gray at the temples, and his gaunt face also had a two-day shadow with a lot of silver. He was tall and handsome, but tiny red lines around his nose and blood-shot eyes strongly indicated alcoholism. The girl, seen close up, couldn't be a day over eighteen. The Wolf kissed the back of her neck. Joe balled a fist against the urge the punch the lecher's lights out.

"My name is Joseph de los Santos," Joe said instead.

"Ramone Villalobos," the Wolf replied. "Call me Ramone."

Nova would be here in about one hour. She would likely be as disappointed in this dissolute contact as he was. "I'd like a room," Joe said, eager to find out whatever was essential from Ramone Villalobos, and then make an escape. "Right away if possible."

"Sure, sure," Ramone said. He shoved the girl off his lap and stood. "Cummon. I'll get you fixed up." He patted the girl's behind. To his buddies he said in English, "The singin's over. I'll see you later."

Joe picked up his luggage and followed Ramone Villalobos toward the reception desk.

Chapter 21

The dead jungle fowl—a rusty-red and glossy black cock with an impressive red comb—kicked its last. Its blood-spattered body lay in the dirt of Escurra's fighting pit, its gray feet sticking into the air.

The winning bird's owner rushed into the ring and snatched up his wild-eyed male. The win qualified the owner to be one of the lucky men to bring a game fowl to the big fights on Christmas Eve, only two days away. Betting during Escurra's famous Christmas Eve fights was always heavy, the winnings much more substantial than what the bird's owner would pick up tonight.

Tomas Morinigo Escurra rose, bored. He signaled Rodrigo and Juan to follow him. His main office was in his home, the Casa Grande, but for convenience he had turned two of the first rooms in the long shed that held the pen cages into a passably comfortable spot to spend time away from the house and the women. Fortunately, his wife and youngest daughter had gone with Felipe's wife, Escurra's oldest daughter, to New York. All three of the women in his life would be out of the picture until after New Year's.

Escurra kept a tight hold on the key to the shed office. Only he knew that built into its dirt floor was a safe holding two hundred and fifty thousand U.S. dollars, a kind of insurance. Over ten years ago he had dug out the hole right under his desk chair, mixed and poured the cement himself, installed the safe and thrown a rug down to hide the heavy wooden cover. But he didn't keep all his emergency reserves in one place. He kept the diamonds in the safe in his office in the Casa Grande.

A big man with wide shoulders and a beaked nose that fit his name from the fighting days—the Eagle—Escurra had purchased an especially outsized swivel armchair. He sank into it as Rodrigo slumped onto a battered armchair. Juan leaned against the wooden wall, crossed one ankle over the other, pulled out a toothpick and proceeded to work it over his gums.

"I've changed my mind," Escurra said to Rodrigo. "I was gonna have two Guarani men fight each other, but I did that last year. I got a great idea. I'm gonna have the black American kid fight a Guarani kid. Can you imagine that! The betting will be hot."

"I don't know, boss," Rodrigo said. Escurra knew that Rodrigo felt comfortable disagreeing with him occasionally on small things. After all, Rodrigo's brother, Felipe, had married Escurra's oldest daughter. After checking Escurra's face to be sure he wasn't stepping on his dick, Rodrigo continued. "Doesn't it figure that a Guarani of the same age as the Negro would whip the Negro's ass? Who would bet on the American?"

"Get me a beer," Escurra said to Juan, who immediately peeled himself from the wall and went to the ice chest. "You're wrong about that. The Guaranis are short. You haven't seen the American. He's tall. And heavier. And blacks are tough."

"Well, if you say so."

Escurra popped off the beer cap and swigged down a cold slug. "You and Juan steal me a Guarani kid tomorrow. Fifteen or sixteen years old."

"Okay."

The sound of a car motor intruded. Escurra waited, watching the door. Felipe came in. Pepe, one of Felipe's men, followed, both of them dressed in gaucho clothing and looking as if they had been out wrangling cattle. They smelled like it, too.

"Hey, *hermano*," Rodrigo said. The brothers exchanged a quick, intimate clasping of hands.

"Beers for everyone," Escurra said to Juan.

Juan hustled.

Escurra didn't like the frown on Felipe's face. "Why the fucking black look?" he asked.

Felipe sat down, took a beer but didn't open it. He just looked at Escurra with jittery eyes. Escurra's sense of something wrong strengthened. He waited, letting Felipe stew.

Finally, Felipe said, "We killed the first hostage, like you said. And the photos are on their way."

Felipe kept squirming. Escurra waited him out, feeding his subordinate's distress.

"The thing is, the Americans' tour guide leader got loose right afterward. He ran into the jungle. Pepe and Carlito and Luis went after him. Pepe had to kill him."

Escurra leaned forward, palms down on his desk. Fucking idiots! "My orders were that no one was to touch a hair on the head of any of the Americans without my permission."

Felipe grew even more frantic. "But he ran into the jungle, Tomas."

Escurra looked hard at Pepe. "Did Felipe explain my orders to you?"

Pepe, who had also been given a beer and who had opened it, now let his arm drop. He didn't seem able to find his tongue.

Felipe said, "They couldn't let the bastard escape."

Escurra swiveled his attention back to Felipe. "You really think some soft American could escape through the jungle?"

No smart comment came back from Felipe since the idea was obviously stupid.

Escurra looked back at Pepe. "Who killed him and how?"

Finding speech at last, Pepe said, "We, I, had to stop him."

"So instead of running him down, or tracking and cornering him, you shot him? You shot my valuable hostage?"

"Yes, Señor Escurra. I'm sorry."

Sorry wouldn't teach Escurra's other men to follow his orders without question. Escurra opened the center drawer of his desk, put his hand on the butt of the Colt .45 he kept there, pulled it out and placed a shot in the center of Pepe's chest.

At first, Pepe simply looked surprised. Then he dropped the beer and then dropped to the floor himself.

Felipe jumped to his feet, his face red. The gaze he turned onto Escurra could strip skin off had it been a knife. "Fuck you, Tomas. I've known Pepe since I was five years old. All he did was make a mistake."

"What you need to understand, Felipe, is that everyone

is useful. Brilliance is in knowing how to use a man. Don't forget that! My orders are never to be disobeyed." Escurra looked to Juan. "Go outside and close the door. Tell everyone at the cockfight that we were just fooling around and I shot a hole in the floor by mistake. But you tell my men exactly why Pepe won't be around any more."

He put the gun back into the desk drawer. Tomorrow he might use it for target practice before he had Juan clean it.

"Sit down, Felipe! Rodrigo, haul this body out of here and stash it in one of the pens. Later tonight you and Juan can dump it in the river for the piranhas."

To Escurra's satisfaction, Juan's, Felipe's and Rodrigo's faces were still rigid with a look of horror. All three would quickly spread around what the penalty was for disobeying the Eagle, a lesson Escurra had learned he needed to reinforce every now and then to keep the men in shape.

Chapter 22

At seven o'clock, a taxi let Nova off in front of the Tropica. She was running behind schedule; her flight out of Rio had been delayed an hour and forty-five minutes. Several bad experiences had taught her that air travel within every South American country was never reliable, but that didn't prevent frustration when it happened.

No longer fuming but still churning over the loss of time and anxiety for the hostages, she stomped into the building and up to the reception desk. Mercifully, the humidity here seemed to be half that in Manaus. "Do you have a room for me?" she asked. "My name is Nora Smith."

"Yes, yes," said a sleepy-eyed, sixty-year-old man.

He slid a registration book to her, along with a pen. She slid her passport across to him on the counter and he placed it in a file for passports before turning to the wall behind him. He fetched a key from the message box for room 302 and passed it to her.

A teenage Guarani boy materialized from somewhere. He snatched up her overnighter and was about to take her shoulder bag when she shook her head and smiled at him. His return smile showed beautiful white teeth against his dark brown skin. The desk clerk said, "Ms. Smith, our owner waits for you in his office. The boy can take your bag to your room. I will show you to the office."

The man led her down a hallway toward the back of the building. He stopped at a closed door and knocked. "Come in," said a baritone voice in English.

The receptionist headed back to his post. She opened the door and stepped inside.

Joe and another man sat opposite each other and sideways to her. She felt oddly comforted simply at the sight of Joe. But when the two men turned her way, her heartbeat came to a full stop.

"Well, I'll be damned," said Ramone Villalobos.

She blinked, a reflex to determine if she was hallucinating.

"I was getting very worried about you," Joe said.

His words registered, but her tongue remained frozen, her mind stunned. She couldn't think what to say.

Joe tried again. "You're almost two hours late."

"Fancy meeting you here," Ramone said.

He was still handsome. Tall and erect. He wore cowboy boots and jeans and she noted that he now had a tattoo on his arm, a wolf's head. She couldn't find her voice, the shock of seeing this bastard was too great. The room felt like it had fallen into suspended animation.

Joe leaned toward her. "Are you all right?"

That voice she loved finally broke through the shock barrier. "Yes. Perfectly fine." She looked at Ramone, hoping he got the message. She was perfectly fine.

She noted now that Ramone's eyes were bloodshot and his cheeks gaunt. Maybe the years hadn't been kind to him. Maybe he hadn't sailed through them all too well. After all, he'd ended up working for the Company in Asuncion, Paraguay. How rewarding for a lifetime of service could that be?

He held a coffee mug and used it to point to another big chair next to Joe. "Sit yourself down, Nova. I had no idea they were sending you. Quite a coincidence, no?"

The CIA deputy director, Claiton Pryce, whom she strongly suspected had been involved in choosing her for this op, knew a lot about her past. He certainly knew from her files that Ramone Villalobos had recruited the fresh-out-of-prison Nova Blair to work for the Company. Pryce also knew that Villalobos was a womanizer who had dropped out of her life within that same year. Did Pryce know that Ramone had dropped out after convincing her to love and trust him? Pryce couldn't know that Nova had been haunted in her dreams for years by futile searches to find Ramone, to make him love her, to heal the wound to her trust, but Pryce knew that sending her to Asuncion would throw her into Ramone's presence. Maybe Pryce didn't know that she and Ramone had been lovers, but still, she should have been told that he'd be here.

Ramone had been the last man she'd trusted. Until Joe. She trusted Joe, but in his own way he'd also let her down. In the end he couldn't accept her as she was. Seeing Ramone stirred up old memories and fears.

Joe stood. "You look like you need a hit. It isn't cappuccino, but it's damn good coffee." He strode to a table where a sleek coffee brewer stood.

She took the chair Ramone had indicated, noting that the office at least was neat and welcoming in a male sort of way. The dark wooden furniture and desk were finely made from Brazil's beautiful jacaranda. She scanned the walls and not surprisingly found tasteful wildlife prints of raptors and big cats. That had been another shared love he had used to seduce her—her love of nature.

She turned to accept the coffee from Joe and the photograph behind Ramone's desk caught her eye and froze her again. *The Girl and the Bees.* One of her earliest photos that had appeared in *National Geographic* and won several awards years after Ramone had taken off. And here it was, behind his desk.

She studied him. Even under his deep tan she could tell that he was blushing.

The whole scene struck her as surreal and she laughed, a sharp, bittersweet chuckle.

Joe sat again. He checked her face and then Ramone's. "So, you two know each other?" he asked.

"A long time ago," Ramone said. "Nova and I worked together in her first op for the Company."

"Ah," Joe said, and then took a long sip from his coffee.

This wasn't where the conversation ought to be. "What do you have for us?" she said to Ramone.

"Two sources said that Gomez still works for Felipe Martinez on Martinez's legitimate enterprise, the big cattle and cotton spread, but no one has actually seen Gomez for quite a while. So the tie to Martinez might not be as strong as we've been thinking. The ranch is located roughly a ten-minute drive outside of Ciudad del Este, on the Paraguay side of the Paraguay/Brazil border. We don't know if Martinez involves any part of the ranch in his weapons smuggling. The entire ranch operation may be legit."

"I've got some ideas about tomorrow," Joe said. "How long will it take us to get over there?"

"I've arranged a private flight for us tomorrow at first light. We'll have rooms in a place I've used before in Ciudad del Este. The *Loro Azul*. The Blue Parrot. Do you know that Martinez is married to the daughter of Tomas Escurra?"

The big rancher? "Tomas Morinigo Escurra?" she said. She looked at Joe, who shook his head. Apparently this little tidbit had not been in any of the material they'd been given.

"That's him. Escurra is the crime boss of this whole region. Like Martinez, but he's into cotton and cattle and a bunch of other legitimate things as well. Five years ago, Martinez married his oldest daughter."

To the picture she had sketched in her mind—that Gomez worked for Martinez and so Martinez had been pulling the strings of the kidnapping—she did a quick redrawing. The scope of the op must expand at once to include Escurra. They had another cup of coffee. Escurra's place, Ramone said, was a half-a-million-acre minikingdom slashed out of jungle on the Brazilian side of the tri-border area, not far from Iguazu Falls.

She looked at Joe. "I have a good friend who is the manager of The Royal Hotel Iguazu. Right at the falls. Brazilian side. Fabulous views." She looked back to Ramone. "I've checked and Bebe still works there. The first thing I want to do is talk to him. Bebe knows everything going on and everybody who is anybody in the area."

"I'm bushed," Ramone said. She wasn't surprised. His bloodshot eyes made her suspect a very practical reason for why he'd been drinking coffee when she arrived, instead of his favorite, bourbon.

"I've given you separate rooms on the third floor, but there is a connecting door if you want to talk further," Ramone added.

She checked the sturdy antique clock on his desk. Ten fifteen. Joe had not had much sleep the last few days, so he probably also wanted to hit the sheets.

Ramone set his coffee mug on an end table with a click of closure. "I'll have the man at the desk wake you both at five."

This was always hard for her, having to let others go into that other world, the one of dreams, while she stayed awake for many hours more. It always felt lonely. In prison, though, she'd learned how to work her peculiarity to her advantage. She lived a second life. While they slept she would exercise. Then she would read further into a novel written in Moroccan Arabic, Leila Abouzeid's *The Last Chapter*, the story of a young Moroccan woman's struggle to find her identity in the late twentieth century. Nova read and spoke nine languages now, and keeping them fresh took time.

She and Joe left Ramone's office separately, five minutes apart. Still shaken by Ramone's presence again in her life, she wanted to put herself as far away from him as possible while she regrouped her emotions.

She had barely had time to get out of her clothes and start running a bath when she heard a knock on the connecting door to Joe's room. She wrapped herself in a big blue towel. "Come on in, Joe."

Chapter 23

Joe opened her door and peeked inside. Nova checked that her towel was securely wrapped. He stepped in, leaving the door between their rooms ajar. "So what's with you and Villalobos?" he asked.

Nova knew exactly what he wanted to know—and it wasn't his business. "Like Ramone said, we worked my first op together. It didn't go well."

"What was the op?"

"Drug ring." Not only wasn't she going to share with Joe how she'd been tricked into love and into working for the Company, she'd also been tricked, or forced, into killing two drug-crazed men intent on killing her. That op had made her a three-time killer. Since then she'd done a lot of good, but she thought a shrink might claim that a deep need for redemption was a big part of the drive behind all her work for the CIA.

Psychobabble could be interesting, but it didn't change anything.

Joe threw himself into one of the room's two comfortable armchairs.

She said, "I'm getting ready for a shower."

"Villalobos thought you looked great. I could see it in his bloodshot eyes."

She smiled and took the other chair. "What do you think? Alcoholic?"

"Yep. Although he did start drinking coffee the minute I arrived, right after he'd patted the bottom of a luscious Guarani girl who might have been eighteen."

Ah. Trying to make Ramone look like a bad, lecherous old man suggested a bit of jealousy. "Do you think his drinking will make him a liability?"

"Can't tell yet. So, you going to see your friend Bebe first thing tomorrow, right?"

"As soon as I can. And you don't need to follow me. No one here knows anything about me and I figure the sister cover isn't any use here. We know who the bad guys are. So I'm just a woman visiting a friend."

"Fine, I'll take the direct approach. I go out to Martinez's place, show my journalist credentials and ask for an interview on money laundering and terrorism. Butter him up. Tell him people in town say he knows everything and so on."

"Someone may have died already. Someone else tomorrow. It's more efficient if we split up. I feel sick if I let myself think about it."

They fell silent, she thinking about how much she should confide in Bebe. Joe interrupted. "So, you glad to see Villalobos again? Maybe it will go better this time."

"We need to depend on him more than I'd like. Alcoholics can be horribly unreliable."

"Women would find him hot, right?"

"Stop fishing, Joe." She stood. "I need to shower. And don't you need sleep?"

He hauled himself to his feet. "Okay." He left, closing the door.

Damn! She stared at the floor, and anger at Pryce, which had been on simmer, bubbled into boil. Pryce would be following every detail of this mission. He would have known that Ramone was here. Eleven o'clock in Asuncion meant it would be only ten o'clock in Washington, D.C. She'd prefer that it be twelve or one, some truly annoying hour in the morning.

She fetched her cell phone from the bag and dialed Claiton Pryce's private, secure line. He'd given it to her, one of the many reasons on Joe's list of arguments for why Joe just *knew* that Pryce carried a torch for her. "Pryce," he said.

"It's Nova."

"My God, Nova! Is something wrong?"

"You knew, didn't you, that Ramone Villalobos is our man in Asuncion?"

"What's wrong?"

The sincere distress in his voice shocked her. She regretted her haste in making this call. Pryce had no way of knowing how much seeing Ramone upset her. "I called because I need to know if a hostage was killed today."

"I'm sorry, but we don't know yet. Not likely to know until tomorrow. I've left word to be called the minute we learn of another death. Shall I contact you at that time?"

"No. I'm sorry to have called so late."

"Don't worry about it. I'm delighted to hear your voice. You may call me any time for any reason, Nova."

"I appreciate that. I sincerely do. Good night."

She hung up, shaking her head. Joe and Ramone, an

explosive combination, had triggered a truly unprofessional response from her.

"Get a grip," she said as she headed for the bathroom.

The next day she, Joe and Ramone arrived so early in Ciudad del Este that she had to fight her impatience and actually went to the Blue Parrot in person to check in. She called The Royal Hotel Iguazu. Bebe would not come in until nine o'clock. She ate breakfast and by nine o'clock found herself standing in front of and staring at one of the planet's great wonders.

Chapter 24

A breathless awe crept over Nova. Goose bumps prickled her skin. She had wondered in Rio if she would once again feel it or would she have grown blasé.

It was December twenty-third, two days before Christmas. In Nova's consciousness, Christmas meant twinkling snow, green fir trees draped with baubles and topped by a star, white steam on your breath, the scent of cinnamon in wine and maybe even sleigh bells. Six days ago in Steamboat Springs, she had been closer to Christmas than she was today. This place at the other end of the world from the cheery and crisp traditions of America and Europe could not have a less Christmassy feel.

But what magnificent beauty! Here, exposed to her, its closest point perhaps no more than three hundred yards away, lay the gushing primitive power of nature. A breath of misty air cooled her skin even in the ninety-degree heat.

Nothing in the world compared to this series of some two hundred and fifty falls draped in a curtain extending over three miles in breadth. The massive rush of water crashed downward two hundred feet in two tiers, to a reddish-tan river, and to Nova the ceaseless roar—day and night, never-ending—represented eternity itself.

Iguazu. The Guarani word for "great waters."

The falls were cloaked in jungle-green. At irregular intervals, a patch of tall trees peaked out from behind the water. If jungle covered some of the protruding black, rocky crags, others stood starkly naked in the midst of the torrent. A heavy cloud of white vapor hovered in the air above the lower river. During the rainy season the cloud grew thicker and rose yet higher.

A small, black tourist helicopter with yellow markings suddenly intruded, buzzing at about two hundred feet like a huge wasp across the top of the falls. Nova immediately remembered the time one of the helicopter pilots, after learning that she could fly such a craft, had let her fly his copter over that very route. The views of the sprawling river's approach to the abyss had been almost as spectacular as hanging above the water as it took its plunge over the edge.

Finally, her feet felt ready to move. Hurrying down the path to the left of the three-story, white, Spanish colonial-style hotel, she headed toward the main overlook. Three couples stood in rapturous poses, gazing at a phenomenon that, like the Grand Canyon or a major migration in the Serengeti, must be seen and felt to begin to comprehend.

She saw her first rainbow painted against the white mist and, darting like tiny black rockets flying through rainbow and mist, thousands of black swifts that came to feed on insects. For a moment she lingered in the pure luxury of this stupendous power. Longer would bring on guilt. She strode back toward the hotel's outdoor terrace and café.

The Royal Hotel Iguazu with its European decor was five-star: air conditioning, two swimming pools, four tennis courts, golf course, and all the personal amenities a rich traveler might demand. Some suites had Jacuzzi tubs and small private gardens with their own caged song birds.

Bebe had been the manager for at least fifteen years. She had met him and his wife and daughter ten years ago on a cruise to the Galápagos Islands. Nova had been twenty-four, and the cruise was her first time as a guide to the Ecuadorian islands made famous by Darwin. While snorkeling, Bebe's shy, fourteen-year-old daughter, Solange, had got into a sticky situation, and Nova had performed a minor rescue. Consequently, Solange had adopted Nova, following Nova everywhere and braiding her hair in the same French braid Nova wore at the back of her head.

Nova made her way across plush blue and gold carpets, past a pair of scarlet macaws littering the tile under their brass perch with peanut shells, to the reception area. The concierge, a young woman with dark Spanish eyes and fair skin, said that Bebe was expecting Nova and would be back to meet her in no more than five minutes.

Bebe returned just after Nova checked her watch for the fifth time in as many minutes. He rushed to her, clasped her in a bear hug, which, given his six-foot, two-hundred-pound frame, crushed the air right out of her.

"I am the happiest man in the world to see you, my dear little Nova."

"Hello again, Bebe. It's been three or maybe four

years." He hadn't changed. A Savile Row suit draped his hulking but solid frame beautifully.

He stepped back. "You are as beautiful as ever. This time married?"

She laughed. "No, Bebe. I've told you, I'm hopeless." His dark skin still had a healthy glow as did his coal black hair in spite of his age, which had to be about fifty.

"Never never are things hopeless. Come to my office." He guided her away from the desk. "Your message said you must see me urgently."

He at once offered her a cappuccino.

She grinned. "You still know how to get to this woman's heart."

Using an intercom, he ordered two cappuccinos, then settled behind his massive desk. Beaming he said, "You look extremely fit."

She'd worn white slacks with a silk, icy-pink spaghetti-strap top that left her shoulders and arms bare. Anyone could tell she worked out a lot.

He continued. "So now tell me, what is urgent?"

"First I want to ask how you and your family have been."

His smile drained away, his lips formed a sad, downward crescent. The twinkle in his eyes snapped out. "I lost Sonaria, Nova. She died suddenly two years ago. Ovarian cancer."

"My God, Bebe. She was too young."

"Only forty-four."

Beautiful, fun-loving Sonaria, Bebe's perfect soul mate. Nova didn't know many couples who were profoundly happy in their marriage. Too many, when you got behind the stage decoration, lived compromised lives that didn't match the public show. But not Bebe and Sonaria. Someone had once told her that a great love was a tragedy in the making. Eventually someone leaves, and the survivor's grief would be as profound as the love had been. "I am truly sorry for your loss. Solange must have been devastated."

The two cappuccinos arrived, delivered by the same young, dark haired woman.

"Solange is here, Nova. For Christmas. After we chat, you must see her. She adores you. She is finishing her last year of law school at Berkeley."

"I will, of course."

"But let us focus on now."

She talked, he sipped. "I'm going to be pretty honest with you, my old friend, but not totally honest. I ask you to trust me and let me tell you what I can. Please don't ask questions that I can't answer."

He smiled. "How very mysterious. I shall do my best."

"You know everything that goes on around here. As it turns out, a terrible thing has also happened to me. One of my sisters, Linda Stokes, has been kidnapped."

"Dear God!"

"Not here. Strangely enough, she was taken with nine other hostages from a boat in Manaus. They were on a birding trip."

"I did not know you had another sister." He waited, sipping again at his drink.

She ignored the comment, hoping Bebe would let it slide. "I went to Manaus and did some searching. I had a little help from the Brazilian authorities. One of the kidnappers is a man named Carlito Gomez and he's employed by Felipe Martinez."

Bebe's eyebrows shot up, but he said nothing.

"I also know that most of the kidnappers, maybe even all of them, spoke Guarani. This kidnapping was orchestrated here, Bebe. That's why I've come. I need your help. But I'll understand if you don't want to get involved. This could be dangerous."

"You know, life is very slow here at the falls. I've grown ever so comfortable with my days, not like when you took me to the Galápagos and you saved Solange. That experience taught me something, made me a better man, made me see that the world is a much bigger place than just Iguazu or even Brazil."

She sipped, he talked. "I've grown complacent in my comfort. And I see that people who come here and stay in the familiar comfort of this Western hotel don't grow much, while the ones who venture out do. We—I—don't get many opportunities to get out of the rut and grow. I'm eager to help. Besides, I owe you for saving Solange. But I don't quite understand how I can help. And what will you do if you find her?"

"Now that's one of the questions I can't answer."

A long silence followed as he studied her. He downed the last of his cappuccino. Bebe might have been born in an obscure part of the world, but she knew he read everything he could get his hands on and was as smart as they come. His guests were people from all over the globe, many in extremely powerful positions. That she wouldn't tell him what she intended to do he must consider as more than odd.

"What can I do? Of course I pride myself on knowing a great deal of the ins and outs of my world. But a kidnapping is quite something else. Information about such a thing would be closely held. Ten people taken? That is an enormous operation."

"Yes, but they're asking a huge ransom which, if paid, would be worth it."

"So your prime suspect is Martinez. Have you

considered that Martinez is very close to Tomas Escurra? Rumors, entirely unconfirmed and apparently unprovable, are that Escurra is the big crime boss here."

"I do know their connection. Martinez is the son-in-law. And it seems to me that Martinez wouldn't mount such a major operation without the big man being in on it."

Bebe frowned. "Don't be so sure. Martinez is also powerful and is thought to be his own man, despite the marriage. I think it might be a mistake to assume Escurra's involvement." He tapped his cup. "Do you want another?"

"No. Thanks."

He continued. "I know someone who works in the stable at the Martinez rancho. He owes me a favor or two. I shall contact him today. Have him do some snooping, ask some questions. Early tomorrow I may have something for you. Shall I call you?"

"Call as soon as the man has anything. The minute he does, Bebe. Time is critical. They might kill Linda. But we won't use the phone for details. I'll come here."

"You should know that many police around here are in Escurra's pockets. The chief is my friend. I know he wants to nail Escurra, but you may receive little help from the police if Escurra or Martinez is involved. Better to stay away."

"It's one of the reasons I so need your help and inside knowledge."

"Something else. Tomorrow night is Christmas Eve. Escurra throws an enormous fiesta every Christmas Eve at his hacienda. Everyone who's anyone comes. I myself have gone several times. The parties are great fun, music, dancing, food, fireworks. And on another part of the property, behind three very substantial guest houses—he has a fighting arena where he throws a party for his employees. Rumors are that the entertainment includes cockfights and dogfights. Maybe things much worse. It's an enormous drunken brawl, that's what I've heard. No one in polite society knows exactly who attends the 'outback' parties and no one asks." Bebe chuckled. "It's our local version of don't ask, don't tell."

"If you think of anything else, you will call me?"

"Of course. Before you leave, please, you must stop and talk to Solange. You will find her on the terrace. She was having a late breakfast. I told her you were here."

Nova stood. Bebe came around his desk, and they hugged. Bebe had the safe feeling of her real father. She tightened her grip. He wasn't her dear father, of course, but old feelings of love and security flooded her. "It's good to be with you again."

Doing a recon of the Escurra place was imperative. She retraced her steps to the terrace. She couldn't refuse to see Solange, but she must keep their conversation brief.

She had to ask a waitress to point out Solange Garcia. Stepping up to the young woman's table, Nova said, "Good heavens have you ever grown. I didn't recognize you, Solange. You must be six inches taller. You look like an Amazon."

Chapter 25

Solange jumped to her feet. Nova stood five feet, eight inches tall. Now grown into a beautiful, bronze-skinned Amazon, Solange had to be at least six foot two. Nova smiled to herself, thinking that two days ago she had been on the Amazon River and how most Americans who knew that name thought that Amazons came from South America. The fact was, early European explorers, familiar with Greek mythology, had thought they had glimpsed spear-and-bow-carrying women in the jungle—Amazons they had thought—and so they had named the river after these powerful women of Greek fame.

The Greeks had been fascinated with mounted women warriors from the Black Sea and a frieze depicting a Greek battle with Amazons even graced the Parthenon. In Greece and Turkey, Nova had visited the tombs of several such women: Penthesilea, Derinoe, Melanipe and Hippolyta.

Recalling that Solange's grandfather had come from Norway, Nova thought that might explain the girl's unusual Amazonian height.

"Papa said you were here." Solange's fully mature voice brimmed with pleasure. They hugged. "I just ordered coffee—but please, join me for lunch."

For a second Nova hesitated, a refusal on the tip of her tongue. She must go out to the Escurra place, but eating was necessary. She looked at her watch. Eleven thirty.

Nova took the chair opposite Solange. "I am so pleased to learn from Bebe that you are graduating from Berkeley Law. How wonderful."

"Did he tell you about Mama?"

"Yes. I'm profoundly sorry for your loss."

Solange gestured and a waitress hurried to their table. "A menu for my friend."

"I'm sorry but I'm rushed. Please order something they can put together quickly."

Solange ordered salads.

"Won't you have time to walk with me down to the falls?"

The falls' edge wasn't more than a short city block away. The roar and the mist once more made Nova feel like she had arrived at the throne of the Wizard of Oz. Solange continued as their salads arrived. "The butterflies simply overrun everything this time of year. Yesterday in one water puddle alone, I saw six different species drinking. I was on the path to the Isla San Martin overlook. Papa has told me you love to go there."

"I've had four transcendent experiences in my life, Solange. One in Grand Canyon. One in Africa. And twice here on the San Martin overlook."

Solange frowned. "What does *transcendent* feel like?"

"The overlook is halfway down to the river and very

close to the water. You feel your bones vibrating. It felt like I was being held in the arms of the goddess Gaia—a sense of mind-blowing power and largeness beyond anything I can put into words. I felt humbled, and at the same time I felt one with an immensely powerful force."

Nova forked down the salad as though a gun were at her back. In truth, the gun was at someone else's back. A glance at her watch. Eleven forty-five. If the kidnappers kept their word, in fifteen minutes a hostage would die.

"But I've been rude," Solange suddenly said. "I haven't let you explain why you are in such a hurry."

"I must ask you to keep what I say in secret."

"Whatever you say."

"I've lost contact with my sister. I believe she is somewhere here in the area of Iguazu, but I am sick with worry for her. I was hoping Bebe could help me."

"Star?"

Here she was, lying again, now to Solange. "No. Star is fine. It's my sister Linda."

"I don't remember you having another sister."

"I'm going to the police, I think, after I leave you." She took a last bite of avocado. "And I fear that must be now."

She used the napkin and stood. Once again she hugged the tall beauty. Before leaving the hotel, she asked the concierge if the hotel had maps of the area that included the Escurra ranch. They did not. Her best bet, she was told, would be the tourist office in Ciudad del Este.

On her way to the tourist office, Nova crossed the bridge back into Paraguay. She must also stop at the Blue Parrot to change from the white pants and silk top into something that a bird-watcher might wear: the lightweight, easy-dry jungle-green pants and shirt that many tourists adopted. The sweat already beading on her forehead whenever she stepped outside called for a French braid pinned up off her neck, a bandanna worn as a headband, and her camouflage hat. Her high-top hiking boots were unusual because a GPS transponder had been built into one heel and the other heel contained a single-edged razor blade, useful for cutting all sorts of things. It released into her hand when she touched a spring latch on the front edge of the heel.

She thought about the Hill boy—the diabetic—wondered how the heat might be affecting him. If he hadn't been allowed to take his insulin with him or was kept from taking it, he might already be dead. Lord, everything was taking so damn long!

The woman in the tourist office spoke good American English. When Nova explained that she wanted to do some birding but had lost her luggage with all of her maps and field glasses and cameras, the woman took charge. She said she loved talking to bird watchers, they were such a polite group of people.

She gave Nova a remarkably detailed map of both Ciudad del Este in Paraguay and the outlying land around the falls, including Argentina and Brazil. Outside Iguazu National Park, this rugged part of the world had long ago been broken up into fiefdoms, ranches of one hundred thousand acres being not uncommon. Escurra's was a kingdom of nearly half a million acres carved out of Brazilian territory.

The woman knew exactly where Escurra's house was located and marked it on the map with an *X*. She suggested a place where Nova could buy field glasses and a camera and rent a four-wheel drive. When her helpful tourist agent asked, frowning, if Nova was alone, Nova lied and said, "Three friends."

By two o'clock, she had what she needed and had

changed clothes. She put the four-wheel drive, an open-top Jeep in gear, studied the map for a moment, and headed out of Ciudad del Este for Brazil. She text-messaged Joe. He wouldn't like that she was going alone to Escurra's, but he would have to accept it. Time was against them. Something had to break, and soon. Splitting up increased their odds of getting a lead.

Traffic in the town crawled, but once back into Brazil and onto the two-lane graded dirt road that should take her to Escurra's place, she made better time—she would reach the northern edge of the property, the location of the house, in thirty minutes.

Chapter 26

Given that the dirt road meandered through unfamiliar territory with a wall of jungle on either side, Nova considered that getting lost only once qualified as success. She'd made a right turn too soon and had ended up at a small beach on a branch of the Iguazu River. The road hadn't been marked on the map.

She turned around and when she took the next right, the grading of the dirt immediately improved. Soon gravel replaced dirt. She had to be headed for Escurra's front gate.

The map indicated that a network of roads led to various scenic sights, or tourist trailheads, and small ranches. On the map she had sketched out a route that looked as if it might let her work her way around the property's edges.

At three fifteen she pulled off the road, about two football fields east of the main entrance. Most of the jungle had been cleared away between the road and the house.

Keeping within tree cover, she found a strangler fig with vines wrapped around it like a ladder, which made it easy to climb. Nestled into a comfortable perch amid lianas and orchids, and steadying her arm against a branch, she trained the ten-power glasses onto Escurra's home.

She would give this thirty minutes. From a leg pocket she fetched out a pencil and steno pad and sketched what she could see, estimating distances and occasionally shooing away a butterfly attracted to the salty sweat on her hands or face.

At the top of her sketch she drew the hacienda. Its American Southwest look was familiar: adobe with red tile, two stories and lots of sprawl. Green grass all around it. A square of blue had to be a swimming pool. A separate building with electrical lines between it and the mansion housed one or more electrical generators.

To the south lay three smaller houses. She remembered Bebe saying that Escurra had built three guest rancheritas. A bit beyond the rancheritas, a circular, two-story structure rose, which she took to be Escurra's cock- and dogfighting pit. Next to it stretched a single-story row of what was either one long shed, or a bunch of sheds strung together. Now there, she thought, was a place where a man could hold ten hostages. Well away from all these structures lay five buildings that appeared to be bunkhouses—a few battered jalopies in front, chairs on the verandas, open doors.

She nibbled her eraser's tip as she tried to figure out how to get a look inside the shed. A strip of jungle ran across the property behind them. The sound of howler monkeys reached her all the way from the trees as she penciled in the strip of green.

She checked the map. The ribbon of jungle probably ran along a small tributary of the Iguazu River that crossed through Escurra's property. If she could find where that jungle strip began, she could most definitely use it as cover to approach the sheds from the rear.

Activity near the entry road caught her attention. A battered truck with an empty bed drove through the massive wooden gates and parked at the hacienda. A woman climbed out, went inside and after ten minutes returned to the truck and left the way she'd come.

At twenty minutes of her allotted thirty, Nova felt a rush of anticipation when she heard the familiar sound of beating helicopter blades. Sure enough, a four-seater Bell & Howell swooped in, a clone of the helicopter she'd once flown over Iguazu Falls. It landed on a helicopter pad. Three men hopped out and dashed into the house. At this distance she wouldn't be able to identify them later even if her life depended on it. Which it might.

After thirty minutes, she slithered down and headed the Jeep farther east. The jungle on her right soon gave way to tall grassland and fences designed to keep cattle from straying. Judging from their snowy flanks and scimitar-like horns, the cattle were the same humpback, well-mannered zebu she'd seen all over the Paraguayan Pantanal. A bit farther along she heard a trumpet, and scanning the grass she spotted a lone mounted cowboy on the far horizon. She heard the trumpet sound again. Every zebu between her and the cowboy that hadn't already done so lifted its head. Several started a slow walk in his direction. *Salt,* she thought. Pantanal cowboys used a trumpet to signal their cattle that a salt lick had been refilled and was ready for customers.

When she arrived at a strip of jungle and then a bridge crossing the river, her pulse sped up again. She drove off the road as far as she could into dense undergrowth. How often, if at all, did Escurra's guards check the various parts of the property? If they found the Jeep, they would certainly hunt for its owner. The risk was unavoidable.

Her watch said four o'clock. She moved west rapidly over the gnarled bases of the looming trees, welcoming the jungle's shade. In the perpetual gloom of a tropical rain forest's understory, undergrowth has little chance to get a foothold. Even without a trail she moved quickly over spongy, earthy-smelling groundcover left by decades or even centuries of undisturbed decaying vegetation.

Butterflies. Begonias. She stepped over a quivering line of leaf-cutter ants. Any other time she would have stopped to watch them trudge their way home with their little green sails, bits of leaves to supply their ant farm. But not today.

In the roughly twenty minutes she'd estimated it might take her to reach the area of the sheds, the river—more accurately, it was a modest creek—suddenly expanded into a small lake of perhaps five acres. She doubted the lake was natural. More likely, something Escurra had created with a dam. Why would he want a lake? The size was too small for sailing or boating. Besides, water lilies thrived in big patches; they weren't compatible with boating. Maybe fishing.

She skirted the lake, the sheds in sight about the distance of a couple of football fields away. Along the lake's muddy edge, the jungle gave way to brush, short trees and a swampy shore. Birds, drawn to the water, abounded. Two rusty-red female jacanas picked their way daintily, like prissy ladies, across lily pads on their territories at opposite ends of the lake. A white great egret peered intently into the water, looking to stab a fish with its rapierlike bill. Two black-headed, white-bodied jabiru storks took off, their massive eight-foot wingspans breathtaking as they beat the air.

A startling bang and clatter of the thick brush. A small chestnut body and tiny antlers exploded from the thicket as a red brocket deer took off deeper into the jungle. Nova rocked backward and pitched into the water, her hat sliding off her head.

Her first thought, as she gasped for breath and kicked frantically seeking footing, was, *piranha!* The dreadful little South American fish, half of whose body was teeth and schools of which were known to consume an entire cow in less than two minutes. In panic, she gulped in bitter, warm water. She spat it out, choking, as her kicking feet found something solid.

Piranha could nibble her to a quick and nasty death.

Arms flailing, her feet slipped again on the mud. A caiman slipped from the shore into the water, headed for her at top speed, his long tail making curves in the water, his nose and eyes peeking up above the water line along his crocodile-like body. She guessed him to be five feet of obviously hungry reptile. Paddling to get her balance, she once more found footing and pushed off toward the water's edge but up a slippery, steep bank.

She wasn't going to beat him in this race.

She stripped off the bandanna from her forehead, spun toward the caiman and, when it opened its mouth to chomp down on her arm, she grabbed his snout with all her strength, digging into the mud with the toes of her boots.

She pulled the reptile to her, lifted her arm over his back and tucked his snout, nose forward, under her arm to make sure he could not open his mouth while she slipped the bandanna on. He trashed and twisted, dragging her under. She held her breath, kicked to try to regain her footing, and kept her arm's tight, viselike grip on his snout.

The big weakness of every crocodilian in the world was

its bite. More specifically, the weakness of the muscles that opened its mouth, not the ones that held it shut once it had a good hold on its prey. The latter muscles were formidable. You'd never pry them open. But if you could get a croc's mouth closed and keep it that way, you could win, because it simply would not be able to open it to bite you.

She rolled to the surface and grabbed a lungful of air. He rolled her under again. They were thrashing up so much mud she could barely see, but she wrapped the bandanna twice around his snout, tied a knot, then pulled her knees to her chest and kicked the prehistoric creature away with all the strength she could muster.

Breaking through the water's surface again, she turned toward the shore, praying the bandanna would hold its mouth and distract it long enough for her to scramble up the slippery bank onto land.

The caiman thrashed its head back and forth until she saw the bandanna come free. The beast lay quiet a moment, then slowly exhaled his breath and sank out of sight into the muddy patch they had stirred up.

Well, that was fun. Every muscle in her body was quivering. Her knees felt unsteady.

When she could walk again, she moved down the shoreline. Mud smeared her pants and top. It would soon dry and cake and be hard to explain. She needed to rinse it off.

She did a full scan of her surroundings. Seeing no one, she stripped out of the shirt and pants and walked to the lake's edge. The binoculars weren't waterproof. In all this humidity they would probably quickly fog up. Her notebook and her birding guide were both soggy, but happily the notebook was quite readable.

She rinsed her shirt and pants, then found a rock where she could sit to wait. She hung her clothes over the branches of a bush. Half-naked, she felt more creepy with every passing minute. Her ears strained to hear any snap of a twig that might warn of approaching guards. Without unpinning it, she squeezed some of the water from her braid.

In the few minutes it took her clothes to dry, she heard a plush-crested jay, a saffron finch, and a raucous flock of parrots. A centipede made its slow journey past her from the shady place at the base of her sitting rock to the cool place at the base of another rock a few feet away. Somewhere, maybe not far from her, she knew that a jaguar rested, waiting for night and a hunt. And perhaps not far away, guarding their captives, she might encounter the most dangerous predator species of all.

At ten after five, with plenty of daylight left, she hung the binoculars around her neck, her badge of innocence, and she walked as fast as she could, covering the open ground between the jungle's edge and the sheds as quickly as possible, praying no one would see her.

Chapter 27

Nova strode through calf- to waist-high scrub grass and bushes, and then, perspiration soaking her underarms and trickling down her spine, she hugged the backside of the long, low building. Bars, the kind in a jail, sat like metal teeth in a row of windows built high up from the ground. Hope flickered, elevating her pulse. For what reason other than to keep captives would Escurra need a building with barred windows?

The windows were about three feet too high for her to see inside and nothing lay nearby to climb up on—no boxes, barrels or logs. After listening for a solid minute, and hearing only the beat of her heart and the distant buzz of what sounded like a lawn mower, she decided she might risk peeking around the side of the buildings.

Standing upright again—clutching her binoculars—she strode to the edge of the long building and walked around the corner, her cover story about birding on her tongue.

She found nothing there but a view all the way to the big ranch house. She judged that the nearest buildings she could see, the three rancheritas, were at least a half a mile distant and the big house maybe three quarters of a mile away. This meant that the fighting pit, with its viewing stands, was readily accessible to Escurra, but also private.

Between the rancheritas and the big house lay open ground, most of it covered in lawn. A macadam road lined on both sides with palm tress led from the house to the rancheritas and at the last minute, the road split three ways, one branch leading to each of the guest houses. She could see and faintly hear two men riding lawn mowers.

The macadam road continued on down to the fighting pit. Other than the guys mowing lawn, she'd seen no men, armed or otherwise. Her initial hope cooled.

She decided to check out the ring with its tiers of seats. Maybe she could get some elevation, the better to scan the property. She strode across the thirty feet of empty space between the back of the sheds and the back of the ring. The pit and the viewing stands, deserted and quiet, were constructed of wood.

She climbed to the top row level and, crouching, checked the surroundings. In front of the sheds, two cowboys, unarmed, were wrestling a back tire off of a battered pickup truck. They wore the tall boots, baggy pants and loose blouse of a gaucho. Not exactly the picture of kidnappers on the alert.

When she trained the binoculars on the rancheritas the scene proved equally disappointing. Expensive cars were parked in front of all three, cars of the kind that might be driven by important guests, not thugs: Bentleys, Rolls, Cadillacs.

At their rear, the three houses shared one big swimming

pool. A woman in a white bikini lay on a chaise lounge beside it, soaking up some very late afternoon sun. On the lawn beside the middle house, two kids smashed a badminton bird back and forth.

No one was concealing kidnapped Americans at the rancheritas, and it didn't look like the Americans were being hidden in the sheds either. Still, its interior had to be checked out. She retraced her steps, and then walked to the shed's front corner. Peering around it at the two cowpunchers changing the tire about seventy-five feet away, closer to the shed's far end, she heard them chatting in Guarani.

She straightened, boldly rounded the front of the wooden structure, ducked inside the closest open door, and found herself in a dim and eerily quiet interior. In spite of the heat, she shivered.

The structure reminded her of the rows of horse stalls in a riding stable or at a track. A single, wide corridor, lined with scattered chairs and a couple of tables, ran its entire length. The barred windows on the little chambers where horses might be kept just shrieked that the chambers were cells. Some doors were closed and some open. She picked the closest cell, its door standing open, and went inside. The floor was of well-packed dirt. The walls and low ceiling were rough-hewn, old and dried-out wood. A real fire hazard.

Other than a rusty pan on the floor under the lone, barred window, the little cubicle stood empty. Dark smudges on the walls looked like they might be blood. In one corner she found dog scat. In another, to her surprise, she found different scat with the unmistakable stench of wild boar still on it.

So, he did keep animals for his fights here.

She stepped outside the cell and, proceeding down the

corridor, glanced inside each cell. At the first closed door, she peeked in the window. A beautiful specimen of fighting cock turned its beady dark eye on her, his red wattle wagging.

When she leaned forward to peek into the next closed cell, the rapid barking of a dog with a deep, intimidating voice caused her to lurch back, her heart leaping up into her throat and fine hairs standing up all over her body.

From other cells other dogs took up the cry.

Chaos!

She imagined the cowboys suddenly standing upright and looking at the shed. Would they come to check out the commotion?

Hell! She spun around and raced back to the door where she'd entered. She skidded to a halt and peeked out. One of the men was ambling toward a door at the other end of the shed with a rifle in his hand, his friend watching.

She dashed outside and sprinted back around the corner of the building. No way could she make the sheltering jungle if either man decided to look for a jaguar or some other source of disturbance behind the building.

The unmowed, wild grass stood knee high. She threw herself face down and lay still. Counting. One hundred and one, one hundred and two, one hundred and three. She kept it up. When she hit five hundred, she lifted her head and looked back at the sheds.

Nothing. Either the men had not looked, or they had not seen her.

Now she lit out for the jungle at top stride, swallowing disappointment. She would not be making an excited call to Joe to let him know she'd found their hostages.

Once she reached the cover of the trees, she tried to jog, but the tangle of roots and the oppressive heat worked against jogging. The return trip to the Jeep seemed to take

longer than the trip in. Relieved to have escaped detection
she tossed her field glasses into the passenger seat.

A male voice said, in Spanish, "Stop. Step away from
the auto."

She turned. Two men looking to be a mix of Spanish
and Guarani and wearing jeans, sleeveless shirts, and 38-
caliber Smith & Wessons still in hip holsters approached
in a slow amble.

She smiled. *"Buenos días."*

The older one, a bandanna tied around his forehead
much as hers had been, didn't return the smile. The
younger one—he looked to be no older than fifteen—
flashed a beautiful mouth full of white teeth.

Concentrating on the guy with the bandanna, she said
"Do you speak English?"

He didn't flicker an eyelash.

The boy said in English, "What you do?"

"Birding," she said. She pulled the still-soaked bird
book from her pants pocket and pointed to the cover, a
collage of paintings of the heads of a toucan, cotinga, harpy
eagle and great egret. "Birds," she said again. *"Aves."*

Rapid Guarani passed between them. The boy repeated
"What you do here?"

She leaned into the Jeep and picked up the field glasses
She put them to her eyes and mimed scanning the nearby
trees. *"Aves."* She pointed to the book cover.

The older man's face didn't twitch a muscle. He reached
for the book and she handed it to him. What would he make
of a soaked book? Her pulse started a rapid thump, thump,
thump in her throat. She smiled at the boy, then scanned
their surroundings. She needed a bird now. Any bird she
could show him. Where was a bird when you really, really
needed one?

More quick Guarani and the boy pointed to the book and said, "Water? Why?"

Pointing in the direction of the river Nova mimed what she hoped looked like a woman losing her balance and starting to fall. She unVelcroed another pants pocket and took out another steno book brought for just this emergency. Not the one with her sketches of the house, but one in which she'd drawn sketches of eight common local birds. Under each she'd written the bird's Latin name.

She opened to the first drawing, a black vulture in flight. "Black vulture," she said. She pointed, feeling idiotic, at the sky. Both would know the profile of this ubiquitous big scavenger and would have seen it their whole lives in the sky.

Whether it was the sketches or her familiarity with the book or maybe just her nonthreatening femaleness, an American woman out here doing the dumb things that tourists did, the old guy finally seemed convinced.

After a quick scan of her other sketches, he returned the steno pad.

A few more words of Guarani and the boy said, "Private property. You go."

"Oh, I'm sorry," she said. "Okay. No problem."

They watched her climb into the Jeep. The boy smiled. The older guy, he of the supreme straight face, simply stood with his hand on the butt of his gun.

While she had collected some information on Escurra's digs, as far as anything substantial was concerned she had struck out. Linda, the Bennings, the diabetic boy, all of them—they were hopefully all still alive, wherever they were. She could imagine their fear. It would be dusk by the time she reached the Blue Parrot. She'd done all she could here. She revved the Jeep to the top speed allowed by the road conditions, looking behind once or twice to see if the man and boy were following. They were. They followed her all the way back to the gravel road leading away from Escurra's front gate.

Would they report finding a foreign woman snooping around to Escurra. Probably so. Too bad she'd been caught.

She asked at the Blue Parrot's reception desk and was told that Mr. Villalobos could be found in the bar next door.

She found him seated in a tiny booth alone, apparently behaving quite civilly. "Let's go to your room, Nova," Ramone said. "I'll stop at the café across the street and order in food. I presume you're hungry."

"Starving."

Chapter 28

Joe entered Nova's room through the connecting door. He took a chair by the single window, kicked off his hiking boots and propped his feet on a straight-back chair seat. As she washed her hands and face to cool off, Ramone arrived and took one of two chairs by the small table.

Returning to the bedroom, she said, "Let me go first. I don't have much. Bebe knows someone who works in Martinez's stable. He'll call me when he hears anything. I also rented a Jeep and bought some birding gear and scouted Escurra's place."

Joe shook his head. "You shouldn't do stuff like that without me."

"We're short on time, Joe."

"I know that!"

"Then don't lecture me about staying safe."

"I just meant—"

"I know what you meant, and we don't have time to play this game safe."

"So what did you see?" Ramone asked, cutting off their head butting.

A knock on the door brought Ramone to his feet. He tipped the kid and set the package of food on the table. They drew up chairs. "I ordered *baribari*. It's a typical Paraguay soup. Meat, vegetables, some bacon and dumplings."

Ramone hauled out six beers and also three of something in capped, insulated cups. "If you guys don't want the hot drinks," he said, "we can just dump them."

Joe took a beer, opened it and swigged.

"The hot drink is a local herb tea. Yerba maté. It's supposed to be some kind of elixir, a rejuvenator. A definite refresher." He picked up one of three strawlike silver objects. Each had a little bulb on one end pierced with tiny holes. "You sip the tea through these *bombillas*. The holes are like a little strainer."

She wondered if he ever actually drank anything nonalcoholic except the occasional coffee. She dished the soup into three enclosed paper bowls. "What's in the dumplings? Also a health food?" She couldn't suppress a skeptical raised eyebrow.

"Maize and cheese."

She fetched the tourist company map and her sketches and laid them out in front of them. She drew a finger around the border of Escurra's massive holding. "He owns it all. His house is here." She touched the *X* the helpful agent had drawn.

"If you use the big house as the anchor point, I've sketched other landmarks. Down here—" she pointed "—there is a fighting pit. He apparently entertains with animal fights. Bebe says he always throws a big party on Christmas Eve, and there were some caged dogs. No guards. No trace at all of Americans or of anything going on.

"That's pretty much it, except that two guards caught me off the side of the road where I'd parked. I don't know if they bought my birding cover."

She sat down and sampled a dumpling, then used the odd silver straw to taste the maté. It had a sharp but pleasant taste.

After another swig of beer, Joe said, "I interviewed Martinez. He speaks damn good English but told me nothing about money laundering or terrorists that any man or woman on the street couldn't have told me."

He gave Ramone a sharp look. "I could see how, in this heat and all, a man could get hooked on this beer."

Ramone simply sucked on his silver straw, refusing the bait.

"What about Gomez?" she asked.

"Oh, yeah. We could probably consider that a plus. I covered twenty or thirty acres before I ended up at a corral where seven men were watching a guy breaking a horse to the saddle. Gomez was there. So at least we know that he came back here. No sign of hostages."

Ramone said, "I tapped the lines to Martinez's land telephone. We may get lucky and intercept a local call, maybe to or from Escurra. They sure as hell won't use cell phones."

Nova stood. "The soup was good, Ramone."

He took her hand. She felt a rush of fire up her arm.

"No, no. Sit back down," he said.

She sat. He didn't let go. Warm feelings on her skin intensified. She normally did not blush. Was she blushing now? Could Joe see the fire under her skin?

Finally Ramone let go. She pulled her hand into her lap,

amazed—no, way beyond amazed—that Ramone could still have such a profoundly chemical effect on her.

The man abandoned you! He just walked out of your life!

Ramone dived once more into the brown sack. "I brought *mbaipy-he-é* for dessert. You'll love it, Nova." The way he said Nova with a soft breath was almost like a kiss. "It's an unforgettable mix. Cornmeal, milk and molasses."

Joe said, "Don't forget me, Ramone. I'd also like some dessert."

The three-way tension around them was thick enough to dice and slice.

Ramone handed her a cup of the pudding and a spoon as he continued his report. "I complained to Rio that we want better maps. I said if they want to catch these guys before they kill the VP's niece, they better get keyhole satellite photos of not only Martinez's place but Escurra's. We should have extremely detailed specifics of whatever is on the ground at both places sometime late tonight or tomorrow morning."

Ramone finally took a beer that by now must have warmed up quite a bit, popped the top and swigged. "I have to confess something, just between us."

Is he really going to admit to being an alcoholic?

"You met three of my friends the other night, Joe."

Joe nodded. "Yeah. Cobra, Barbed Wire and Shooting Stars."

Ramone threw his head back and, grinning, hooted. "Dead on! That's my boys. Well—" he took another swig and then continued "—today I asked them to come join us here in Ciudad del Este."

Joe exploded. "What the hell!"

"Don't get your jocks in a knot. We can trust them as much as or better than anyone with the Company. Fact is, we don't have anyone with the Company here, now, to help us. I asked my boys to come because I'm thinking we might need…assistance."

Nova felt as surprised, and alarmed, as Joe sounded. "I don't understand. What are you thinking?"

"I have a little business on the side. Not entirely legal. These are my partners. They're smart. They're tough. And they blend in, which any backup from the Company would not do. And I can guarantee they will keep their mouths shut."

She said, "You shouldn't involve anyone else, Ramone." He had always been a rogue and rule-breaker.

He crossed his arms and set his jaw. "We may need some muscle of our own. I feel better knowing my men are here. If we don't need them, you don't even have to see them. And I won't tell them why I want them here unless I need them. But I want them here and ready."

"What's your illegal side business, Ramone?" Joe asked.

To her surprise, Nova didn't want to know.

"It's not relevant," Ramone countered.

Joe persisted. "It's relevant to me. I want to know what kinds of muscle these guys are."

"Smugglers."

"Drugs?"

"I'm not a fool and I'm not some immoral shit, Cardone."

"Then what is it?"

"Orchids and birds."

Joe laughed. "Oh, they must be really tough guys all right."

Nova didn't find Ramone's confession at all amusing. Clearly he thought smuggling drugs was evil. He wouldn't understand why she found what he'd just confessed just as reprehensible. Drugs were something humans did to each other and to themselves. Killing birds and robbing the forest of its orchids was something humans did to the natural world and the effects were permanent.

"Don't underestimate my men."

Joe held both palms up and face out. "Okay. Fine."

She decided she wanted them both out of her room.

"Let's call it an evening," she said. "Tomorrow we'll have the keyhole data. Langley's specialists will have decided where we should begin searching. Depending on what they tell us, and hopefully something Bebe's contact may dig up, we can decide then how to proceed."

Neither man moved.

"Seriously. Let's call it an evening."

She looked at Joe, then Ramone. Joe gave in and stood. "In the morning, then."

He left, quietly shutting their shared door.

She hadn't missed the pissed look on Joe's face. He hadn't wanted to leave her alone with Ramone. Ramone said, "Want me to go?"

Joe would know when, or if, Ramone left her room. If Ramone stayed, the longer he stayed, the more ticked off Joe might become. "It's been a long time, Ramone." She said it lightly, tauntingly. "I sure did wonder what had happened to you."

"I didn't think you'd continue to work for the Company."

"My ops give me a chance to make payback now and then."

He frowned, clearly stumped. "Payback for what?"

"By the time you left me, Ramone, I'd killed three men."

Ramone snorted and shoved his beer bottle away. "Three bastards, all of whom deserved it."

Candido Branco, in her opinion if not necessarily God's, definitely had deserved it. But she'd never been sure

about the others. She didn't know their background. Didn't
know what got them into smuggling and pushing in the
first place. That old saying about walking a mile in the
other guy's shoes had always haunted her. "Maybe."

"I missed you. I really did."

"Yeah. Sure."

"We do crazy things when we're young. I left. Then I
figured you'd never want me back."

Had he actually thought of her even once after he'd
brought her home from a fancy dinner, bedded her and
walked out never to be seen or heard from again? Not likely.

"It's late, Ramone. I need to sleep." Besides, teasing Joe
by letting Ramone stay even another minute suddenly
seemed disgustingly dishonest. It was also unkind. Did she
love Joe or not?

She stood, and Ramone took the hint. She moved
toward the bathroom, expecting him to let himself out, but
in the bathroom mirror she saw him standing in place,
watching her back. "Good night, Ramone."

At eleven o'clock her cell phone chimed. She put down
the Moroccan novel and heard Claiton Pryce's voice on the
secure line. "I thought you wanted word when we had news
about the hostages. I'm sorry to say that if the kidnappers
are being truthful with us, the doctor, Redmond Obst, has
been killed. They say another will die at noon tomorrow."

Her throat choked tight and she blinked back tears. The
world-famous birder would not add any more species to
his life list. His life had been stolen from him.

She clenched her jaw. "He had a son with him on the
trip. Let's pray the boy wasn't made to witness it."

"By morning we'll have located activity hot spots on
either the Martinez or Escurra property and can direct you
to the hostages. Analysts are primed to work, as soon as

the satellite makes another pass over your area, which should be in about two hours. But it's a huge amount of land to cover."

"I know. I thank you for calling me."

"Good night, Nova."

"Thank you, sir."

Joe knocked on her door early. He was going for breakfast to the small cantina next to the Blue Parrot. They agreed there was no reason not to be seen together. She had already bathed and braided her hair and pinned it up. She slipped on her gold studs, climbed into the green tourist-in-the-jungle outfit and hurried downstairs to join him.

Chapter 29

The Christmas Eve morning air in Ciudad del Este was already at simmer, but men and boys, young women, and several dogs were out and about their business as Nova crossed to the cantina. Tonight, for Escurra's party, it might cool off enough to be pleasant. She wondered how bad heat stress might be for the Hill boy.

The cantina's thick mud walls kept the inside temperature quite cool. Joe, looking like every woman's dream cowboy in jeans and a blue, short-sleeved shirt, greeted her with the smile that gave her more sustenance than food.

"I ordered huevos rancheros for two," he said.

They had shared a special weekend in Ensenada, south of the San Diego border, and agreed that huevos rancheros was their favorite breakfast. She appreciated his attempt to please her and remind her of the good times. She was going to win him over, she could feel it. She smiled and sat. "Nice choice."

A girl in a gaily colored red, yellow, and blue peasant top and flared skirt brought coffee, and, before Nova even had her second morning wake-up sip, their eggs and beans.

Joe said, "I stopped by Ramone's room. Faxes of the keyhole photos still aren't in." One of Ramone's means of communication with Rio was a portable fax machine with wireless Bluetooth technology.

She shrugged. "Analysis always takes so damn long." The eggs were fabulous, probably because the hens here ran wild and ate well.

Her cell phone chimed, the first two bars of "The Rose," from the depth of her woven bag. Bebe sounded excited. "Come right away. This time of the day the drive shouldn't take more than twenty minutes. I will wait in my office."

She reached the hotel by nine thirty. Her large, dear friend rushed around his desk, took her arm and tugged her to a coffee table upon which was spread a map like the one the tourist agent had given her. "There is something very, very strange about this one place on the property. My friend, Netinho, explains that there are watering troughs all over the part of the Martinez ranch where the cattle roam."

"I believe that's common."

"Yes, of course. And here on this map he put little marks to indicate his best memory of where all of the troughs are." Maybe twenty small black dots had been inked onto the paper. "But—" Bebe continued, pointing to a dot quite close to a strip of jungle "—Netinho says that all of the boys are told to stay entirely away from this trough. Only Martinez's manager and a few men, who Netinho really does not like, go there."

"That does sound suspicious."

"According to Netinho, there are rumors among the

long-time gauchos that Martinez runs guns and they think he hides them there or somewhere around there. Maybe it's drugs. Who knows? The thing is, Nova, he could perhaps hide kidnap victims there."

"Did your friend, by any chance, go out and look the place over?"

"He said he was too afraid of Martinez."

"It's not a problem, Bebe. I just needed to ask." She folded the map, then hugged him. "Thanks."

"On TV, I see practically nothing but news about the kidnapping. But they are all still running around Manaus. I am truly puzzled."

"That's one of the things I can't explain, Bebe. I only ask that you tell no one what I'm doing here."

He patted her arm and nodded.

She raced back toward the Blue Parrot, calling Joe and telling him she had a lead, although nothing solid. She arrived shortly after ten thirty. She reached the entry when Ramone, who came out of the cantina, stopped her. "The faxes are in," he said. "Joe and I have already worked them over. But before we go upstairs I want you to meet my friends."

"We're in a hurry, Ramone."

"This won't take long. You need to see the boys and judge them for yourself."

She let him take her arm to guide her to the cantina door, and once again, as he pulled her unnecessarily close, she felt the old attraction. Apparently powerful sexual chemistry did not fizzle with age. She assumed he was feeling it as well, which made the rational part of her mind damned uncomfortable.

She spotted Ramone's three friends at once. You couldn't miss them, the Hell's Angels of Paraguay.

Chapter 30

The sharp smell of male bodies needing a good bath hit her along with the smell of the beer. An old Willie Nelson song, "Momma, Don't Let Your Babies Grow Up To Be Cowboys," entertained the cantina's few patrons. "Compadres," Ramone said, "this is Nova. Like it or not, she's in charge. I think you'll like it."

In charge of what? No way would she involve these men in high-stakes Company business unless absolutely necessary.

"Glad to meet ya," she said, giving them all a power smile with hard eyes that should convey the message that in the remote possibility that they might work together, they would do well to remember that she would, in fact, be in charge.

Cobra nodded. Barbed Wire said, *"Me gusta."* Stars smiled back and said, "My pleasure, *señorita."*

She turned to Ramone. "Business calls."

"Stay here until you hear from me," he said to his men, and then, side by side, he walked with her to the Blue Parrot.

The moment she walked into Joe's room, with Ramone so close he was breathing down her neck, Joe gave Ramone a daggered look. The glance was brief, only a moment, but it burned with the fire of jealousy before Joe switched his attention to her. "We've got something with meat on it," he said. "Come look."

Joe and Ramone had spread keyhole photos of the Martinez and Escurra places over Joe's bedspread, over-lapping and taped into place so the photos formed one composite. Joe pointed to a spot on the Martinez ranch, the very spot she'd discussed with Bebe. Her pulse quickened.

"What we have is a site here, around a watering trough for cattle, that has an unusual wear pattern."

"Bebe's informant told him to watch out for this same location."

Joe continued. "See here. The markings around all the other troughs are uniform—" he passed his finger over several sites on the ranch "—made by the hooves of randomly moving cattle. Each of the other sites has only one truck track leading to and from it. Now this site has several unusual features. First, it's within forty feet of jungle. Cattle tend to be leery of such heavy cover, and the hoof wear pattern here *is* less dense. Jaguars are a serious problem. So it's like someone picked the site for reasons other than accommodating the cattle.

"Then you can see that there's a shack of some kind. About ten by ten. Not big, but none of the other trough locations have any buildings. Just a trough and a salt lick. Then see how there's not only a truck track leading to and from the site by way of the grassland, there's a track that leads directly into the jungle. The canopy cover is too thick to see what's underneath it. Langley is putting infrared eyes on the canopy in hopes of catching any traffic that might be moving under the trees."

"Bebe's informant said he thought Martinez might be running drugs or guns."

"See that little spot," Joe said, pointing.

She leaned closer to the photo and squinted. The tiny dot was hard to make out.

"It's a man. They have an armed guard on the site of a cattle watering trough. A timed series of photos shows that he stands, walks or sits in front of the shack."

"Aha."

Ramone jumped in. "If we get moving now, we can be out there by noon."

She studied the shack again. "You said the dimensions are about ten by ten, right?"

"That's what the analysts calculate."

"So how many hostages could be inside? I'm getting more and more afraid that they split everyone up and our hostages may be spread all over Paraguay."

A long silence settled into the room.

Ramone broke it. "Well, even if the shack holds only one or two hostages, we have to go look. And we sure have to get solid confirmation before we call in Special Ops."

Nova checked her watch and, frustrated to see that it was already ten minutes after eleven, balled her hand into a fist. Fifty minutes until the next killing. Even if there were captives there, it was too late for Special Ops to arrive in time to prevent it. Would this next victim be the Obst boy? Or maybe Linda. Linda didn't have any family with money to pay up. Maybe they would consider her expendable.

She looked to Joe and then Ramone. "I'm going to change clothes and get armed. Let's meet here in four minutes."

The first stanzas of "The Rose" chimed in her woven bag. Leila Munoz, on the secure line, said, "We have current update from the Martinez site. Since dawn, an unmanned drone has been circling it at high altitude. Ten minutes ago Carlito Gomez was seen driving up to the site using the grassland road. He went into the shack. Then a short time ago, a Ford truck drove up and unloaded supplies. Lots of bottles of water and boxes of food. All taken into the shack. It's way too much to reasonably fit inside. The analysts say that the shack is covering an underground bunker. They've confirmed it using ground penetrating sonar."

"This looks good, Leila. Maybe they haven't split the hostages up."

"It looks so good that we're sending in a special operations team on the assumption that our captives are there. The team is on the way. They'll come in low, under radar, across northern Argentina. We don't have permission from Brazil or Argentina, so it will be quick in and quick out, no footprint."

Nova checked her watch. Eleven fifteen. "How soon will Special Ops be on site?"

"Sixty minutes. Seventy tops."

"That's not good enough, Leila. They threatened to kill again at noon."

"Sorry. It is what it is."

"Roger." Nova snapped the phone closed and quickly explained these new developments. "This looks to be the correct location, but the timing sucks."

Joe checked his watch.

Ramone said, "Maybe the bastards won't be prompt in the timing of their next execution."

They fell silent. She crossed her arms, sucked in a deep breath and let it out. "That doesn't work for me."

Chapter 31

Joe strode to the bedroom window and looked out at the ugly view of rundown clapboard buildings across the street from the Blue Parrot. He turned back to face Nova. "Are you thinking what I'm thinking?"

"We often think alike," she answered.

Ramone added his two bits. "All of us are thinking the same thing." A wry smile twisted his lips. "Somehow I just knew I would need the boys. Instinct. I say we go out there ourselves. Right now. We'll beat Special Ops by at least twenty minutes."

Joe nodded. "We crash the bunker, secure the captives and wait for Special Ops to pick them up."

"We are agreed, then?" Ramone said. "Do I go get the guys up here?"

"Agreed," Nova said. "Go get them."

Ramone headed for the door.

She cut him short. "Look, these guys smuggle birds and orchids. They look scary as hell, but do they have weapons and can they use them?"

"I brought them, Nova, because the answer to both questions is yes. They come from mean backgrounds, but they're good men."

"Okay. Go."

Ramone strode out, closing the door behind him.

Nova punched in the number for Leila and told Leila of their intent to raid the Martinez bunker. "I'm pretty sure SO isn't going to like the idea. But you need to be in direct contact with them," Leila said. "Here's the number. The line's secure."

The nameless voice at Special Ops command center listened to Nova, put her on brief hold, and then came back. "You are to wait. Do not engage."

"We can't wait. They threatened to kill another hostage at noon."

"If so, you are already too late, and the risk of going in with an inexperienced team puts all the hostages' lives at risk. You are ordered to wait."

"We have three experienced CIA operatives and three other good men." She hoped that Ramone's judgment was right about that, otherwise they might, in fact, trigger a killing disaster.

"But you are not a team, and none of you is trained in hostage rescue. It is too risky."

"Do you understand?" said an entirely different voice, a voice carrying much more authority. "We are talking about the niece of the vice president of the United States. You are *not* to engage."

"If we don't go, and go right now, someone may die. Maybe not the niece, but there are other people there, too.

They also count. We'll secure all of the hostages and then wait for your team to pick everyone up."

"If you disobey this direct order and someone dies, you will serve a good long time in prison."

She chuckled. Threatening a stretch in prison might intimidate some people, but it wasn't as if she hadn't already been there and done that. She wasn't seventeen any more; she could survive prison now with one arm tied behind her back. And what was the point of working for the Company if she didn't save every life she could? "I don't have time to argue. I take orders directly from Langley, and I haven't heard from them."

She snapped the phone shut.

Joe was grinning at her. "What was that?"

"We're ordered to lay off. They consider us too inexperienced."

He laughed and threw himself into the armchair.

She sat down at the small table. "I can't think of any way Martinez can know that we are on to him. Total surprise is on our side."

"If nothing else, the fact that they only have a single guard outside the shack and he wanders around all over the place sure indicates they're not on alert."

"I'll take out the guard. Then all six of us go inside and we work it from there."

Joe drew a long, deep breath. "I could take out the guard, Nova. As you point out, it's just one guy."

"You know what I'm going to say."

"If you do it, I'll look like a total pussy to Ramone and the thugs."

"You know a lone woman will be less threatening. If something goes wrong, how can I, or even you, justify sending you to take him out when we could have used me?"

He shrugged, then flashed those beautiful white teeth. "You get all the fun."

"Come on, Joe."

"Okay, okay. But let me be the one to insist that you do it. Let it look like it's my brilliant idea."

She rolled her eyes up. "You guys and the macho image thing."

"Don't knock it. It's critical to male survival."

"Okay, you can explain the whole plan to the boys."

"I love you, you know."

"Please, Joe. Let's not go there now."

Ramone knocked once and bounded in, the three "boys" on his heels. "We're ready. We've got sidearms and automatic rifles in my Land Rover. What's the plan?"

Nova's phone chimed again. Everyone sat, covering all the chairs and half the bed. She ignored the call.

Ramone frowned. "Aren't you going to answer it?"

"I think it's Langley. I don't want to talk with them. I'm going to tell them I missed the call. I was busy."

She turned to look the three boys over, orchid and bird thieves and who knew what else. They did look tough.

She gave the boys a big smile. She thought about their careers as orchid thieves. "Okay, men, this is your chance to do something good."

Chapter 32

For some crazy reason Nova remembered that it was noon on Christmas Eve as she drove slowly toward the remote watering trough and shack on the Martinez ranch. This might qualify as the most bizarre Christmas Eve day ever. Pulsing, blazing heat from the sun beat down on her head like a hammer. She wore the tourist birding outfit with binoculars hung around her neck.

Her Glock lay tucked under the driver's seat. She didn't anticipate needing it to take out the guard, but who knew what waited for them inside the shack.

Her cell phone chimed. A text message from Joe said that his team was in position. There had been some worry that when they closed in on the trough from within the jungle they would find that the canopy hid something bigger than the shack, like a camp of armed men. Apparently, no such bad scenario had materialized. So now the guys were in place, ready to pounce the moment she cleared the way.

She gave the Jeep gas to cover the remaining distance. The faces of Linda, the Obst boy, and Colette Stone kept popping into her head. One of them might already be dead. Or the Hill kid. Or maybe Nancy Benning.

Stop it! Concentrate.

She slowed and braked to a stop beside the water trough, twenty feet from the shack door. The guard, with his rifle cradled across his chest, walked toward her. She stepped out of the Jeep, smiled at him, and waved. She pointed to the trough and to the canteen in her hand. *"Agua,"* she said.

He wore just the faintest smile. She felt certain his attention, which should have been on his weapon and the potential need to use it, was directed to her breasts. She waited until his stroll brought him to within ten feet, then dropped the canteen, charged him and hammered home a karate chop to the vulnerable spot over the carotid artery on his neck. He went out like a slaughter-house cow, thudding to the ground.

She rolled him off his old AK-47 and kicked the weapon toward the jungle. From one of her pockets she pulled out a half-empty roll of duct tape and peeled off a strip already cut to the size to cover his mouth. The next two strips she peeled off were cut to size to secure his wrists and ankles.

Joe and the boys sped up in two Land Rovers. Cobra and Stars stuffed the guard under the shade of her Jeep.

As already discussed at the Blue Parrot, Joe would take the lead. "Remember," she said. "This is my op. We don't kill unless we have to."

Joe tried the shack's door. It opened. No lock. No nothing.

Quietly, the team moved in. A ten-foot by ten-foot metal

trap door lay open in the center of the dirt floor. Seven cement steps led down to a cement passage. The six of them stared down for a moment, then Joe went first, followed quickly by Ramone, then Nova, then the boys.

An eight-foot-wide passage at the bottom led toward a lit room. The room's far wall stood some thirty feet from the door. Nova sucked in a big breath of cool air and the smell of cool, damp cement. The temperature was probably the fifty-five degrees Fahrenheit, typical for underground caves—divine relief. Such a large underground space of solid construction indicated a business that was significant and permanent.

With handguns at the ready, they moved in a bunch with impressive quiet toward the door to the room. Nothing on their clothing rattled, no footsteps echoed. The "boys" were performing damn fine so far.

She could make out the stout legs and top half of a wooden table where someone had been playing cards. A male voice spoke loudly and stridently in Portuguese.

They burst into the room.

About fifteen feet away to her left, the bug guy, Dennis Chu, stood blindfolded against a wall. To her right, three men, one of them Carlito Gomez, stood watching as a fourth man harangued Chu with what were apparently intended to be last words, because the thug's Colt .45 was aimed at Chu's head.

They had agreed to take out any men they encountered without setting up an alarm since they had no idea how large or small the bunker might be or where the hostages might be located within it.

Joe, Ramone and Nova rushed across the fifteen feet separating them from the man with the Colt .45. Cobra, Barbed Wire and Stars rushed the other three men.

The executioner, completely stunned by the onrush of

three green-clad strangers, hesitated one second too long. He didn't shoot Chu and he didn't even have time to yell or turn his gun on his attackers. Joe knocked him out with a gun blow to the temple. He went down with a loud thud, his gun clattering dully on the cement floor.

Ramone pulled out duct tape and peeled off a strip for the guy's mouth. Joe taped the man's wrists and ankles. Glad that the only sounds from the other side of the room were one smothered yelp and some soft scuffling, Nova hustled to Dennis Chu. "You're okay," she said softly.

She pulled off his blindfold and helped him sit. It didn't take much effort. He more or less collapsed in a heap and she squatted beside him.

"Be absolutely quiet," she said. "Where are the others?"

"In…" tears started rolling down his cheeks "…two more rooms."

She stood and checked the action. All four of Martinez's men were now secure and no alarm had been raised. Trained Special Ops could not have done it better.

But apparently the rest of the hostages were in two separate rooms. The only other exit from this room was another cement corridor that ended in a T after about six feet. This room held four bunk beds, sleeping spaces for eight, and also a propane stove and refrigerator, so there might easily be at least four more men to take out. The sound of a generator permeated the background, persistent but not too annoying.

She held up two fingers and signaled that they were to split and that Joe would go with Cobra. Stars would guard their backs. Ramone and Barbed Wire should stay with her.

Once again in a bunch and with Joe leading, they headed into the next corridor.

Chapter 33

With Cobra at his back, Joe hurried silently down the fifteen or so feet toward another big room. He could already make out that it served for storage: boxes and crates had been stacked in neat rows, ceiling to floor, along the wall he could see. A sizable arsenal.

Stooped, his Glock at the ready, Joe rushed into the room.

To his right, three bound captives sat on a cement floor, their backs to the wall. A single guard had been sitting in a chair and apparently getting ready to clean his gun because he held it in his hands. He turned it on Joe and fired.

Following Ramone, with Barbed Wire at her back, her heart racing and her senses taking in sounds, smells and sights, Nova heard a gunshot just before she and her teammates burst into a room packed with crates and boxes. She scanned left and saw only more boxes. She scanned right and saw three bound women—and a guard with raised gun.

The guard aimed at her, fired and, in that strange world of slowed-down time that she had experienced more than once, she saw something else. Something amazing. Ramone, seeing the gun aimed at her, launched himself into the path of the bullet.

She saw Ramone's action with total clarity, saw the bullet strike him and his body shake at the impact, saw him reach for his chest and then glide in a flowing, gentle movement to the cement floor.

Seeming to have all the time in the world, she pulled the trigger on the Glock twice, aimed directly at the guard's heart.

Joe ignored the slight sting where the guard's bullet grazed his shoulder and plowed into the son-of-a-bitch's midsection. They crashed onto the floor. He sensed Cobra coming up beside them, and before either Joe or the guard could strike a blow, Cobra bent over and cold-cocked the guard with his fist. "You don't get all the fun," Cobra said, grinning as Joe pushed himself off the guard and to his feet.

Cobra pulled out his own handy roll of duct tape and secured the guard's wrists.

One look told Joe that he had found the two Bennings and the Obst boy. To Cobra he said, "Protect the hostages."

He ran back into the corridor, Stars behind him. Two shots, Joe thought, anguished. *The one at me, and another. Let Nova be okay.*

The guard who had fired at her and hit Ramone fell forward and hit the cement floor with a sickening thud.

For a moment Nova's mind went blank, a strange, confused moment. It was as if she had stripped some kind of gears in her head and her mind could not decide what to do: check the hostages or go to Ramone.

The paralysis passed as Barbed Wire knelt beside Ramone. Nova turned to check the hostages. She had found Linda, Nancy and Colette. They sat on the floor, bound and with eyes still wide in terror, but apparently unhurt.

She should go to find Joe immediately. He might need help. But something deep and primitive gripped her and moved her to Ramone. He had taken that bullet for her. She knelt, praying that she would see him smile and hear him say, "It's not too bad."

His eyes were closed and blood seeped from the corner of his mouth.

"Goddamn it," Barbed Wire said. His next two words were in Portuguese. "Shit. Fuck."

Joe burst into the second big storage room to find Nova and Barbed Wire kneeling beside Ramone. *Jesus, Joseph and Mary.* Ramone looked to be dead or dying.

A guard, lying facedown on the cement, also looked to be dead. Against the wall sat the rest of their hostages. He started untying them.

Colette Stone was the first to rediscover her voice. "Who are you?" she said in a choked, dry whisper.

"We're here to free you."

"There are others. I think in another room here."

"We've got them. You're all safe."

She bowed her head. "Thank God."

Joe stood and looked at Nova. She had taken Ramone's head into her lap.

Wait a minute, he thought, suddenly puzzled.

Something didn't add up. The bug guy. Then three people in the first room. Three people here. That added up to seven. But there should be nine. Two were missing.

Chapter 34

Ramone's pulse beat so faintly that Nova had at first thought he was dead. She had lifted his head into her lap, searching his face, a bit of hope surging through her. Some part of her realized that Joe had come into the room, that she didn't need to leave, that the situation must now be stable.

She took Ramone's hand in hers. "Hang on," she said, putting all the conviction and urgency she possessed into the words. "The Special Ops team will be here soon. They'll take care of you."

Her voice must have reached him. He opened his eyes, blinked, recognized her.

"You shouldn't have done it, Ramone."

"Had to." He tightened his grip.

Little vignettes of the good times with Ramone flashed through her memory. How he had taken a hard young woman recently out of prison and made her laugh at jokes for the first time in five years. His earnest attempts to give her passion in their lovemaking and his tender patience with her when she said she wasn't capable of enjoying it. Ramone had introduced her to nature photography, a love that in the years to follow would sometimes be the only thing to give her joy. And now he had taken a death blow meant for her.

She pressed against the wound in his chest. It seemed to have no effect at stopping the blood. "You're tough. You hang on!"

"Loved you. Really did. Should never have left."

"Don't talk."

"So, so sorry."

In the background she could hear the now-freed captives hugging and laughing. The other Americans, obviously freed by Joe and Cobra, had come to join them, and in the cold, sterile concrete bunker, these people felt like party time.

God, life was ironic beyond anything a human being could ever dream up or even comprehend. Ramone was dying; the red pool rapidly collecting around his body terrified her. The captives were deliriously happy. A man who was single-handedly responsible for recruiting her to this bizarre life was dying in her arms, and he had finally told her he was sorry for treating her in a way that had scarred her for years.

The sound of running feet drew her attention to the door. A team of five black-clad men rushed in, handguns drawn. They halted, scanned the scene and visibly relaxed. Joe approached the team leader.

"Glad you're here." He nodded toward Ramone. "One of ours needs help stat."

Two of the men came to her side, clearly preparing to carry Ramone out of the bunker. The collecting pool of blood continued to widen.

Nova shook her head. "Check him before you move him."

One of the men complied, opening up Ramone's shirt. She wanted to look away but couldn't do it. She had to know.

"We need to stabilize him." He called to another teammate. "Get some plasma!"

Ramone's grip, which had held firm, relaxed.

"Don't go," she said.

Ramone took in one more shallow breath, and then nothing.

Hot tears rolled from her eyes and down her cheeks.

"You can't do nothin' for him now," Cobra said, pushing the Special Ops guys aside.

She laid Ramone's head down onto the concrete, rose and stepped away. She turned her back on the scene, sensing that Cobra and Stars were lifting Ramone. She brushed at tears. Sucking in a deep breath, she finally mastered them.

When she turned back, Cobra, Stars and Barbed Wire disappeared into the corridor, carrying their boss and friend. Joe stepped up to her. "We have a big problem."

"Which is?"

"The Hill boy isn't here. And Colette Stone tells me she's pretty sure they killed the guide, Kimball Kiff. He got loose and ran out and they never brought him back."

"Suleema Johnson's grandson isn't here?"

"Right."

Nova strode to Ronnie Obst. The kid was rubbing his eyes, clearly fighting tears running down his cheeks and dripping off his chin.

"The bastards killed my father! My father is dead."

She put a hand on his shoulder. "We want to help your friend. What do you think has happened to Alex?"

Colette Stone came up to Ronnie and put her arm

around his shoulders. The woman who had looked so fresh and bright in the smiling photos Nova had studied looked haggard and ten years older. Smeared patches of dirt covered her white culottes and top. But her azure-blue eyes looked at Nova with frank clarity. "Alex was never kept with us. From the time they took us off the airplane, they immediately took Alex away in a separate car."

"Who is 'they'? These men here?"

"No. We never saw the two men or Alex again."

Ronnie searched Nova's face. "Do you think they've killed Alex?"

She shook her head and told him the truth, both because it was the truth and might also reassure him. "I doubt it very much, Ronnie. No. Your friend is alive. They didn't bring any of you down here just to kill you. Do you know if he had his medicine with him?

Colette said, "None of us were allowed to talk to each other until we arrived here. There is no way for us to know."

"Look everybody," one of the Special Ops team said with authority, "we're here to get you out, and we have to move it. Follow me out of this bunker."

Nova joined Joe, who was talking with the special ops team leader. "This is Bill," Joe said by way of introduction.

"Nova," she answered, and shook Bill's hand. "We need to ask questions of the other guards." She nodded toward the man still lying facedown on the floor, pushing away any thoughts of a wife, mother, children, or even a pet dog that he might love. "I'm sorry to say, I had to take this one out."

Bill turned, and she and Joe followed him back to the first room. The hostages and three of the Special Ops team were apparently already above ground. One towering, black-clad, iron-jawed African American stood guard over their captives, who had been lined up and seated in a row on the floor.

Nova looked at Joe and nodded to Carlito Gomez. Gomez needed to be intimidated as much as possible, at least for starters. This called for Joe's appearance and demeanor, not hers.

Joe went directly to Gomez and ripped the duct tape off Gomez's mouth. To his credit, Gomez didn't complain. "Who is the boss here?" Joe asked in Spanish, leaning over the seated man.

Gomez nodded to one of their five kidnappers, a wiry man with a heavy five o'clock shadow. "Luis," Gomez said softly, apparently hoping that pointing out the boss would get the very angry-looking American off his own back.

Still in Spanish, "Where is the other boy?"

Gomez kept his gaze fixed on the floor.

Joe struck Gomez a solid blow on the jaw, snapping his head to one side. "Where is the other boy?"

Gomez answered in good Spanish. "I will be killed if I tell that."

"I'll kill you if you don't tell."

She could see Gomez clench his jaw tightly. She moved in and nudged Joe aside. Time for the good cop. She stuck with Spanish. "You know these people you have taken are very important. You know we want all of them back. I can offer you anything you want if you will tell us where the other boy is."

"I don't know. Ask Luis."

"I'm asking you." To give him a bit of time to think about her offer she asked a different question. "Where is your boss, Felipe Martinez?"

It seemed Carlito realized it would be unbelievable to her or anyone that this operation could be on Martinez's property without Martinez's knowledge. He said, "He's gone to a big celebration."

Escurra's party? "At the Escurra rancho?"

Carlito nodded and looked sideways at Luis, who was glaring at Carlito and, had his mouth not been taped, would probably be screaming at his subordinate to keep his mouth shut. Isolation from the pack might help loosen Carlito's tongue. "Bring Carlito into the other room," she said to the big African American soldier.

Leaving Joe behind, the three of them moved back into the room where she had shot the guard. Seeing his dead friend on the floor opened Carlito's eyes wide. The soldier shoved Carlito into a chair.

Nova came close to him, stuck her face inches from his. "Anything you want, Carlito. We need to know where the other boy is."

"Anything?"

Right on! Just how much would he ask for? "Pretty much anything that's legal. I won't kill someone for you or go to bed with you."

"Will you fly me out of Paraguay? Right now. Take me with you. If you leave me here or even put me in jail, Martinez will find and kill me."

"Sure. I can promise you that if you know where the boy is."

"Will you take me to Spain and give me a thousand U.S. dollars?"

Clearly Carlito had no real appreciation for how little a thousand U.S. dollars could buy him, even in Spain. "I can't promise Spain for certain. But I can swear that I will see to it that you are accepted by a Spanish-speaking country and that you have the money."

"How can I trust you?"

"Why would I lie? You are nothing to me and nothing to my government. The boy is very important. Stop stalling. Either you know where he is or you don't."

"He was taken right away to the Eagle."

"The Eagle? That's what people call Escurra, right? Escurra has him?"

"Yes."

"Where does he have him?"

"On his ranch."

"But the ranch is huge. Where?"

"I don't know, but I think the Casa Grande. Luis said once that he wished he would be spending his time watching over the other boy instead of having to sit in this hole in the ground. It made me think the boy might be at Señor Escurra's fine place."

Nova looked at the Special Ops man and said in English, "Keep him separate from the others. They don't need to know he talked."

She returned to Joe and Bill in the living and sleeping room and told them that the Hill boy was possibly at Escurra's ranch house. With Joe and Bill, she quickly went back outside into the heat, leaving the gagged guards in the soldier's care. The Special Ops men had already hustled the Americans into a transport helicopter.

Cobra approached. The boys had put Ramone's body into one of the Land Rovers. "We're taking him back to Asuncion with us," Cobra said. "Did you get what you want? I hope it was worth it."

"You all did something fine. You know that. We've rescued seven people and we're going to rescue another one. The Special Ops guys will help us now."

"You know that Ramone had Sam monitoring Martinez's phone calls, the landline."

"Yes."

"Well, did Ramone tell you that this Luis has called Martinez every hour on the hour saying that everything is fine? And during one of the calls Martinez said he expected to hear from Luis on schedule all night. The calls were all to the Escurra ranch."

She didn't know if Cobra would like it or not, but she was truly grateful for their help. She put her hand on his arm and said, "Thank you. I want you to let me know where Ramone is laid to rest."

A nod. A sad smile. "The boss thought helping you was worth it."

With that, Cobra returned to the Land Rover, and he and the other boys took off.

Bill said, "It's time for us to get the hell out as well."

"You can't go yet. We don't have Alex Hill."

Chapter 35

Bill shook his head. The Special Ops team leader widened his stance and crossed his arms. "We've retrieved seven of our nine targets, most especially the VP's daughter. We need to get out ASAP. We're not hanging around."

"We can't leave the boy behind," Joe snapped at him.

"You can take out the people we already have," Nova said, "but we're not writing the boy off."

Bill shrugged and looking at Joe said, "What do you suggest?"

Joe looked at her. "So?"

"I don't like to think out loud, and we're going to have to do some serious calculating." She looked at Bill. "All right. Take them out. But I want you to call first and get permission to come back to extract us once we find the boy. You make that call while Joe and I start thinking how we'll find him."

"Okay." Bill moved off several feet and spoke into his communicator.

"First off," Joe said, "we need to have at least one Special Ops guy stay here and make Luis send his everything-is-okay messages to Martinez. We should have kept the guys here. One of them could have done it."

"It's just as well we don't get the boys any more involved than necessary."

Joe looked at his watch. "It's one thirty. First things first. We need to get onto the Escurra property. Search the house. If we're lucky, Alex will be there. If not, we have to have a plan B and C."

"What I can't figure out is why they would treat Alex differently."

"I've been beating my brains out over that one myself," Joe said. "If we knew that, we might know better what kind of treatment they could be giving him."

"I can't get out of my mind that he's a diabetic and presumably without the ability to eat the foods he needs. God forbid that they have him stashed in some hot place."

Bill strode up, a determined look in the bearing of his squared shoulders. "Okay. I have permission. We'll take these folks to the *Ronald Reagan*. It's our base just outside of Brazilian territorial waters. When you locate the boy, you can call. We'll come in again, with only one copter."

Joe said, "We're going to need someone to stay here with this guy Luis. We have to be dead certain he makes his call in to Martinez regularly."

"I can leave James. Twenty-four hours only. Then he abandons the bunker and Martinez's guards and we pick him up."

"Okay," Joe said. "I'm going to go down right now and

see to it that Luis makes a call. He may already be past his scheduled call time." Joe went back into the shack.

Nova shook Bill's hand and held it just a bit longer than necessary. "We'll be depending on you. And thank you."

"It's my job," he said, but he grinned at her.

She watched the helicopter take off. It disappeared over the jungle canopy as Joe returned to her. "Luis is cooperating nicely," he said. "I get the feeling his men don't much like Martinez. Luis calls on the half hour, so this call-in was only eight minutes late. Martinez chewed Luis out, but I don't think any alarm was sounded."

"Unless they had some kind of special agreed-upon signal for indicating that something's gone wrong."

"What can I say? These guys are big-time operators. We just have to plan for the worst and hope for the best."

"Yeah. Look, it's hotter than hell out here. You've got maps of the Escurra place in the Land Rover. Let's take them back into that deliciously cool bunker."

Nova collected up the playing cards and Joe spread the maps onto the table. James had found a beer in the refrigerator and made himself comfortable in a chair where he could keep an eye on the bound guards. For a while Nova stood beside Joe, both of them thinking in silence. Finally she said, "He's having this big party tonight. Maybe we could find out who's catering the whole thing and I could go in as a cook's helper, or serving girl."

"You can't be serious."

She laughed. "No. But a ploy like that might work if this was the States."

"Probably not even there. Mobsters have their catering service employees fully vetted. Besides, this guy very likely employs so many people he won't need outside help with the cooking or anything else. He wouldn't need me to park cars, either."

Again she smiled. Joe's sense of the ridiculous was one of the very best things about him to love.

Love. There it was again.

"I know a way for sure that I can get into the house, but we'd have to wait until this evening. I hate having to wait."

"If we find the kid, an extraction at night will be best in any case. The place is going to be crawling with people preparing for the party. How *could* you get in?"

"Bebe has been invited. He could take me as his guest."

"You're certain he can bring a guest?"

"Not certain, but I think so. I can call and find out."

"Call."

Bebe answered immediately. "Yes. Of course. No problem. I've brought people before. You come see me when you are ready. We will go together from the hotel."

"We're on," she said to Joe as she snapped the cell phone shut.

"What if the kid isn't at the house? This Escurra has other homes, some in Paraguay, in addition to this place in Brazil."

"But they brought everyone else here. Why not Alex as well?" She started folding up the maps. "Let's drive back to the Blue Parrot. I have to pack what I'll need."

"Fine. After you pack we can work on plans B and C."

"Basically we only have twenty-four hours of surprise on our side—the rest of today and half of tomorrow—because after James leaves, the calls from Luis will stop and someone will come out to find out why."

Joe walked her to her Jeep. He closed the driver's door for her, letting his hands rest on the top of the doorframe, temptingly close. He said, "I loathe to suggest another worry, but how much do you trust Ramone's boys?

Ramone is dead. They could make a lot of money selling what they know to Martinez or Escurra."

She put her hand over Joe's. She didn't need to. She just couldn't stop herself. "They smuggle birds and orchids and look like they could do battle with the devil himself, but Ramone vouched for all of them. I think they loved Ramone. I don't think they'd do anything to dishonor his memory."

Joe's fingers curled around hers. "I love *you*. And I hope you're right."

Joe loved her. That had not changed. They had never talked about children, and that was the only really compelling reason to marry. Security for children. And children didn't appear to be all that important to Joe. When this op was over, she would win him back. Things could be like they had been before.

Joe drove back to the Blue Parrot at top speed. He kept kicking himself for telling Nova that he loved her. She hadn't said a thing. She sure didn't say, "Okay, I'll marry you," although that's what he wanted to hear.

The words had just popped out of his mouth, and he knew why. He'd seen her tears when Ramone died. He knew, just knew, there had to be something more than one op between Nova and Ramone. Why would she cry?

Would she cry if *he* died? That's what he'd been wondering.

Chapter 36

At quarter to six, still dressed in the green birding outfit and boots, Nova entered the now festively decorated lobby of The Royal Hotel Iguazu. A mammoth fir tree, imported from a cold climate, dominated the two-story room. Its angel-crowned peak looked down on a treescape of twinkling white lights, fake snow, and hundreds of sparkling red and green Christmas bulbs. The soft strains of "O Holy Night" provided background music and was accompanied by the strong and distinctive scent of cedar.

She went directly to Bebe's office carrying her woven bag and a small backpack with the dress she would wear to the party. Inside the bag's lining she had packed the Glock, the GPS transponder, the lightweight camouflage bodysuit and climbing shoes, and the miniature camera/tape recorder/cell phone. The obvious contents, should the purse be searched, were lipstick, a mirror, money, cell phone, a small but powerful flashlight, and a packet of tissues. Of course, she could worry about the extra weight of the Glock…but she wouldn't.

Bebe closed the door behind them and after hugging her said, "Did you find them?"

"Yes, Bebe." They took seats opposite each other, she on a sofa in front of a low coffee table and he in a comfortable armchair. "Your friend's information was correct. The shack he described actually covered an underground bunker where Martinez probably stores weapons and ammunition. Maybe drugs. We didn't check it all out. We found seven of the hostages, and the team sent to rescue them wanted to depart ASAP. Now we must find someone else."

"Was your sister with them?"

"Yes. I found Linda. But another boy is still missing."

"You're not going to tell me who is helping you, are you?"

"I can't say much more, Bebe."

"CNN and MSNBC and all of the Brazilian channels still talk of practically nothing else. Everyone says maybe the Americans will send troops to invade Manaus."

She laughed.

"Why must you go to Escurra's party?"

"Because we think Escurra has the boy hidden somewhere on his ranch. Most likely somewhere in his big house."

"You don't look well, Nova. Are you okay?"

"Of course. I'm fine."

But she wasn't fine at all. She kept having flashes of Ramone holding her hand and then letting go. The effect was profoundly shocking and sobering. One minute you could be alive and the next millisecond you could be dead. Contemplating this fragility of life was eating at her, as if urgently trying to remind her of something important.

"I won't press you. Tell me what you want me to do."

She explained some of the plan she and Joe had devised, an awful lot of it being sheer improvisation once she penetrated the big house. She did not mention Joe. Then she asked, "What is the earliest we could arrive at the party?"

"The party will not start until eight o'clock. It's a thirty-minute drive from here. We can leave at seven thirty."

"I'm exhausted, Bebe. I hate to impose, but could you find a small room for me where I can rest? I also need to shower and change clothes."

He accompanied her to the registration desk, arranged for a room in double-quick time, and then he walked her to it. "You don't need to babysit me," she said as she opened the door to room 311. "I'll be fine. I'll meet you in the lobby at seven thirty."

"I'm not babysitting you. I've seen you in action. You never need to convince me you can take care of yourself. It's just my pleasure to be at your side."

Bebe took her hand and gave it a continental kiss. A warm glow of affection for him and recognition of his affection for her flushed her skin. He turned quickly and strode away, a big, dear man who, she was quite sure, must have made his wife extremely happy. Certainly Solange adored him.

The moment she was safe inside the room, she text-messaged the room's number to Joe, who was waiting outside in his Land Rover. She wedged a piece of notepaper taken from the bedside stand in between the door latch and the jam just enough to be sure the door could open without a key and closed it.

She shoved the woven bag under the bed, then sat her backpack on top of the bedspread. She laid out the white silk top and pants, picked not only because they could breathe well in this topical heat and looked elegant enough for a party, but because they folded down into virtually nothing. She would finish the outfit off with wedge sandals, pearl-drop earrings and the gold locket with mother-of-pearl front that held a tiny GPS transponder.

The bathroom, with brass-plated fixtures and black marble, exuded the same air of money as the rest of the hotel. She could not get out of the green pants and shirt fast enough. She dropped them, along with her pants and bra, onto the floor and started the shower, temperature on the cool side. She used the jasmine-scented shampoo.

She'd just rinsed her hair a last time when the shower door opened. Joe grinned as his eyes exaggeratedly explored her from her forehead to her toes.

She splashed a spray of water at him. His grin just broadened.

"You are rude, impolite, uninvited and should be whipped," she said, meeting the challenge of his grin with a defiant smile of her own.

"Whipped! Sounds good. And you are still gawdawful beautiful."

"Get out of here!" she demanded, thinking what it would be like for him to strip and get in with her. They had once made love with memorable results in the shower on Capri.

He shrugged. "Okay. Whatever you say. Then make it snappy."

After she finished, while he showered she slipped into a black, hotel-supplied bathrobe and dried her hair. She'd wear it straight and loose, pulled back behind one ear. When it was dry she stretched out with a sigh on the queen-size bedspread which, like the bathroom, was also done in black and white.

Joe came out with no towel around his waist—was he taunting her again, or reminding her of what she had given up? He'd put a gauze patch over his grazed shoulder at the

Blue Parrot and had managed to keep it dry. "Do they supply two robes?"

She pointed to the closet.

"Your friend Bebe is pretty ballsy to do this."

"He says it will give him a chance to grow. Something about not liking to be in the same old rut all the time."

"Pretty nice rut."

"The hotel is beautiful and the people who come here must be interesting. But Bebe is quite sad. I don't know, maybe he's even subconsciously reckless. We're asking him to mess with the most powerful man in a thousand square miles. Bebe lost the wife he loved two years ago. Now he has only his daughter, Solange."

Joe stretched out on the other side of the bed, his hands clasped together behind his head. Nova could barely keep her thoughts on their conversation. He *had* to be taunting her. He could have sat in a chair, couldn't he? It might not be so comfortable, but surely he must know that every inch of her body longed for him to cross the line between them and peel back their robes.

"So he has a daughter?"

"I talked with her yesterday for a short time. She's grown very beautiful."

"You know, my brother got married."

"Really!"

"I like the woman. And I bet they get right down to having kids."

Nova had wondered how Joe felt about kids. Now would be the perfect moment to ask. The question formed, but for some reason she held it back.

He continued to stare at the ceiling and then said, "I still want you so much it sometimes hurts, Nova."

She felt her throat tightening. She kept her gaze fixed

on the ceiling. "Sometimes I think it was stupid for us to split up. I can't even imagine wanting anyone else."

Joe sat up, closed the space between them and kissed her, a gentle, short kiss. Then touching her chin he said, "Me neither."

"We could be adults," she said, grinning. "We could kiss some more and make up."

He kissed her again, this one long and lingering but still tender. He tousled her bangs for a moment, then gave her his very best killer smile. "Why don't we take the big leap, like my brother."

She shook her head and returned the smile. "I read somewhere that married people take each other for granted. Why not stay single and keep things fresh and exciting?"

"I saw the way you cried when Ramone died. Would you ever care for me that much?"

She touched his lips, and tracing one eyebrow said, "Don't be silly."

"What was it between him and you?"

"We—I—don't want to go there, Joe. It was a long, long time ago."

"Then he must have made one hell of an impression a long time ago."

"Let's talk about now and let the past be the past."

"Okay, babe." He opened her robe and kissed one breast, teasing the nipple. She closed her eyes and inhaled deeply, savored the tingling. He kissed the other breast. "Marry me. Now or as soon as we can arrange it."

Her eyes snapped open, the mood immediately broken yet again. "Why won't you lay off the marriage thing?"

He sat back. "Because I love you. I want to spend my life with you, however long that life may be. With no one else but you."

She felt suddenly short of breath. She wasn't winning him over. She hadn't even made a little dent. "I can't marry you, Joe. Why can't you understand that?"

"Would you have married Ramone?"

Alarm mixed with anger, warming her cheeks. She sat up. "Ramone is one of the very reasons I don't want to marry. He loved me and he left me, and I had no say in the matter. I spent time in prison, another place where I had no say in what I was allowed to do. Marriage is a major way to get yourself all tied down, can't you see that?"

The light in Joe's eyes flared like someone had breathed on glowing coals, all tenderness in them burnt up. "I can see that I could die without ever having been married or having kids. And I don't want that."

She stood—on her side of the bed—and stared at him.

He stared back.

Something needed to fill the silence.

She clenched her jaw. "I am never going to give up my independence."

"Fine." Joe rolled off the other side of the bed. "So, let's get dressed."

Chapter 37

Joe had tried to convince Nova that he should be positioned somewhere on the Escurra property near the house so he could be closer to her if something went wrong. She'd insisted that there were no good places to hide near the house on the north side and that on the south side, he risked being seen because that's where all the party action would be. He finally conceded that it was better that he wait on the road just north of the property, where she had done her scouting. "If you have to," she'd said, "you can reach the house from there in a quick thirty-second dash."

Bebe drove his year-old black Mercedes sedan carefully, such a contrast to Joe who drove a car like he was still flying jets off a carrier. Nova sat in the front passenger seat clutching her cell phone. Escurra's Casa Grande lay not more than half a mile ahead when the text from Joe came in.

I'm in place.

Bebe gave the Mercedes a bit more gas and they arrived within moments at the front of the imposing home. An attendant took the car. No host or hostess greeted them. They walked inside and were immediately offered a selection of canapés on a tray. "There are drinks in the bar, directly ahead of you," the pretty young waitress said in Spanish.

Music always set any party's mood and "Joy to the World" played by Mannheim Steamroller flooded the large entry hall. They passed a few chatting duos and trios as they strolled deeper into the house. They found the bar in a room with two pool tables, four video game booths, and a mechanical bucking bronco, which no one in this crowd was using—yet. The night, she thought, was still young.

She'd accepted a gin and tonic, her favorite drink in hot climates, and Bebe took his first sip of a Campari on ice when Escurra himself entered the bar/game room.

"My friends," he said in Spanish, loud enough to capture everyone's attention and cause all chatting to subside. "I must leave to attend the festivities for my hired hands, but I will be away from you only briefly. Enjoy. I shall return."

Several guests called out *"Feliz Navidad,* Tomas," as Escurra made his departure.

Nova handed her drink to Bebe. "I have to see where he goes. I'm inside now. You should leave. Go to your car and get out of here."

"I will not leave you here alone."

"You can't help me, Bebe. I will worry if you are here. Please don't ask questions or argue. Just leave."

She hurried after Escurra, hoping Bebe would comply. Escurra's leaving the house called for a substantial shift in plan. She had not expected Escurra to leave the party, a mistake. Of course he would attend both parties, the one here and the one for his men. Making mistakes like that could be costly if not disastrous.

Catching up to him was easy because he stopped in each room to deliver the same message that he would return. She followed, well back, and finally watched him walk out the open front door. From a tall window beside the door, she watched him climb into a golf car and head south. He was heading for the fighting pit.

She nibbled her lip, her mind calculating. Should she follow, or use this opportunity to search the house, the original plan, and then follow if she didn't find the boy?

Her instinct was to follow Escurra. But everything Carlito had said indicated that Alex was being kept in a nice place, which probably meant the house. Certainly not those sheds by the fighting pit. She'd already checked most of them out. She pushed instinct aside. "First things first," she said softly.

She couldn't just stand here looking out. She moved away from the door slowly. Earlier in the afternoon, the CIA had faxed the Casa Grande's building plans to the Blue Parrot. She and Joe had figured that if she started from the kitchen on the extreme east side and worked her way through the whole place, both floors, she could cover it in ten minutes, provided she encountered no hindrances.

Someone had abandoned a nearly empty champagne glass on an end table. She picked it up and headed toward the kitchen. On the way, she stopped to look in every room, even those close to the party.

There were men who appeared to be guards every now and then, but they simply smiled at her. This was way too easy. They did not have the demeanor of men hiding anything. They behaved like they were there to make sure that none of Escurra's valuable possessions got lifted. The house seemed to be entirely open to the guests, who could apparently explore wherever they wanted to.

She wandered into the kitchen, taking the cooks by surprise. But even most of them just smiled at her. She helped herself to a bit of roast beef and strolled back out, heading for the stairs to the second, top floor. Escurra's office occupied the middle room.

A guard stood at the foot of the stairs, and while Nova was wracking her brain for a means to distract him, a woman approached him and said that she could not find her purse. He escorted the woman toward another guard, and Nova raced up the stairwell, her heart pounding, unable to resist a tiny smile.

Still, this was much too easy.

As she stepped into the second floor hallway, the hair raised on the back of her neck. No guests here. The music and bright lights were all down below. The recessed doors along the hall were cast into deep shadows. If she encountered guards here and if Alex was being held up here, she would not likely receive smiles.

She heard the sound of flushing water before the second door down opened. She shrank back into the shadow of the first doorway. Felipe Martinez strode out of the bathroom, passed her and ambled down the stairs.

Peeking out from the shadow and seeing no other guards, she turned around and opened the door to the first room. From her bag she took out the high-beam flashlight, did a scan and found an empty bedroom.

She checked every room on the floor, including Escurra's big office with its overstuffed brown leather furniture and massive rosewood desk. Like the Casa

Grande itself, his decorating taste ran to American Southwest. He'd probably watched too many Western movies.

Alex Haley Hill wasn't in the house. No basement had been indicated on the building plans. She needed to get out of here, change clothes and go after Escurra. Pushing aside crushing disappointment—perhaps the boy had died—she decided to follow the feeling in her gut this time.

A second stairwell lay at the other end of the hallway, and clutching her champagne glass she marched down it and past the guard assigned to keep guests from going upstairs. She smiled, and though he looked both puzzled and pissed he also managed a stiff smile. They had probably all been told to act nice.

Outside she told the only car boy present that she was waiting for someone, and when he drove the next car away to park it, she strode briskly toward the pool cabana.

Guests surrounded the pool, and tango music set an entirely different mood. She walked to the generator house. Oleander, in fragrant bloom, had been planted around it to hide it. To the steady thrum of the generator's electric pulse, she undid the lining of the woven bag and quickly changed into the lightweight, green-and-tan camouflage outfit and the folded boots. She took off the gold locket and replaced that GPS device with one that fit into her navel, then put the GPS locket into the hiding place in the lining.

The silk outfit she folded and stuffed into the bag, along with the wedge heels. She checked the Glock to be sure it was loaded and ready, and decided to keep it concealed but ready for action in the bag's hidden compartment.

Crossing the bag's strap over one shoulder and under the other arm, she bolted toward the first of the lighted rancheritas. To her right, a few lights beamed into the night from the bunkhouse, but it looked mostly deserted.

Halfway to the first rancherita, she heard the sounds of shouting men.

Chapter 38

All three rancheritas were lit up. but Nova could not see or hear signs of life in any of them. Surely by now all the guests at the party, but these folks were not likely to be big into energy conservation so she wouldn't expect them to turn off the lights.

Recalling that she had been unable to look into the tiny windows of the cells in the shed because she couldn't find anything to stand on, she scanned the yards. She filed away for future reference the memory of two motorbikes in one yard—in her experience, motorbikes often came in handy. But not now, when she needed stealth. Instead she stole one of three bicycles from the yard of another rancherita.

Silently, she pushed the bike behind the houses and past the pool, and then hopped on and peddled toward the animal shed. The moon still hung low in the sky and was only half full so she probably wouldn't be seen, the black bike and her camouflage blending into the background. But if her peddling movement or the subtle sounds of her wheels or the bikes' chain caught someone's attention, she would be a sitting duck.

Ancient trucks and Jeeps lined the road, but everyone seemed to be inside the arena. She zipped behind the end of the shed farthest from the fighting pit. The shouting sounded like a riot in progress. She pushed the bike to the first window, leaned the bike against the wall and climbed up to stand on the seat. Inside, a wild boar ran in what looked like a crazed circle.

She found the same in the next two pens. At the fourth window she looked inside and saw nothing. She started to climb down when a hushed voice said, in English, "Is someone there?"

Nova was so startled she nearly fell off the bicycle. She peered harder into the gloom. "Who's there?" came the same hushed voice of an American boy again.

"Are you Alex?"

"Yes. Who are you?"

An enormous wave of elation swept through her. Only then did she realize that no matter what she had kept insisting with her conscious mind, she had believed that Alex Haley Hill was already dead. *Sometimes fate is kinder than we expect.*

He stood, emerged from shadow and moved closer to the window. He was fully clothed in jeans and an extremely filthy white shirt. He not only wasn't dead, he didn't look ill. They must have let him use the insulin.

"I'm getting you out of here."

"There is another boy," he said. "In the cell next to mine. Did you see him?"

"No. My job is not to get anyone else away." The question flashed through her mind, Why would they have another boy?

"You can't leave him." The words spilled out of Alex, like he'd been dying to say them to someone. "They're going to make us fight to kill each other. If you leave him, I think they'll kill him."

"Alex, just sit tight. Please, don't make any fuss. I have to leave, to call in Special Forces to get you out. Do you understand?"

"Okay."

She was impressed with the kid's smarts. He didn't beg her to stay or beg her to get him out right this minute. He seemed to comprehend his situation and hers. And he cared about the other boy. She decided then that she liked Alex Haley Hill very much.

The clamoring voice of at least two barking dogs broke their contact. She swung her head in the direction of the sound and saw two Doberman pinschers galloping down the back side of the shed toward her.

"Shit!"

She dropped down onto the bicycle seat, turned the bicycle away from the dogs and pedaled like crazy. Near the other end of the shed she looked back. Two men dressed like ranch hands with guns in their hands sprinted toward her behind the Dobermans. She pedaled harder and started to turn the shed's corner, nearly running over a man dressed like a gaucho. He grabbed the handlebars. The bike stopped dead in place and Nova tumbled to the ground.

Before she could rise, one dog sunk his teeth into her pant leg and started shaking. She kicked at the beast with her other foot, wishing she was wearing her heavy hiking boots rather than the flimsy climbing ones.

One thug grabbed the dog's collar and pulled the Doberman off her. It continued to snarl. She rolled onto her back. The man glared down at her, his enormous mustache drooping like great black cigars down each side of his mouth. The other ranch hand had caught onto the collar of the other dog to hold it back as it barked.

If it weren't for all the screaming and yelling in the fighting pit, the dogs' clamor would have been drawing a crowd. The gaucho grabbed her by one arm and hauled her up. She thought about attacking him. One she could take. Even two. But the odds were against her with three, two of them with guns. The guy with the drooping mustache asked in Portuguese who she was. When she didn't reply he switched to Spanish. *"Quien esta?"*

She shook her head.

Mustache and Gaucho exchanged heated words in Portuguese, the gist of which seemed to be that they weren't sure whether to treat her like a woman or like a threat. Squeezing her arm, Gaucho shoved her toward the end of the shed nearest the fighting pit. The two ranch hands kept their grips on the dogs. They didn't put away their guns.

When they marched her into what appeared to be a shabby office—five chairs, desk, three filing cabinets—she wasn't surprised to see Felipe Martinez. He hadn't made himself comfortable behind the big desk, though. The desk and the huge swivel chair behind it were probably reserved for Escurra.

Martinez sat in a big leather armchair with his cell phone pressed to his ear. Seeing her, he said in Spanish, "I'll call you back" and snapped the device shut.

All four men now studied her intently and silently. She had to be quite a sight. The tight camouflage outfit, her hair braided up in back, the nice touch of pearl studs in her ears, and the dark brown woven bag across her chest.

"Go get the Eagle," Felipe said to Gaucho, who immediately left.

Felipe gestured toward the bag. Mustache helped himself to it. He dug a big, dirty hand inside and came up with her silk outfit, her cell phone, the wedge heels and her makeup kit. The men watched as he placed all the items, including the flashlight and tissues, on the desk.

She mustered long-practiced control to keep her breathing steady and her look innocent, but the hardest thing was to keep her gaze off the handbag. Would he find the Glock? Could he feel that the weight was too heavy for a woven bag holding only some makeup, clothes and a flashlight? Maybe not. How often would this rough man have a woman's purse in his hands?

Giving her a squint-eyed look, Felipe asked, in Spanish, "What are you doing here?"

She smiled and shook off the hold the Gaucho still had on her. "No *Español*."

"Search her," Felipe said.

Things would now get unpleasant. She noted that Mustache, apparently delighted by the prospect of searching her, stepped toward her, then discovering he still held her purse, he laid it on a chair beside her.

The camouflage outfit was skintight, not loose, so a search didn't take much time. But Mustache seemed to savor every minute of running his hands over her shoulders, down her sides, between and under her breasts, especially slowly between her legs and finally down to her ankles. The only way they would find the GPS inserted in the hollow of her navel would be to have her undress.

Before their brains could fix on that idea, Escurra burst

into the office. Every last one of the men, including Felipe, gave him immediate and full attention, doubtless moved by respect, fear or maybe both. Nova used a foot to scoot her purse out of the chair onto the brown dirt floor.

"She's not armed," Felipe said.

Escurra caught sight of the stuff on his desk. He walked to it, and while the men followed his movement, she kicked her purse with her heel toward the dim corner of the office as hard as she could without moving the rest of her body or looking to see if she'd been successful in hiding it. Out of sight, hopefully out of mind, she prayed.

Escurra snapped her cell phone open, turned it on, and discovering that everything was in English, turned to her and said in English, "Didn't I see you at my house dressed in this pretty little thing?" He held up her spaghetti-strap top.

She stuck with silence.

The man could frighten with just his appearance, to say nothing of his powerful reputation. Big shoulders, deeply set dark eyes and a hook nose. He'd been given his nickname, the Eagle, because the largest eagle in the world, the harpy eagle, made its home in Brazil. Escurra sure had the penetrating, dead-level gaze of the eyes of an eagle. Or perhaps, more relevantly, of a sociopath. In her career with the Company she had interacted closely with three such men, and she had read somewhere that virtually all sociopaths, whether they were charismatic ones beloved by many people or notoriously evil, shared the same trait—dead eyes. Their lips smiled, but their eyes never did.

Escurra strode to her. He towered over her. He used thumb and forefinger to feel the quality of the camouflage material.

"Are you American?"

When she didn't answer, Felipe said in English, "They caught her out back."

Escurra pushed her into the chair. He started to pace from her to his desk. "She came here with Bebe Garcia." He turned to Felipe. "Go to the Casa Grande and get Bebe. Be discreet. But bring him here. Right now."

Felipe stood. Escurra turned to Mustache and commanded in Spanish that he stop the cockfight. From the door, Martinez said, "Are you sure that's wise? Don't we need all the cover we can get? The more people here the better."

Escurra nodded. "You're right. We let the fights continue. But we have a serious problem. Someone with access to some fancy camouflage material is on to us."

Chapter 39

To his man who had until now remained silent and done nothing, Escurra said in Portuguese, "Move the American boy to the cave immediately. And make sure you double the guards. Tell them to maintain strict radio and audio caution."

Nova fought down panic and disappointment. She had found Alex only to be caught, and now Escurra was moving Alex to some damn cave. Of course, the Company had doubtless tasked an eye-in-the-sky satellite to watch every move on this ranch. It would most likely pick up and follow any transfer. But if they disguised Alex, the analysts would have no way to know what was happening, and there were probably close to a hundred vehicles coming to and going from the ranch tonight. Bad luck.

Now in the room with her were only Escurra, Mustache and Gaucho. She calculated the odds of being able to escape from three men, at least two and possibly three of them armed, and quickly chucked the idea.

Bebe would surely be long gone back to the hotel, so what would happen when Felipe returned without him?

Escurra started pacing again. He was rightly alarmed. A big noose was slipping over his head and his animal instincts knew it. He pulled out his own cell phone, stopped and studied it. She guessed he was trying to decide whether he could risk a call out or not.

Apparently deciding he must take the risk, he punched in a code. She listened as he talked in Portuguese. He was talking to Luis in the bunker on Martinez's place, and she felt grimly pleased because James clearly was still on the job and Luis was still producing convincing assurance that everything in the bunker was secure and quiet.

When Escurra rang off he told Mustache and Gaucho to watch her, saying that he was going back to the pit to watch a fight between a mastiff and a boar until Felipe returned. It seemed that a lot of money was riding on the match, and Escurra, having never seen a boar go up against a mastiff, didn't want to miss the action.

The two ranch hands grinned. Mustache asked if maybe he could go with Escurra and just let Gaucho watch the woman. Escurra's eyes burned a hole right through his underling's skull. "Look at how she's dressed. You think this is just some woman?" He stomped out.

Mustache was clearly disappointed that he'd miss the blood and gore. For a brief moment, as she listened to the still roaring voices of men, Nova suffered a loathing of the opposite sex. It passed quickly enough. Her father would have been repulsed. So would Jean Paul König. So would Bebe. So would Joe. The sickness to take joy in death and blood didn't infect all men—it just sometimes seemed that way.

When Felipe returned, he came with two captives: Bebe and Solange. Nova felt nauseated and swallowed hard. Bebe and Solange looked bewildered, especially Solange.

Felipe had apparently been required to pull his weapon at some point to convince them to accompany him. They looked around the grungy office, taking in the dirt floor and then Nova dressed in camouflage. She could imagine their dismay. *Why, oh why, Bebe did you not leave? And why, Solange, did you come to this damn party?*

"Solange decide to join us at the party. A surprise," Bebe said.

Felipe and Gaucho shoved Bebe and Solange into chairs.

Nova swallowed back her urge to scold Bebe with, "Why did you not go home?" Scolding would do no good now. "I'm damn sorry I got you into this."

Escurra strode into the office and signaled to Felipe, who closed the office door. The roaring outside continued, barely diminished.

"So, Bebe," he said in English. "Who is this woman? She came with you."

Bebe, though his face was pale, summoned courage. He said nothing.

Escurra pulled a nasty little folded knife from his pocket, pressed a spring and the knife sprang open, its blade maybe three inches long. He cut Bebe across one cheek. Not too deep, but it would be painful.

Nova balled a fist and bowed her head.

"I asked you, Bebe, who is she?"

Again Bebe said nothing. Nova's mental wheels raced. This could escalate into a nightmare. She had to do something. But what? Confessing to Escurra would serve no purpose, just get them all killed for certain.

Escurra placed the knife along the edge of Solange's chin. Nova leaped out the chair and Felipe slapped her back down into it.

"Her name is Nova Blair," Bebe said swiftly.

"Fine. Now we are getting somewhere. That's her name. Who is she? Who does she work for?"

"She's a friend. A travel agent. She told me her sister has been kidnapped and she is looking for the sister."

Escurra looked at Nova with his dead eyes, then back to Bebe. "How do you know her, Bebe?"

"She is a travel agent. We met years ago in the Galapagos."

"I find that hard to believe. Look at her, Bebe. Do travel agents dress like that?"

"I don't know why she's dressed like that, Tomas. She just told me she is looking for her kidnapped sister. That's all I know, I swear."

"Who did she come with?"

"Alone. She's alone." Sweat covered Bebe's pale face.

Escurra cut a line along Solange's chin, another shallow cut but bright blood sprang from it.

Nova felt her own face burning and perspiration trickling down her back. She made a promise to herself. If—no, when—she got loose from Escurra, she would come back and pay him back for that cut to Solange.

"You can get a good cosmetic surgeon to fix that, Bebe. But the next ones I make will be deeper and across her cheeks. I want to know who this Nova came with."

Chapter 40

With tears running down his cheeks, Bebe cried out to Escurra, "I swear to you on my daughter's life, this American woman came to me alone."

Thank you, thank you, Bebe. In spite of his terror for Solange, Bebe remained a damn smart man. Keeping Escurra in the dark was their best and only hope. Bebe knew Nova had to be with others, but he didn't know who they were so why even give Escurra the idea that she might not be alone.

Martinez yelled, "Then why is she here? How did she learn about us?"

Escurra strode to Nova and planted himself squarely in front of her. With one of those big hands, he slapped her so hard her head snapped backward. He then put the tip of his little knife to her cheek.

She heard Solange gasp. Solange was also crying, but silently.

The time had come for some creative lying. And some convincing acting. "Don't, please don't," Nova begged. She had missed sending her every-five-minute text to Joe. He would be alarmed.

"Talk, then."

"Bebe is telling the truth. All that he knows. I came to find my sister. The man helping me is from Asuncion."

Escurra pressed the knife to her skin, it stung, and she knew he'd drawn blood. A little warm trickle down her cheek seemed to settle at the edge of her chin.

"He's a...a long-time lover. He saw everything about my sister on television, and he called me and said that he knew where a bunch of Americans were being held captive. He said he figured it had to be the ones on the TV."

Martinez exploded. "What the fuck!"

"Shut up, Felipe," Escurra commanded, his voice a low growl. To Nova he said, "Go on. That doesn't begin to explain why you are here and dressed in fancy camouflage."

"When I got here, to Asuncion, he said that you—I guess you are Tomas Escurra—he said that Tomas Escurra was the big man in the tri-border area. That if anyone had organized a kidnapping this big, it was you."

"What's your friend's name?"

"He doesn't have to be—"

"Did you hear me?" Escurra said, leaning close to her and yelling. "What is your friend's name?"

"Ra-Ramone Villalobos."

"So how would this Villalobos come by all this information? I don't believe you."

"It's true. I don't know how he got this idea. And maybe he's wrong. Maybe this is all a big mistake."

"Why did you believe him? You've come a damn long way."

"Ramone, well, we've known each other a long time. He has…contacts. You know. Criminal elements."

"I don't believe you."

The little knife pricked her chin again.

"Pl-please. Ramone traffics in exotic birds and orchids. I figured he could know what he was talking about and I'm desperate. I just want to find my sister. Clearly she's not here. You can let us all go. I'm sure Bebe and Solange will say nothing." She looked at Bebe. "Isn't that right?"

Escurra pulled a pinch of the material of the camouflage outfit on her arm. "How do you explain this?"

"Well, like Bebe says, I'm a jungle tour guide. I know my way around. I thought I could get in here with Bebe's help, and then look everything over myself. No one at home would listen to me. They think I'm crazy to think the Americans are down here."

Escurra backed away and leaned against his desk, one ankle crossed over the other.

Felipe Martinez sent his boss a defiant look. "We can't let any of them go."

"I told you to shut up, Felipe," Escurra shot back.

The room fell silent, then Escurra shifted to both feet again. "Juan," he said in Spanish to the guy with the huge mustache, "get stuff to tie them up and gag them."

Nova felt a cold hand slide over her heart. Escurra hadn't bought her story. He knew she was lying, probably because of the camouflage outfit, and he'd decided they were all to die. It was just a question of how and when, not whether.

Escurra looked to Martinez. "The story is just crazy enough to be at least partly true. You call our best man in Asuncion. Now. Wake him up. Have him find out about this Ramone Villalobos. But first call Luis again and make certain that everything is secure there."

Juan of the huge mustache returned carrying thin nylon rope and some rags. Martinez left. Juan and the Gaucho set to work securing her, Solange and Bebe.

As soon as they had been bound and gagged, Escurra said, "You know, I had planned something special for my boys tonight. I always give them something special on Christmas Eve. I had planned a fight between a Negro and a Guarani, but the Negro is no longer with us. So I think I'll offer them instead a really special treat. A cat fight."

When Escurra said cat fight, the first image that popped into Nova's mind was a jaguar. But as Escurra continued to grin at her and then Solange, his meaning clarified.

It solidified horribly when he said, "None of you is going to leave here alive. But I can make it easy or hard on the old man. I'll put you two females in the pit. The boys will love it."

Solange twisted in her seat, straining against the rope. Bebe sat absolutely still. And even though it was well after midnight, Nova began to perspire again.

Seeing the discomfort on the three faces of his captives, Escurra laughed. Nova wasn't at all surprised that the humor did not touch his dark eyes, which remained dead, flat and cold.

To Juan and the Gaucho, Escurra said, "My money says that the big mixed-race bitch will tear the heart out of the soft, white tourist agent."

Chapter 41

Joe sat perched in the tree that he imagined Nova herself might have used to spy on Escurra's place. He had kept his binoculars on the house to the point where his arms ached. She had faithfully text-messaged I'm Okay until five minutes ago, and five minutes was their agreed upon maximum lag time. He felt smothered in panic.

"Dammit, Nova. I wish to God you had quit this life after Italy."

He flipped open his cell phone and connected with the Special Operations command tasked to extract the Hill boy. "Give me the position of the Dove."

"Here's how it will be," Escurra said, looking from Nova to Solange. "I take you to the pit. Give you both a machete. The fight's to the death. Don't fight and I'll signal Juan. He'll be with Bebe."

Escurra looked hard at Solange. "Juan will torture your father slowly. If you fight well, I'll kill Bebe cleanly when your fight with the American woman is over."

Solange looked at her father with terrified eyes. Nova thought, *You sick bastard.*

Escurra grabbed Nova and pulled her out of the chair as he signaled Gaucho to take Solange. Nova went easily, her mind clear as a crystal but lacking so far any possible idea of how to get them out of this. Solange twisted and moaned behind her gagged mouth as the Gaucho dragged her out of Escurra's office. Juan remained behind with Bebe—Bebe's torturer and executioner.

The shouting of the men packed onto the seats of the fighting pit doubled when Escurra appeared among them, and it actually doubled again when Escurra and the Gaucho hauled her and Solange into the center of the dirt ring. *The dregs of the dregs.* The stench of alcohol mixed with the odor of sweat and blood. The nearest drunken viewer had to be twenty feet away, and big brown patches of drying blood dotted the dirt floor.

Escurra signaled, and a minion dressed like a Texas cowboy with a ten-gallon hat and chaps rushed up to them carrying two machetes. Nova guessed this dual to the death between two humans had probably been Escurra's grand finale for his boys for years. Escurra lifted Solange's hand and put a machete into it. Nova reached out and grabbed hers from the cowboy. The crowd roared.

Solange had stopped crying and had stiffened her back. She would not look at Nova. Chances were good that Solange had decided to fight, and fight well, in the hope of sparing her father a slow, tortured death.

"If either of you take off the gag, I will shoot you both

dead," Escurra said. Escurra and the Gaucho backed away. Nova stared at Solange, who stared back, her expression unreadable. Solange rushed Nova, and swung the machete, a hard but poorly aimed swipe that Nova easily dodged. Escurra yelled from the view stand, "Either fight her, tourist agent, or I send a signal to Juan." Solange swung again. Nova used her machete to block the swing, and returned it with a half-powered and poorly aimed swing of her own. The crowd booed.

Twice more Solange charged, and Nova could tell that the blows weren't meant to hurt her. Poor Solange. Nova had both training and firsthand experience. So this fight was no fight, more like a potential execution, but she sure wasn't going to kill Solange.

A thought struck, a possible way out, at least a stall. Nova switched the machete to her left hand. She lunged toward Solange, whose gaze of course followed the machete, and struck Solange a karate chop to the carotid on the girl's throat, praying that she hadn't hit too hard.

The blow was right on target. Solange halted, blacked out and went down.

The crowd roared, Nova couldn't tell whether from approval or dismay.

Nova checked Escurra. He'd remained seated, but Gaucho strode toward Solange, a ten-inch Ka-Bar serrated knife clutched in his hand. Nova moved back, to put herself between Gaucho and Solange.

"I forgot to tell you one of the rules," Escurra yelled. "If someone gets knocked out, we kill them on the spot. Then I pair the one still standing with the Guarani."

Not Solange! No way! Nova flung herself at the Gaucho and with a quick machete swing, she knocked the Ka-Bar from his hand and cut at least two fingers with it. He howled, clutched his hand and spun around.

Every man present was now on his feet, and five more men ran toward her. She went into full defensive aikido mode, stunning the first man to reach her with a forward kick to his solar plexus. Letting momentum carry her around, she planted a back-kick into the side of the second man. He spun away and crashed onto the dirt.

With the machete, she hacked a slice out of the calf of the third man, but was brought crashing facedown into the dirt by the last two men, one of whom sat on her back. The other flung himself across her legs.

"Stay away," she heard Escurra shouting to the men in the seats. "Stay away."

Then she recognized his boots in front of her face. He stooped over, grabbed her braid, pulled her head up and looked in her eyes. "Just who the hell are you?"

The astounded look in his wide eyes pleased her. She couldn't manage to come up with saliva, but she made a spitting motion and sound.

Escurra dropped her face back into the dirt. Solange was regaining consciousness. Escurra roared at two men, "Lock all three of them in a pen!"

He remained in the fighting pit addressing his boys as she and Solange were manhandled away, telling his men that they had seen blood, just not the blood they had expected to see. The two men banged on the door to Escurra's office. It swung open and they pushed Nova and Solange inside.

Bebe stood in front of the desk, unbound. Juan lay on the floor, bound and gagged. Joe stood behind the door. He slugged the first man, who let go of Nova as he fell to the floor. She spun around and karate chopped the thug

holding Solange, who also hit the floor as Joe used his gun
to knock out the first guy and then the second.

Nova hugged Joe and whispered into his chest, "Once
again to the rescue."

Chapter 42

"We can't waste time tying them up," Joe said, searching her face. They had two options: kill all three men to deprive Escurra of their help or let them live. Joe, a military man, was always of the view that all opposition should be "taken out," but ever since the German operation he knew Nova's preference. He knew that when she was in charge of an op, killing was never her first choice. He wanted to know her choice now.

She looked at Solange and Bebe. "C'mon! We have to run like hell."

She grabbed up her bag from the corner and sprinted out of the office, turned away from the pit and headed for the cages that held Alex and the other boy. She pointed to the one she thought must hold the boy. "Get him out of there, Joe!"

The cage doors weren't locked. A simple hotel-room-like hasp had been screwed to the outside. There just wasn't a handle on the inside. She pulled open the door to Alex's cell. As she feared, he was gone. "We have to get out of here!" she said.

The five of them dashed toward the shed's far end, Nova leading and Joe bringing up the rear, his Glock in hand. If their getaway wasn't clean, if someone were to see where she was taking them, Joe would shoot to kill.

She looped the bag's woven strap across her chest and raced across the field that separated the shed from the jungle, looking back frequently to make sure everyone was keeping up. Joe had freed a short Guarani boy who was dressed only in jeans. No shoes. No shirt. The boy kept tight on Nova's heels, obviously in good physical condition and unbothered by rocks or twigs underfoot.

They reached cover. Maybe they hadn't been seen. The moon sliver that stood high in the sky made the dash across the field possible, but now the jungle smothered them in darkness. She and Joe gathered everyone close. Joe said, "I can't see a damn thing."

"Escurra and his men can't either. And I have a pretty good feel for how to get us back to the road."

Nova put her arm around Solange's shoulders and held Bebe's hand. "We're going to move together. I know it's dark, but we can't stay this close to here."

"They will come with lights," Bebe said.

"When they figure out where we've gone. But I think we have some time. Escurra has to wish a Merry Christmas and good night to all his thugs and come back to his office to even know we've escaped. Then they have to think: did we head for the big house or maybe just steal a car? Their very last thought will be that we'd head into the jungle at night. And even if they try to search for us now in the dark, even if they have lights, finding our trail will be next to impossible."

"They won't search at all at night," Solange said. "Everything human in the jungle stops at night."

Telling them to stay no more than a couple of steps apart, Nova led them down near the lake, which they skirted. Her eyes soon accommodated to the severely reduced light. She could not risk using the flashlight and she could see shapes well enough to lead the way, but the sounds and near total darkness kept her nerves on edge. Once they heard a jaguar's catty yowl. When they stumbled upon a bunch of caiman, the intimidated reptiles wiggled themselves into the lake.

Beyond the lake now and back into the jungle, heading for the spot where she had earlier parked the Jeep, Nova paused to let them nurse the bruises, stubbed toes and scratches they were collecting. While Joe called the SO co-ordinator, she spoke to the Guarani boy in Spanish and was delighted to discover that they could communicate. His name was Vitor.

Joe said, "Escurra's thugs took Alex to a cave. I have the position. When we stop, we'll look at a map. Special Ops will plan a raid to extract the kid."

They moved on. Escurra might have a hard time figuring out where his captives had gone, but he had to know for certain now that Nova had help. When they reached the place where she'd hidden the Jeep, she stopped. "We spend the rest of the night here, close together."

Bebe and Solange fell to the ground, exhausted. The Guarani boy said he knew where he was now and was going to go home.

"Can you help us?" she asked. "Stay a minute, please. We need to look at a map to see where they took the other boy." He nodded solemnly and sat down, legs crossed.

Joe pulled out one of their maps and a flashlight. Nova

sat to his right, Vitor to his left. After a brief study, using the coordinates SO had provided, Joe said in Spanish, "There should be a cave about here."

"Do you know this cave?" Nova asked Vitor.

"Where are we?" Vitor asked, gesturing at the paper. Nova traced the map as she explained. "You were held here. We came past this lake and this is the river that runs across the property. And this road—" she turned and pointed in the direction of the road "—is right over there, not too far."

It was clear that the region where Special Ops said Alex had been taken was on the other side of the river, but not all that far from where they were right now. "I know the cave," Vitor said. "Do you need me to take you there now? I want to go home."

Nova looked at Joe.

Joe said, "Yes. If you can take us there now, that's what we should do, because we want to be there when people come to rescue our friend."

The boy stood. "Then let's go."

Nova smiled and took his hand. "Let us rest a moment more, please."

Vitor sat back down and asked Joe if he could look at the flashlight. Joe shrugged and tossed it his way. The boy started tinkering with its different levels of lighting.

She struggled to decide whether to take Bebe and Solange with them. Special Ops did not have permission from Brazil to be in the country. The idea was to extract Alex secretly. If Bebe called a friend to pick up him and Solange now, at least one other person would be involved. The more people involved, the greater the risk of a leak with possible serious political repercussions. But she could not leave Bebe and Solange here alone.

She would take them to the cave site where they would

all spend the next couple of hours together, until the SO team arrived. Then, after she, Alex, and Joe left, Bebe and Solange could call a friend to pick them up. By that time tomorrow they could surely concoct some believable story about why Bebe and Solange were alone in the jungle.

Well, they would try to concoct such a story. That would be quite a challenge.

She explained the plan to Bebe and Solange. They both confessed to being very tired, but agreed that if she set a slow pace, they could walk the distance to the cave. Solange was having the worst time of all because she wore only flimsy dress heels.

Vitor led the way. Nova sensed from the swing of his shoulders that he took pride in being able to help. They made the road, crossed the bridge and reentered the jungle.

She estimated the hike to the cave site took another forty minutes. Only once did everyone drop to the ground and huddle together in terror—when a jaguar roared so close that Nova thought it must surely be attacking. But nothing happened. The smell of that many humans was more warning than temptation.

With Vitor's help, they picked out a slightly elevated spot with good cover overlooking the mouth of the cave. The boy said, "I'm going home now."

She sensed Joe pressing the flashlight into the boy's hand. "It's yours, Vitor."

The boy was standing at her shoulder. He turned the light on and she could see on his face for the first time a grin, a shy one. *"Muchas gracias, señor."*

He left, moving back into the darkness, toward the road. She couldn't resist the momentary thought she always had when she met children and young people in the third world: *What will his life hold?* She and Joe had saved him from an early death. Perhaps fate had other good things in store for him.

Joe contacted SO again. "How long?" he asked. A team was in the air, on its way, but it looked like it would be close to dawn before its members arrived, she figured only forty minutes away now. No one seemed ready or able to sleep on the damp earth. They fumbled their way over the above-ground roots of a massive fig tree and found back rests.

She explained that they needed to come up with a cover story for why Bebe and Solange needed someone to pick them up—why did they not just go back to Escurra's place for their own car? And why did they spend the night in the jungle—or had they spent it somewhere else?

"I'm too tired to think," Solange said. Nova could hear her settling down.

"I am too, Nova," Bebe added.

Nova wiggled into the most comfortable position she could manage, and used the trick of going mentally into her "favorite place," the place she always went when she wanted to sleep or bad things were happening.

The shriek of a macaw jolted her into consciousness followed almost immediately by the sound of an approaching helicopter.

The dawn light now revealed the mouth of a cave surrounded by vines and roots, and leading from it a well-worn but narrow trail. And kneeling beside the cave's mouth, hidden from the view of the approaching Special Ops helicopter, were four of Escurra's men, two with stinger missiles on their shoulders. Escurra had figured out that someone big was on to his operation and he'd prepared.

"Oh God, Joe," she moaned. "Call them. Tell them those bastards know they're coming!"

Chapter 43

Suleema stood with tears streaming down her face in front of the Christmas tree that her daughter, Regina, had put up in defiance of what Regina most feared.

"They will find Alex," Regina had insisted as she'd helped Clevon haul the seven-foot tree into their living room. "So when he comes home we'll have to be prepared for Christmas."

The tree was so beautiful. The lights twinkled and the angel hair glowed with the color of the bulbs behind it: soft red, green, blue, yellow. *I thought when Raymond died that my heart would never heal and it could never break again. But maybe this is just different. This time I'm not breaking. I'm being crushed to death.*

Last night, near midnight, the Marshal's Office had called to let the family know that a successful rescue attempt had taken place and most of the hostages were now free and on their way to their families. But not Alex.

Suleema had awakened when she heard Regina scream, and she ran from the guest bedroom to Clevon and Regina's to find her daughter walking in a circle and tearing at her hair. The scene of the distraught woman in her pajamas looked like something out of a horror movie. When told that Alex alone was still missing, Suleema herself had broken into sobs. Thank God for Clevon, strong and calm, even though his heart was in agony for his son.

Hearing footsteps coming down the stairs, Suleema swiped the tears away. She thought she ought to turn and smile bravely at Regina and Clevon, but a smile was completely out of the question. She just stood staring at the tree.

Clevon put his arm around her shoulders as Regina went toward the kitchen saying, "I'm going to make coffee. And then we are going to have breakfast. And we are going to continue to hold to faith that Alex will come home."

Clevon gave Suleema a comforting squeeze. "She's right, Sulee. We have to have faith."

Suleema patted his hand. "Yes. Faith."

Keeping faith was important to help bring Alex to them, but faith could not help her resolve the dilemma eating at her for nearly six days now. In two days, on the twenty-seventh, the Supreme Court would hand down its decision on Sharansky versus the U.S. government.

She had decided to vote as she'd originally intended, against the government and for the lieutenant governors and the people of the United States. Actually, for the people of the world.

I must make the call now. Whatever the cost.

Clevon let her go and shambled toward the kitchen.

Suleema wrung her hands. The trade-off some villain had forced upon her was between Alex's life and letting offensive weapons be put into space to create God only knew what kind of hellish future.

She bowed her head and closed her eyes. *Dear Lord, I have decided to sacrifice my grandson, my posterity. I'm not sure I can ever live with myself again, even if Alex does come back to us alive. You sacrificed your own son for others. I guess maybe you would say I shouldn't do less. I do know that these weapons have no business leaving our planet. Lord, give me the strength to do this. And live with myself afterward.*

She turned from the tree and walked down the hallway to Clevon's office. She knew the phone number for the Marshals by heart, had memorized it days ago, perhaps preparing herself for this moment. Some traitor wanted to rig the court.

She called and recited her story twice, and was told by the second marshal she talked to that someone would be out to speak with her within the hour. "You do understand," he said, "that this changes entirely how everyone's been looking at the case. This suggests that money is perhaps not the chief motivation for the kidnapping. The kidnapping and ransom demands may have been convincing cover for securing your vote. We may need to look somewhere right here at home to find the true forces behind this mess."

After she hung up, she searched her feelings and realized that some small weight had come off her heart. She was not alone with her secret now. The authorities could start looking for whoever had terrorized her. Presumably whoever was behind the whole scheme. And her vote, her sacred duty to her country and its people, would reflect her conscience, not her fear.

She smelled coffee. Regina, her strong, beautiful daughter, had put on music. To the strains of "O Holy Night," Suleema headed for the kitchen.

Chapter 44

Too late. It was too late to send a warning to the Special Ops helicopter. Nova watched, horrified, as one of Escurra's four guards fired off a stinger missile.

The helicopter exploded with a massive *kabloom!* into a ball of red and black smoke that twirled toward the ground. Two of the guards standing in the tennis-court-sized clearing in front of the cave's mouth sprinted off toward where the craft would hit or get hung up in the trees.

Solange was hugging Nova, her fingers like a vise on Nova's arm.

Joe rose. "Bebe. Solange. Stay here!"

Running in a crouch, he sprinted toward the cave. Nova extricated herself from Solange's grip. "Stay," she repeated. She pulled the Glock from the bag as she ran after him.

The remaining two guards stood about fifteen feet from the cave mouth, sideways to Nova and Joe. She watched as Joe squatted behind a tree, pulled a silencer from a pocket on his pant leg and fixed it to his Glock.

He aimed and fired. A clean headshot dropped the closest guard. A second shot took out the second guard even as he was staring in surprise at his companion.

Joe stood and ran at top speed toward the cave, and Nova kept right behind him. They didn't have much time. When they reached the cave, she said, "Go get him. I hope to God he's here. I've got your back."

Joe disappeared inside.

Breathing hard, her pulse thrumming at the crook of her throat, she backed up closer to the cave's mouth and knelt behind a shoulder-high boulder. A minute passed, a long, long minute.

Joe finally emerged from the cave tugging the Hill boy with one hand. *Yes!* She felt a rush of elation as Joe ran with the boy back toward Bebe and Solange.

One of two guards who'd gone after the helicopter returned. She fired twice, then sprinted after Joe and Alex. Neither man went down. Shots rang out. The guard's aim wasn't very good. She was still in the open. While still sprinting, she returned fire.

Then reached the trees.

Joe and the others ran for their lives, back the way they had come, toward the river. Solange, with her dreadful shoes, slowed them down and Bebe wasn't leaving Solange's side. Nova stuck the pistol into the bag, ran harder, caught up and yelled, "You have to take off the shoes, Solange. I don't care if it hurts like hell."

Joe and Alex were way ahead of them. Four shots rang out. The two guards had decided to pursue them, but no one had yet been hit.

Solange kicked off the shoes, and their speed picked up.

Joe led the way on what Nova took to be a pell-mell scramble with no particular direction, leaping and stumbling hand-over-foot to cross massive tree roots and avoid clinging vines.

Once she heard Alex yell to Joe, "I'm too tired. I have to stop."

Joe yelled back. "We can't stop, kid. You can do this." He pulled Alex to his feet, and the five of them ran on.

Ahead she could see light through the trees. They had to be coming close to the river. She was trying to keep track of direction, noting landmarks and distinctive vegetation. The ground had been more or less level. No one expected the mini-ravine, and all five of them tumbled down fifteen feet of brush-enshrouded ground.

Ahead of them, though, lay the river. They leaped up and rushed to it. Panting, Joe said, "We get to the road. We can hide there. I'll call for someone to pick us up."

With Joe leading and Nova bringing up the rear, they wove their way back and forth around ancient wood obstacles, keeping the river in sight to avoid getting lost in the darkness of the forest.

Suddenly, Alex, a couple of feet in front of her, stopped. She bumped into him. For the first time she noted that he was pale. No. Not pale. His face, a milk-chocolate brown naturally, looked drained of all color and massive beads of sweat raced down his skin. His eyes closed and he dropped to the ground as though he'd been shot.

But there had been no sound of shooting for at least a minute. She didn't doubt that the guards were pursuing; they would have to explain to Escurra that they had tried everything possible to prevent the boy's escape. Could they have a silencer?

"Stop," she yelled to Joe.

She knelt beside the boy, looking for any signs of a wound. "Alex! Alex!"

Nothing but weak eye movement behind his lids.

Diabetic! Coma. Shock.

Whatever they called it. Alex was having an attack from the stress of running and the heat. She ran her hands over his pants pockets, praying she would find his kit, or at least a packet of glucagons tablets, but he had absolutely nothing with him.

Joe knelt beside her. "He's in shock," Joe said. "He's run out of sugar."

"He doesn't have any glucagon tablets on him."

"Shit! We find him and then we kill him!"

"He needs sugar. Fast. Give me your knife, Joe."

Chapter 45

Joe slipped a Ka-Bar from a sheath strapped to his right calf. Nova grabbed it and stood. He said, "Where are you going?"

"I saw two or three sugar apple trees not too far back. Fruit was ripe and low enough I can reach it. Hang on."

"Do you need me?"

"No. Keep guard. Escurra's men may show up. I'll be right back."

She remembered exactly where the trees were. Typical of trees growing wild in a jungle, there were only two, not a grove, about fifteen feet tall. Ripe fruit hung heavily on both. A troop of squirrel monkeys were stuffing their mouths. At her approach they shrieked and took off to watch her from nearby, higher trees.

The ripe fruit, green on the outside and a creamy white on the inside, hung low enough for her to cut off six quickly. With their many conical segments, they strongly resembled an oversized hand grenade. She cut off six and only then realized that her bag was missing. *The fall!* When she'd tumbled down the hill, the strap must have broken.

Juggling all six apples, she ran back. Alex was mumbling when she again knelt beside him. Solange and Bebe hovered, Bebe holding his arm around his daughter, probably imagining how he would feel if it were his child lying on the forest floor near to expiring from lack of sugar to feed her cells.

Nova split a fruit, plucked out a segment and expelled the big conical seed. "Can he chew?" She handed the fruit to Solange. "Separate out the seeds of more of this."

"Alex," Joe said. "You have to chew this."

Nova squeezed some of the juice into Alex's mouth. His tongue licked. She squeezed the last of it. Again his tongue licked and he swallowed.

Solange handed her another segment and she squeezed again. One by one they fed him the juice until his eyes flicked open. Joe helped him sit up and handed him a whole piece of the sweet-smelling fruit, which Nova knew to be delicious. Alex gobbled it down and held out his hand for another.

Within less than fifteen minutes, the crisis passed. No guards had shown up. Before they went on, Nova took Bebe with her and collected another six fruits, just in case Alex should need another sugar fix.

"After I saw you," Alex explained, looking at Nova, "they moved me and took away my travel kit and didn't feed me. I'm going to need food and insulin again soon."

"I know," she said. "We're working on it."

Not much farther along they found themselves in a tiny clearing along the riverbank. A canoe had been pulled up onto land and Joe borrowed it, Nova silently blessing the fates that the current ran with them.

Solange sighed as she sank down in the center and inspected her battered feet. Joe used the single paddle to keep them on course while Nova communicated with Special Ops. She explained, keeping her tone and words formal, what had happened to the SO helicopter. She knew how close the SO guys were. There was going to be terrible sadness and also recrimination among them over the downing of that team; they should never have come that directly anywhere near the cave. She explained that she and Joe planned to get back to Joe's Land Rover and use it to return to Martinez's place for an SO pickup. Her contact agreed. They discussed timing. He shared the information that word was out about the earlier rescue.

After she hung up, she told Joe, "They're pissed that the Brazilian authorities have found out that most of the hostages have been rescued. Carlito talked to someone aboard the *Ronald Reagan*. The word is also out that Escurra is involved."

Joe shifted the paddle to the other side of the canoe. "Bad news for us. We need to get out of here fast, before things get complicated."

When they reached the road, Joe steered them onto the riverbank, and after they clambered out, she checked his watch. Seven o'clock. The sound of a motor shocked them into silence. "Hide!" Joe said. "Except you, Bebe. If it's anyone who might not be one of Escurra's thugs, stop them if you have to throw yourself in front of the car."

Bebe grinned. "This is Brazil and we are far from any city. I will not have to throw myself in front of the car."

It turned out to be a rancher from a small spread headed into town, his truck bed piled high with cotton bales. He smiled and waited patiently for Joe, Nova and Alex to climb aboard the pile, while Bebe and Solange slid inside with him.

In less than eight minutes they reached Joe's Land Rover. After thanking the rancher profusely, they climbed inside, and Joe had them back on the road in double-quick time, heading for the Martinez ranch.

They had no choice but to drive past Escurra's entry gate, there being only one road, and a car came out, racing after them. "It's Martinez's brother, Rodrigo," she said, "and three other men." The car was a garish, yellow Thunderbird.

The Land Rover lurched into higher speed, Joe's foot pressed hard on the gas.

"Plan B," she said. "We do need to get out of Brazil ASAP. Let's turn off at the next big road. There's a hotel on this side of the Brazil-Argentina border with a helicopter pad. They give tourists rides over the falls." She snatched a look behind them. The yellow Thunderbird was narrowing the gap between them. "I flew out of there once. We can borrow the helicopter and get to the Martinez place much faster."

"How close?"

"We need to try it, Joe. It's the best option. And I have to tell you, I lost the Glock."

When they turned onto the road, clearly labeled with a big green and blue sign with the hotel's name on it, they were still ahead of Escurra's thugs, but just far enough to be out of shooting range. Apparently Escurra's men had souped-up the Thunderbird.

"Turn right, turn right," she yelled. The Land Rover fishtailed into the right turn. The hotel itself sprawled off to her left. The helicopter pad, assuming there still was one, should be just around the next tree-lined bend.

Nova looked back again. The Thunderbird was hidden behind trees lining the road, but now she could clearly hear its motor's roar. She strained forward, holding her breath and praying. She checked her watch. Seven thirty. No tourist flights were likely to be scheduled before eight or nine o'clock. What if the key wasn't in the helicopter? Where had it been kept before? She tried to remember where the office for the sightseeing flights was located. They might have to break in.

They rounded the bend and there sat the helicopter, tied down and waiting. Not a soul in sight. Office about fifty feet away. "Let us out at the pad," she said. "If we're lucky, the key will be in the ignition."

The Land Rover's brakes squealed as Joe jerked them to a stop. He yelled, "Everyone out," at the same time she yelled, "I'll check for the key."

She opened the helicopter's Plexiglas door and checked the ignition, under the seat and in the visor. Alex had climbed into the front passenger seat. On his own he'd opened the single map compartment. "No key, Nova," he said.

With her hand on the door she turned and yelled to Joe, "No key."

The yellow Thunderbird roared into view. Joe fired off three shots and the car braked to a dust-spraying stop. The four thugs climbed out, squatted behind their car and started laying down fire. She didn't think they would shoot at the helicopter, not with Alex in it. But she couldn't be sure, and neither could Joe.

Joe was returning fire. Nova sucked in a deep breath and sprinted in a zigzag to the office. As she threw herself through the open doorway, she remembered exactly where the keys had been kept. Under the counter, under a statue of Arnold Schwarzenegger dressed as the commando in the movie *Predator*.

Chapter 46

The helicopter key, all these years later, still lay under the little statue. Nova grabbed it. Zigzagging to the sounds of gunfire, she sprinted to the helicopter. The pad sat just feet from the rim of Devil's Throat, one of the most spectacular parts of the falls. She could hear the roaring and knew the water lay roughly two hundred feet below the rim.

Bebe had untied the last of the four hold-downs. He scrambled into a seat from the passenger side as she leapt into the pilot's seat and shoved the key into the ignition. The machine responded. Blades began to churn.

Escurra wasn't with the men firing at Joe. Escurra presumably still thought he could hide behind his respectability and his paid protection, but the Brazilian feds were on to him. He'd soon get his.

Joe got a good line of fire, and Rodrigo, Felip Martinez's brother, went down, a new hole between his eyes.

Finally the gauges indicated that the helicopter's blades were up to speed. Leaning out the window, she yelled, "Now, Joe."

He stood, and then twisted and fell, his right leg collapsing under him. She couldn't tell how badly he was hit, but he would need help. She opened the door, but before she could jump out, the three remaining thugs behind the Thunderbird charged toward Joe.

The moment seemed to stretch out forever as she realized she must either take off without Joe, or all of them could be taken captive again.

He looked back at her. "Go!" he yelled.

I can't leave you!

"Go!" he yelled again.

The paralysis broke. Discipline took over—fear for the three people in her care. She slammed and latched the door and lifted the bird, aiming it toward the big drop-off, to get it out of the line of fire as fast as possible.

Her three passengers twisted to watch the action on the ground just before the helicopter dropped below the rim; Nova kept her eyes on the canyon. All of them put on the headphones with built-in mics.

"They were on top of him," Solange said.

Tears welled. Furious, Nova bit her lip. *No crying!*

An extraction at the Martinez place was out; no way would she leave Brazil without Joe. It would be safe to take Solange, Bebe and Alex to the hotel to wait there. And she would use the helicopter to come back to find Joe. She needed to call Special Ops.

"What time is it, Bebe?"

"Just a little more than half past seven."

Alex touched her arm. She kept her eyes on her flight path. "Thank you," he said simply.

"We'll soon have you to some food and some medical care."

What if they kill Joe? I can't imagine the world without him. God, if I could only go back right now!

"I have to tell you something important," Alex continued. "That guy, Escurra. He's not the one who set it up for us to get kidnapped."

"I don't understand."

"It was someone else. I heard him on tape."

"I'm totally not understanding you, Alex."

"Escurra had me in his office. They kept me there or in a bedroom at the beginning. They took pretty good care of me. I had my insulin. I wasn't even tied up. I could play games on an Xbox he had in there. They just said it was impossible for me to run away because there was nothing but jungle everywhere, and everyone on the place worked for him and I'd die without my insulin. I figured they were right since I'd seen the jungle for myself when they drove me in.

"I was in the office when Escurra got in a big argument with this guy who married Escurra's daughter."

"Uh-huh. Felipe Martinez."

"They never caught on that I understand Spanish. My two cousins live in Puerto Rico. I visit all the time. I'm really good at Spanish and it was fun for me to listen to them and them not to get it.

"Well, this Felipe guy said they should get more money by blackmailing Red Dog. That's the name they used, in English. Red Dog. And Escurra says, 'I been thinking Red Dog is more interested in something else than just ransom.' So I knew the Red Dog guy was one of them. In fact, they talked like the whole thing had been Red Dog's idea.

"And Felipe says, 'We can blackmail him because I've

got him talking on a tape. Right here.' So Escurra asked him to play the tape."

Nova suddenly had the bizarre feeling that the whole kidnap experience must have unhinged Alex. His tale seemed fantastical. But after what he'd been through, maybe it was understandable. She sure wasn't going to accuse him.

"I did something I could probably have gotten killed for, but I wanted to get some proof to screw both these guys and maybe even Red Dog. Like if I got ransomed. So I turned the Xbox up real loud. I walked away from it, and when Felipe came to turn down the volume, I stole his cell phone. Right out of the jacket he'd dropped on a chair.

"You know, I think these guys figured I was stupid. I don't know, but whatever. I stole Felipe's cell phone and I recorded the whole tape thing, with Red Dog and Felipe. And then some stuff with Escurra afterward. But not much. I decided I better hide the cell phone before Felipe missed it. Maybe he'd think he left it somewhere else. I guess he did. I never heard anything about it."

They were approaching The Royal Hotel Iguazu's helicopter pad. The hotel's tourist helicopter occupied the pad so she was going to have to set down on the lawn. "That's a pretty wild story, Alex."

"You don't believe me?"

"I suppose so. Right now I need to concentrate on landing."

The landing went smoothly. A couple of uniformed mechanics materialized quickly. Bebe told them to watch the helicopter and then escorted a bedraggled Nova, Solange and Alex to his office via a back entry. By the time they were inside, the clock on Bebe's wall said eight o'clock.

"I have to make some phone calls," she said. "Would you all please just wait here a bit. The feds will be here soon."

Alex planted himself in front of her. "You have to believe me. I did record them. The cell phone is probably still there."

Alex had been through a lot of stress. Could he be delusional? Or just making the story up to sound heroic? "Where, Alex?"

The boy frowned and leaned forward, giving her a hard look that said, pay attention. "It's in the office. There's two big sofas in there. I shoved it down under a cushion of the sofa closest to his desk."

Alex sounded rock-solid and clear-minded. She recalled how he had been concerned for Vitor. "Okay. You know, kiddo, I do believe you." She touched his cheek, and he smiled. "I still have to make calls. I'll be right back."

She left the office and out another door into a pretty alcove where a wrought-iron bench sat in front of a wall of red, yellow and purple orchids.

Pacing, she called Special Ops and told them the pickup at the Martinez place was off, that she had to go back to locate an agent, and she'd get back to them with another extraction time and place if necessary. They agreed and said they would stand by.

Then she called Claiton Pryce's private and secure number.

Chapter 47

The deputy director of operations of the CIA answered immediately. "Pryce," he said.

"It's me. Nova."

"I've been expecting a call from you. It's outstanding that you and Cardone pulled out the VP's niece and all the others. Great job."

"Not all of the hostages. But I just brought out the last one, too; Alex Hill."

"I'm not surprised."

"Mr. Pryce—" She choked up, saw the image of Joe falling and the men rushing him. *Hell.* "I had to leave agent Cardone behind to get the boy and two others to safety."

"That's rough. He's a top man."

Pryce sounded upset but not really distressed. She detested him for a brief moment for that failure. "Now that the others are safe, I'm going back for Joe. I just hope they don't kill him." *I'm praying they haven't already killed him.* "I have some other information that I don't know what to make of. It seems crazy, but it comes from the boy and he seems remarkably credible for his age."

"Yes?"

She told him Alex's story about Red Dog and the hidden tape.

When she finished he said, "I believe it, Nova. And here's why. You know that Alex is the grandson of Supreme Court Justice Suleema Johnson. She told us yesterday that someone is blackmailing her to vote a certain way on a case that is to be handed down in two days. The threat is to kill her grandson."

Surprised but also filled with a sense of pieces falling into place, Nova slid down onto the bench. "That would explain why they kept Alex separate from all the others. He was their bait for something other than the money."

"This is big, Nova. Whoever Red Dog is, he's a traitor and he is on the inside of our government. We have to get him. And it sounds very much like the boy's cell phone recording might be the key we need. Hold the line a moment. I need to confer."

She crossed her legs but couldn't lean back or relax. She bent forward, shifting her cell phone to her other ear. Pryce was probably in his office or perhaps in the situation room. And he was right. Whoever had set up this elaborate plot stood to gain something enormous, probably financially, but maybe equally important, politically. She couldn't think of anything more treasonous than trying to fix the Supreme Court.

Finally, three minutes later at quarter past eight, Pryce came back on. "We need to get that recording at all costs, and we have to secure it fast because the Brazilian feds have been told that Escurra was behind everything. The Brazilians are on their way to Escurra's place right now. They should arrive within the hour. You must go back to Escurra's house, find that recording and get out. If they beat you there they'll sew up the location and do their own searches and we won't get the recording soon, if ever."

"You want me—"

"I'm giving you a new assignment, an order. You go back to Escurra's place ASAP, secure that recording and bring it out of Brazil."

"I have to find Joe."

"Did you hear me? Your job is to get the recording. Joe is in charge of taking care of Joe."

She stood, the heat of anger warming her neck. If she could have shot Pryce through the heart, she would have. Instead she pulled in a long, deep breath.

"Under no circumstances are the Brazilians to take control of it."

Her voice low, her words slow, she said, "I'm not leaving Joe."

"Nova, I know you care for him. He's a good agent. We don't have better. But the CIA is Joe's life. He would tell you to go get the goddamn recording, and you know it."

Silence spanned the thousands of miles between them, but Pryce was right. She could go back, no question. She had the helicopter and she sure knew the Escurra layout, knew right where the office was, knew the very sofa that Alex had described.

Finally she sighed and began pacing. "The partygoers should probably all have left late last night or early this morning. I think I can make this work."

"You will have any support you need. I know SO is standing by. I hear they lost a team."

"Yes. I saw the helicopter go down. And I'm on this." She told him she'd keep him posted, said goodbye, and snapped the phone closed.

She was going to leave Joe to his fate. Maybe death. Again the image rose in her mind of him falling to the ground, his face as he yelled to her to, "Go!" Tears she'd been fighting from the moment she'd left him behind rushed free and down her cheeks. She sobbed. Her anguish finally spilled into the only words that seemed right. "I'm sorry."

How dumb had it been to say she wouldn't marry Joe? She dropped her head, wrapped her arms around her as if to hold back the sobs.

Just how stupid could one control freak be? She was free. If she didn't marry him or anyone else, she'd be free the rest of her life. But she didn't want freedom from Joe. No number of compromises and risks were too high a price to pay if…if he found a way to get out alive.

The line from Kris Kristofferson's "Me and Bobby McGee" slipped out. "Freedom's just another word for nothing left to lose."

She stood. *If he lives, and he wants me, he'll never get rid of me, I swear.*

Back in Bebe's office she said, "I need a helicopter pilot, Bebe. I have to go back to Escurra's place before the feds get there."

Solange said, "Why don't you wait. Papa called the local police. They are on their way to arrest Escurra right now. Let them take care of it."

"What!" Nova turned around to Bebe. "Is it true? The locals are on their way out there?"

"Yes."

"Oh, Bebe, that makes a big problem twice as big. I have to beat them to Escurra's place. I'll need a helicopter pilot who is willing to take potentially lethal risks. I'll pay him whatever amount of money he asks. I have to have him now. And some clothes. A gun. And a chicken."

Chapter 48

Unfortunately, the American agent simply would not talk. They were not going to learn from him who they had to look out for, they would not be able to tell Red Dog where the danger for all of them lay. They were out of time.

Escurra stood up from his desk in the Casa Grande just as Felipe planted another blow to the man's cheek, opening a second cut.

Juan had been mostly leaning against the wall and watching the beating since he returned from the helicopter site with this stubborn North American bastard and handed him over to Felipe and the two of them had brought the agent to Escurra's main office. Juan took a toothpick from his shirt pocket and set to work on his teeth. Felipe shouted at the bound man. "You killed my brother, you shit! Who are you working for?"

Escurra said, "You're not going to get anything out of

him, Felipe. At least not by beating on him. He's clearly been trained to withstand this kind of interrogation."

Escurra strode toward the door. "I'll be back shortly. We have to get away for a while, but I must have cash to use for payoffs until everything is sorted out. Don't kill him. We may need a hostage."

He left, heading for the office at the fighting pit.

At eight thirty, the borrowed helicopter took off from The Royal Hotel Iguazu with the hotel's senior pilot, Ernesto, at the controls. "I'm retired Brazilian military," he said in response to Nova's question about whether he'd ever flown a helicopter in a dangerous situation. "I can do anything you need to have me do. And given what you agreed to pay, I gather this could get quite exciting." He grinned, a cocky smile that stuck a painful stiletto into her heart because the smile was so like Joe's.

"Right now," she said, "we need to make top speed to the coordinates I gave you on the Martinez ranch."

"What is the significance of the ugly peasant woman outfit and the caged chicken?"

She smiled grimly. "Disguise."

She punched in the number for her Special Operations contact and asked for the location of the GPS hidden in one of Joe's boot heels. It was currently in Tomas Morinaga Escurra's house!

Yes! She let a little ray of hope warm her heart. Joe must be alive! If he were dead, why would they take him there? And even better, that's right where she needed to go as soon as she picked up James.

She punched in the number for James, the macho African American SO watching over Luis. James answered immediately and assured her that everything at the

Martinez bunker remained secure and he was anxious to get lifted out.

"We have a new assignment," she said. "After we talk, you can call your commander and have him validate that you are to help me, but I need to know if that bunker full of munitions has RPGs, plastique, and the stuff to set it off."

"Roger," he said, sounding quite happy. "Do I get to blow stuff up?"

"If all goes well. So please round up all the explosives you can carry, an RPG, and a couple of rounds for it. I'll pick you up in—" She checked her watch. It was now 8:33. "—in about six minutes. We're in a real hurry."

At eight-forty, right when she'd estimated, the hotel pilot sat them down fifty feet from the Martinez bunker and James threw some gear in the backseats and then climbed in himself.

"Okay, Ernesto," Nova said, "Escurra's ranch."

It had been only twenty-five minutes since Bebe had called in the local authorities. Even if the local police took off at once, an unlikely probability, they could not be at Escurra's place yet. She estimated that she might be as much as twenty minutes ahead of them. She began explaining her plan to both men.

Kneeling on the floor of the fighting pit office, Escurra threw back the rug that covered the safe lid and twirled the dials of the combination lock. He kept two hundred and fifty thousand U.S. dollars cash in there and had to replenish it often as demands for bribes and payments rose and fell.

He packed the money into a briefcase, then raced his Jaguar back toward the house. That's where the diamonds were—he had never kept all his backup assets in a single stash. He was going to need a lot of money to bribe his way out of this mess. Escurra punched his helicopter pilot's number on his cell phone. The pilot had the best room in the bunkhouse and was always on call. He answered immediately.

"I'm leaving!" Escurra announced, his voice harsh because of the pressure to hurry. "Ten minutes at the most. Get the helicopter warmed up. There will be three, or maybe four of us."

Ernesto zoomed the helicopter on a direct path to Escurra's ranch.

"Look over there, Nova," James said, pointing out the back window on their side.

Five cars in a caravan were tooling down the single road leading to the ranch, appearing and disappearing behind the mass of green trees that lined the road on both sides. "Local police?" she asked.

"Sure are," Ernesto replied.

She checked her watch for what must be the hundredth time—8:51. Not good. She estimated that she, Ernesto and James were maybe fifteen minutes ahead of the Brazilians. How could she get the recording and Joe out of there in fifteen minutes?

Ernesto sat them down on a spot on the road north of the ranch's boundary, which she knew could not be seen from the house. If she cut straight south through the jungle running from this spot, she could be at Escurra's fancy entry gate over the road leading to the house in under two minutes.

"Guys, it'll take me ten minutes or less to get into position near the house. When I signal, do your thing."

"Roger," both men said at the same time.

"You be careful, little lady," Ernesto said.

James already knew she was more than able to take care and just gave her a thumbs-up as she climbed out.

Escurra heard the sounds of his helicopter starting up as he strode into his bedroom and went to his wife's jewel box. The thought had occurred to him on the way back to the Casa Grande that she sometimes failed to put even her most valuable jewels in the safe in his office, where he also kept his most movable asset, the diamonds, no matter that he had told her repeatedly she must do so. Most especially he had told her she must do so when leaving this country, like now.

Sure enough, she had not obeyed this time either. When he got all this mess sorted out and his wife was back with him and his life was back to normal, he would find a way to punish her for this lapse so she would never forget.

He grabbed up the six pieces that held exquisite emeralds, sapphires, pearls and a huge ruby and stuffed them into his jacket pocket.

Carrying the chicken in a wooden cage and stooped over so that the front of her bright red and green peasant skirt trailed in the dirt, but walking briskly nevertheless, Nova found herself within a hundred feet of the ranch house nine minutes after Ernesto and James had set her down. She text-messaged to James: In position.

Both of Joe's cheeks throbbed from the cuts Felipe had opened, mostly because Felipe wore a big diamond ring on his right hand. The gunshot wound on his leg had been mercifully slight. It had finally stopped bleeding but still throbbed. Escurra's son-in-law paced like a caged bear back and forth in front of Escurra's big desk and had been doing so ever since Escurra walked out.

The office door opened and the Eagle burst in.

"We have to get out of here!" Felipe yelled. "Why were you gone so long!"

"I wasn't gone long. Don't yell at me!"

"I can't stay here."

Escurra had said earlier that Felipe wasn't to kill their hostage. But Joe wondered how long that position would hold. He had heard the sounds of a helicopter warming up. Escurra was going to make a break. Either they would kill him or take him away to God knew where. The nasty little argument between them was the first chance he'd had to take advantage of some confusion.

His arms bound behind him but his legs free, Joe leapt to his feet and made a pretend dash toward the door, his injured leg shooting pain with each step. As expected, Juan unstuck himself from the wall and landed a punch to Joe's midsection.

Gasping for air, but in full control of his fall, Joe went down on both knees, bent slightly forward, reached down to the heel of his right boot, sprung the lever and palmed the razor blade.

Juan dragged him, still bent-over at the waist, back to the chair and shoved him into it. Joe set to work on the half-inch rope binding his wrists.

Chapter 49

Hearing the impressive blast of Escurra's helicopter going up in flames, Nova dashed behind the wall of oleanders lining the road. She stripped off the peasant dress covering her jumpsuit, opened the cage door to set the chicken free and then ran at top speed toward a service entrance into the hacienda's garages.

She sprinted past five cars—two Humvees, two black Mercedes Benzes, and a gorgeous silver Rolls-Royce—and then cautiously opened the door to a hallway that she knew had a laundry room on one side and a food storage pantry on the other. Seeing no one, she plunged farther into Escurra's lair, her first goal being that sofa in Escurra's office and her second, to somehow find Joe and take him out with her.

Joe was sawing away on the ropes at his wrist when an explosion caused him to cut himself, he hoped not too deeply. The blast couldn't have been far from the house, maybe fifty to a hundred yards.

He checked the time on the clock on Escurra's desk—8:52.

"Fucking dogs," Felipe said. "It's gotta be the police."

Escurra said, "Juan, Felipe, both of you go see what the hell happened. Make sure the helicopter is okay."

Both men left at a full run.

Joe sawed harder, watching his captor hurry to a picture on the wall opposite his desk and swing the picture back, revealing a safe. Escurra opened it, pulled out four dark blue velvet pouches, opened the strings holding one closed and spilled diamonds into his palm. Quickly, he poured them back into the pouch and closed it. He tucked all four pouches into a briefcase stacked full of what looked to be U.S. greenbacks.

"Ah. Diamonds," Joe said. "I'll bet your buddies don't know about the diamonds, do they?"

Running past a downstairs powder room, Nova glanced outside to see the blown-up helicopter still burning, dark black soot of the fuel mixed with red flames. She heard the next explosion almost immediately as she ran toward the entry hall. That would be the poolside bathhouse.

Escurra barged across the room to his office window, yanked back the closed drapes and looked out. "Mother of God!" he bellowed. He turned and fumbled a 9 mm Beretta from his desk drawer.

Joe said, "My partner is going to take you down so fast you'll think you've been hit by lightning."

Just a bit more, Joe thought. *Dammit, just a bit more and I'm free!*

His instincts, agent and animal, were yelling that it had to be Nova.

Nova sprinted into the specious downstairs entry and collided with Martinez, who had come running back into the house. She rebounded, and Juan, who was with Martinez, grabbed her gun hand, snatched the gun and twisted her arm up behind her back. He pointed her own gun at her head.

"You again!" Martinez said in English. "Stupid bitch. You should have stayed away. But fine. We can use another hostage."

"Listen, Martinez," she said.

He wasn't listening. They were shoving her up the stairs, all three of them practically running.

"Listen to me. I can offer you a deal. I'm with the American government and I'm authorized to offer you anything I want. Let me go. Just stop right now and leave me and go and get out of here."

"And go where? The police are here. Where the hell can I go?"

"They're not the police. They're not the Brazilian feds. Not yet. They're my men, and I can take you out of here with me. If you want, I can get you out of Brazil to any place you say."

She didn't know if Juan understood English. Maybe she should be offering the deal to him. They turned right, in the direction of Escurra's office. The sound of another massive explosion rattled the glass of the windows. That should be James using the RPG to take out the fighting pit.

"Prisons in Brazil suck," she hurried on. "Everyone knows that. Help me get away, and I'll take you. I'll guarantee you aren't charged with the deaths of the Americans."

"You can't do that."

"I swear, I can." Probably not true, but maybe he'd fall for it.

Another explosion.

She figured both Escurra and Martinez should be pretty shook by now. Martinez opened the door to the office and Juan, still holding the gun to her head, shoved her inside after him. She felt like heaven had opened and shown the light of life on her when she saw Joe sitting, arms bound behind his back, on a chair in front of Escurra's desk. A warm, liquid joy bubbled up from deep inside her chest.

"Hey," Joe said. "Better late than never."

"It's never too late."

"Shut up," Martinez growled.

Like an unleashed bolus from a catapult, Joe sprang out of his chair and charged toward Escurra. Before Nova could turn on Juan, Escurra had raised a gun in his hand and aimed it at Joe. Nova went rigid. Time slowed and in a sudden tunnel vision that was focused on the gun aimed at Joe, she could see Escurra's trigger finger tightening.

She waited for the shot that would blow away her life.

It didn't come. Escurra yelled at Joe to stop, and being still too far away to reach Escurra and having no sensible alternative, Joe complied.

Escurra moved quickly to stand behind Joe, pressing the tip of a Beretta to Joe's temple. So far, both she and Joe were alive in this crazy standoff, but the police would soon arrive and she might lose any chance to take possession of the recording. Assuming that it was still hidden in the sofa. She could *not* let Escurra take her away from the house.

Felipe said, "The police will be here soon. We can't get away."

"Fuck," Escurra said. "Then we bargain with these Americans. We get guaranteed passage."

"What's to bargain, Tomas? They've got us. They aren't going to let us get away. They won't care about these two Americans. Hell, if the Americans get killed for any reason, they'll just say we did it. They've wanted to get you for a long time."

"You're talking shit! We fight it out."

A gunshot cracked beside her head, and Nova shrank into herself. Escurra, an amazed look on his face, dropped the gun at Joe's head and clutched his chest.

Felipe had shot Escurra.

Nova was momentarily too stunned to move. She conquered her surprise, though, before Juan conquered his. She stuck Juan an upward blow under the forearm of his gun hand, his hand flew up, the gun cart wheeling across the room. With her other hand she gave him a paralyzing karate chop to the throat. He went down and out.

Martinez strolled across the floor to stand over Escurra, who was bleeding profusely from the mouth. Escurra stared up at Martinez with the baffled look of a hurt lover, his life ebbing fast.

"I know you of all people will understand, Tomas," Martinez said. "Everyone can be used."

Chapter 50

"Holy shit!" Joe stood looking down at Escurra as the Eagle sucked in his last breath. Nova rushed to the sofa where Alex said he'd stashed the cell phone. She threw off an end cushion and then the middle one.

There lay the tiny silver and neon-blue treasure. All right! She snatched it up.

Joe had shifted his still amazed gaze to Martinez. Martinez looked at Nova.

She ran from the sofa to Joe, threw her arms around him, pressed her head against his chest and hugged him with all her strength, as if that would ensure that nothing in the world could ever take him away.

Martinez said, "We don't have time for that kind of shit! The pigs will be here soon. You said you could get me out of here. Out of Brazil."

Hard as it was to do, she unlocked her grip on Joe. She

fished out her cell phone, flipped it open and punched in Ernesto's number.

Joe shrugged. "What's going on?"

"Come pick us up directly behind the house," she said to Ernesto. "It shouldn't be dangerous. The two top men are out of the picture. The low level thugs will be puzzled, but not likely to blow you away."

Ernesto's "Roger" came back at once.

"We're leaving before the authorities get here?" Joe asked.

"It's complicated. I'll fill you in on the fly. We need to get this cell phone to Leila in Rio ASAP." She turned to Martinez. "Make it fast. Keep in front of me."

At dusk in Rio, with night rapidly approaching, Nova held Joe's arm as they strolled into the lobby of the forty-story Copacabana Beach Sugarloaf Ipanema Hotel. They registered as Mr. and Mrs. Smith, the aliases they used in the operation in Italy and for which they had passports.

After delivering the cell phone to Leila in person, they both had showered in bathrooms of the small gym at the CIA offices. Martinez was being kept in a CIA safehouse until he could be gotten out of the country. She hadn't bothered to say goodbye to the killer and secretly hoped the U.S. government would break her promise and put him in prison forever.

In the elevator, her stomach growled. "Sorry," she said in response to Joe's lifted eyebrows and smile. While they were both cleaned up, they hadn't taken time to eat.

When Joe had called for reservations, she heard him ask for a first-class suite. He'd said after he hung up, "I would have asked for the presidential suite but we'd never get Langley to pay for that."

Now they walked into an ultramodern living room of

glass and brass and white rugs and furniture. A flock of white gulls with gold wingtips soared skyward in the sculpture hung over the whitewashed stone fireplace. She wondered when anyone would ever find a need in Rio to actually use the fireplace.

"This suite is fantastic," she said.

"Langley should be pleased at what a bargain I'm getting with their money."

They laughed. My God, she had come sickeningly close to never hearing Joe's laugh again. She kissed him on the cheek.

Joe tipped the bellman as Nova strode to the sliding glass door leading onto a private balcony and opened it, letting in a balmy sea breeze. The balcony ran not only in front of the living room but in front of not one but two other rooms. The only view was of the now darkening sea, and the only way for anyone to see into any of the three rooms would be to fly by in a blimp or helicopter or light plane.

A little exploring revealed that the suite not only had his and her bedrooms, it had his and her bathrooms. Joe pulled Nova into his arms in one of the bedrooms. "Not likely we'll be using all that bedding and linen in the other half of the place, is there?"

The kiss, wanted for so long, began with just the slightest pressure of his lips and then teasing of his tongue, and then she opened her lips to let his tongue enter her mouth.

"We have at least two days," she murmured. "Maybe we'll use up everything in the place. Maybe try both beds. The sofas."

"Hell," he said. "The beautifully carpeted floor."

Her empty stomach rumbled again. "Hell, Nova." He smiled and touched one of her eyebrows. "You want me to order food?"

She pulled him close again and started unbuttoning his shirt. It didn't take him a millisecond to start on hers. They shed bits of clothing—shoes, slacks, belt, bra, underwear—on a kissing walk to the bed.

"Should I get a condom? I have one."

"I've only been with one man since you, and he wore a condom every time."

"So, there was someone after me?" He scooped her onto the bed.

"But he wasn't you. He never could be anything like you, Joe. There's no one else for me."

"Well, for what it's worth, I haven't been with anyone since you."

She shook her head. "I don't believe that."

"Sure you do. I never lie to you."

With a tenderness that made her ache, that set fire deep inside, Joe lavished kisses on her. Maybe he'd been fantasizing about this moment for months. She had.

She pushed him onto his back and leaned over, letting her hair fall across his chest, deliberately giving him a dark, silky touch that she followed with kisses. She worked her kisses lower until he moaned when she took his erect penis into her mouth.

"Babe, I'll come too soon if you do that," he said.

"It won't be too soon."

She felt him let go, and she gave herself up to making him give out low sounds of pleasure. She felt his skin grow slick under her hands as she caressed every part of him that she could reach until he came with a wrenching moan and arching of his body.

"Jesus," he said, as he relaxed.

She fetched from the bathroom a warm, wet cloth, and then lay down beside him, waiting for him to fall asleep. He liked to fall asleep after. Not long. He'd wake again in a few minutes. She would spend the waiting time visually exploring his body. Ah, yes. Looking at his body, another pleasure she had come close to never having again.

A loud boom awakened her with a start. Joe leaped from the bed, ready to get his gun. The first boom was followed by four others, and outside, four starbursts of color exploded across the night sky.

Fireworks!

She rose and they walked hand in hand to the window and watched the show. She slid the door open so they could see and hear better, and he put his arm around her. They watched the whole display, standing there naked as newborns. She'd stayed on Copacabana before and never had fireworks. Maybe this was something Rio did for the tourists in the week between Christmas and the New Year. Or maybe, she thought with a wry smile, fate had decreed to this show to celebrate the union of Nova Blair and Joe Cardone.

When he took her back to the bed, he returned the favor she'd given him.

Later they turned on music. Some pianist was playing "The Way You Look Tonight," when Nova ordered a late snack of vichyssoise, champagne and caviar.

Joe sidled up, holding one of their white, fluffy pillows. "Feel this."

She ran her hand over it.

He said, "Is it cotton? It's incredibly soft."

"Lots of fine threads," she explained.

He sailed the pillow across the living room where it landed next to the fireplace they would never use. "Love these digs," he said. "I've almost forgotten last night sleeping in a jungle. A gigantic difference in a few hours."

Food arrived, and they sat at the table by the living room window to eat in gold-colored, velvet bathrobes. Joe said, "Maybe we'll just spend our day tomorrow right here. I can skip the beach and the sea."

"Works for me. And I have something else I'd like to do."

"Which is?"

"I think I'd like it if maybe we started thinking about wedding plans."

At first he just sat still. Then came a slow, very special Cardone smile. And then a lifted champagne glass.

She lifted hers. Her feelings about marriage hadn't changed. The idea still scared her mouth dry if she thought about it too much. But she had said more than once, to herself and others, that to get what you want in life you have to step out of your comfort zone. *No big risk, no big reward.*

Joe toasted. "To a partnership for life."

They downed their champagne, the whole glass, looking into each other's eyes as they sealed the pact.

He stood and pulled her to her feet. "Come with me." He guided her to the fireplace and, with his arm around her waist, threw his glass into it. It shattered in a tiny tinkling explosion.

She leaned into his side, as if to make them one, and with a second tinkling explosion, her glass joined his.

Chapter 51

Nova sat beside Joe in a situation room at the CIA headquarters in Langley, Virginia. On the desk in front of her lay today's *Washington Post,* in which an article on page two informed readers that the highest court of the land had handed down its decision in the case of Sharansky versus the Government of the United States.

Suleema Johnson had been, as expected, the swing vote, siding with the lieutenant governors of seven states and the citizens of the states they represented that the space over their heads was part of the commons. The atmosphere did not belong to the government. The federal government could not put offensive weapons, or any weapons, into that space without the consent of the people. Perhaps this court, or the World Court, would be asked to decide at some future time whether space above the atmosphere belonged to any earthly government. But that would be a fight for another day.

How relieved Suleema Johnson must be, Nova thought, that she did not have to pay a devastating price for her faithfulness to her responsibility.

Claiton Pryce was also present and at the moment chatting in a corner with his secretary and Nova's friend, Cleo Johnson. Nova had made friends with Cleo during Nova's initial training days in Virginia, and over the years they had remained fast friends. A striking African American, Cleo was a snappy dresser with an equally snappy sense of humor. Pryce laughed at something Cleo said.

Joe leaned close and whispered, "I wish they would get on with this. I want you back in bed."

She grinned and squeezed his leg under the table. "Patience, hot dog."

Also in the room were Pryce's second in command in the operations division, Dan Gray, an analyst who spoke Portuguese and the brand of Spanish used in Brazil, and a technician with a punk-style, very un-CIA haircut who was in charge of setting up a real-time link with Leila and Oscar in Rio.

"Okay," the communications technician said. "We're all set."

Leila and Oscar were now visible on a big-screen TV monitor, seated side by side in the secure room at the CIA in Rio. Nothing they said could be recorded by listening devices, and whatever they transmitted would be encrypted. Pryce and Cleo took seats.

Nova and Joe had been given a transcript of the recording, both the original Spanish and the translation into English, but this would be the first time they or these people at Langley would hear the actual recording. She and Joe had simply guarded the cell phone, untampered with in any way, until they had delivered it to Leila.

The Spanish translator pushed the play button on a recorder loaded with a copy of the original. Right away Nova recognized Martinez's voice and then the voice of Escurra.

And then came the critical section of tape holding the voice of Red Dog.

"Oh, sweet Jesus," Cleo said at the very moment Pryce said, "Shit."

Everyone in the room looked at them.

Pryce said, "Goddamn, I know who that is."

Cleo was nodding rapidly. "It's him, Mr. Pryce. I couldn't be more certain. I've put him through to you hundreds of times."

Pryce's second in command, Dan, asked the obvious. "Who?"

"That's Skippy Boynton or my name isn't Claiton Pryce. It would seem that the chief aide to our Secretary of Defense is Red Dog."

The room fell silent, Nova thinking what probably everyone else was also thinking. If Skippy Boynton was corrupt, how far up did the corruption go? Was it possible that the Secretary of Defense himself had been involved in a scheme to blackmail a Supreme Court justice over the deployment of weapons in space?

Certainly if voiceprint identification verified what Pryce and Cleo felt to be true, the career of Skippy Boynton was not only over, the guy would spend years into the foreseeable future in a federal prison cell.

"Everyone here is to treat this as top secret," Pryce said. "Nothing you have heard can be discussed outside this room. Leila, Oscar, you understand."

"Absolutely," Leila said, her head nodding in the monitor.

"Of course," Oscar agreed.

Pryce stood and looked at the communications tech.

"You get hold of copies of Boynton speaking ASAP. I want a comparison of the voiceprints yesterday."

Pryce stomped out, followed by Dan Gray.

Cleo and Nova hugged. "I want you to come to the wedding," Nova said.

"Ah, honey. You need have no fear. Cleo will be there."

Four Days Later—New Year's Eve—8:00 p.m.

Suleema stood on a step near the bottom of the stairs leading down to Clevon and Regina's living room. She'd stopped a moment to savor the view. Alex and his friend Ronnie sat, legs crossed, on the floor playing some wildly inventive space game on the Xbox Clevon had given Alex for Christmas. The boys had picked a quite reasonable volume so as not to be too intrusive, but still the sounds of blasts and clanks and zaps reached all the way to the stairs.

The two families had shared a sumptuous roast lamb, New Year's dinner. They had all agreed it would be a quiet time together because Mrs. Obst remained shocked and grieving for her husband and Ronnie for his father.

Suleema studied Mrs. Obst for a moment. She and Clevon and Regina were eating dessert, talking and watching their boys. That her boy lived, Suleema figured, was the thing that would ease Mrs. Obst's grief as she moved into a new year and a new life without the man she loved.

I am so blessed, Suleema thought as she went to join them in the joy of chocolate cake.

"What kind of wedding dress shall I wear?" Nova said to Joe. They were curled up together in bed in his condominium in Washington. No party. No night on the town. They had lives filled with parties. This New Year would begin where it ought to begin—just the two of them. They had been making love or talking for most of the last four days.

"What kind do you want to wear?"

"It's a problem, don't you think?" She laughed and nestled closer. "I sure can't see me in virginal white."

"Don't take this wrong, but I once envisioned you wearing red or black. Red for seductress. Black for warrior."

"No, Joe. It won't be red or black. What horrible ideas."

"It was a joke."

"My mom would expect me to wear a white one, long and fancy. After all, I've never been married and she doesn't have a clue what my life is like. I think it would sadden her if I just wore a suit."

He rose on one elbow and kissed her. "I think I'd like it to be something soft, that moves with your body. But I'm sure you'll find just the right thing. You always do."

Epilogue

Nova ran her fingers over the tight bodice of her wedding gown, a floor-length chiffon in the palest green color her seamstress had been able to find—"seafoam," Star called it. Nova definitely had the jitters. With a nervous finger she touched the single emerald set in the center of a string of pearls, Joe's gift to her along with matching earrings.

The material of the skirt did move with her body in the sensuous way of water lapping gently on a shore. There was a slight breeze today in San Diego, and since the wedding was outdoors in Balboa Park, the dress would be "flowy," Joe's only stated preference.

Star's gown was of the same material and cut like Nova's, but of a deep emerald green. It looked fabulous with

Star's red hair. Nova watched as Star stepped in front of the floor-length mirror in the dressing room the Prado Restaurant provided for brides. The white terrace below the restaurant, with its white wishing well and stunning background of eucalyptus, palm, cypress and sycamore trees, was a favorite wedding spot in San Diego. Nova imagined that hundreds, if not thousands, of couples had pledged their love here. The sounds of a harp and a string quartet, now playing Vivaldi's "Spring", reached into the dressing room.

She stepped behind her sister and put both hands on Star's shoulders as the two of them studied each other in the mirror. "You are a stunning matron of honor."

"Ah, but I do not outdo the lovely bride." Star turned. "It's time for me to put on your veil." She fetched the veil, so thin it looked more like a green halo, and put it over Nova's upswept hair. "I still think Joe will have a fit when he sees you in green, not white. Although I'll admit, it's almost white."

"Joe will love it. I just hope Mother is over her disappointment. Maybe when she actually sees it."

Star stepped away from the completed bride, shook her head and smiled broadly. "It works, Nova. What with your green eyes and all the trees out there and everything, the seafoam is perfect. You're happiest in a jungle, so why not green?"

"His family may think I'm nuts."

"They're from Texas. They'll just think it's a wacky California thing."

"I like them, Star. His brothers, my new sister-in-law. She's very sweet. His mother is so different from ours. It creates a sort of balance. She's of the earth and land, not the world of diplomats and wealth that Mama came from.

And his dad is just as solid as his mom. I think I'm already in love with his dad."

Nova turned to the mirror and studied the finished creation. This was the day most girls dreamed of and women lived for, and a day she had always believed would never be hers for many reasons, among them that under-cover agents often didn't marry, even those with no psychological hang-ups against it. Their lives were too full of lies. If they did marry, they rarely had big weddings, and in that, hers and Joe's would be no exception. Penny was here, really her only close friend. Having lots of friends was impossible when a huge hunk of the life you claimed to be living was a fraud. Penny had been in seventh heaven fixing her hair this morning in an airy mass of soft curls atop her head that matched the mood of the gown.

Star handed Nova her long gloves and started pulling on her own long green ones. "I wish Stephen and I could get away for a vacation. Even our honeymoon was only a weekend in Vegas. And then it was kids and work. Marrakech, Morocco, sounds so fabulous and exotic."

Nova worked her fingers into the gloves. "It's a place we figure no one can reach us for any reason." She stroked the gloves up both her arms. She'd only worn long formal gloves twice before that she could recall, except when she and Star had played dress-up as little girls.

Her brother-in-law was giving her away, and of course Star and Stephen's kids—Bryan, Blake, and Maggie—were here. Nova and Maggie had shopped for Maggie's dress together and laughed themselves silly. Somehow Nova had still avoided any discussion of children with Joe. Maybe someday she'd have her own little girl. But that was something for the future. Joe understood that just getting married had Nova genuinely scared.

Deirdre and Cleo had flown in for the dinner last night. And then there was Joe's family and his friend Benjamin from flight training in his pilot days. That was it. They would keep the fiction that Joe worked for IBM as a traveling troubleshooter, and he would move in with her in San Diego.

"Okay," Star said. "That's the beginning of the song before the wedding march." She handed Nova the bouquet of white roses bound with green ribbon. "Let's go."

They walked out into a beautiful, spring midmorning. Cottonball clouds broke up a perfect, robin's-egg-blue sky. Star stepped onto the ivory runner that led from the dressing room to the bower, where a Catholic priest and Unitarian minister waited to share the ceremonies, walking stately between five-foot-high, lit wrought-iron candelabras draped with the same wispy cloth as Nova's dress.

Her brother-in-law, Stephen, stepped to Nova's side with a big grin. He'd confessed at last night's dinner that he would have bet a bundle that Nova was destined to be single for life, and that he would never have been happier to lose a bet.

A dramatic pause of silence, and then the musicians began the wedding march, solemn with tradition and the weight of many vows. The guests rose and looked her way, every last one of them smiling. Her hand on Stephen's arm, her heart pounding, and then suddenly Joe dressed in a tuxedo in her vision, waiting for her, no smile, only a quiet glow—sure that nothing else in all the world really mattered, Nova walked down the aisle into a brand new adventure.

* * * * *

A special treat for you from Harlequin Blaze!

Turn the page for a sneak preview of
DECADENT
by
New York Times *bestselling author*
Suzanne Forster

*Available November 2006,
wherever series books are sold.*

*Harlequin Blaze—Your ultimate destination
for red-hot reads.
With six titles every month, you'll never guess
what you'll discover under the covers...*

RUN, ALLY! Don't be fooled by him. He's evil. Don't let him touch you!

But as the forbidding figure came through the mists toward her, Ally knew she couldn't run. His features burned with dark malevolence, and his physical domination of everything around him seemed to hold her like a net.

She'd heard the tales. She knew all about the Wolverton legend and the ghost that haunted The Willows, an elegant old mansion lost by Micha Wolverton nearly a hundred years ago. According to folklore, the estate was stolen from the Wolvertons, and Micha was killed, trying to reclaim it. His dying vow was to be reunited with the spirit of his beloved wife, who'd taken her life for reasons no one would speak of, except in whispers. But Ally had never put much stock in the fantasy. She didn't believe in ghosts.

Until now—

She still didn't understand what was happening. The figure had materialized out of the mist that lay thick on the damp cemetery soil. A cool breeze and silvery moonlight had played against the ancient stone of the crypts surrounding her, until they joined the mist, causing his body to thicken and solidify right before her eyes. That was when she realized she'd seen this man before. Or thought she had, at least.

His face was familiar. . . so familiar, yet she couldn't put it together. Not with him looming so near. She stepped back as he approached.

"Don't be afraid," he said. His voice wasn't what she expected. It didn't sound as if it were coming from beyond the grave. It was deep and sensual. Commanding.

"Who are you?" she managed.

"You should know. You summoned me."

"No, I didn't." She had no idea what he was talking about. Two minutes ago, she'd been crouching behind a moss-covered crypt, spying on the mansion that had once been The Willows, but was now Club Casablanca. And then this—

If he was Micha, he might be angry that she was trespassing on his property. "I'll go," she said. "I won't come back. I promise."

"You're not going anywhere."

Words snagged in her throat. "Wh-why not? What do you want?"

"If I wanted something, Ally, I'd take it. This is about need."

His words resonated as he moved within inches of her. She tried to back away, but her feet were useless. "And you need something from me?"

"Good guess." His tone burned with irony. "I need lips, soft and surrendered, a body limp with desire."

"My lips, my bod—?"

"Only yours."

"Why? Why me?" This couldn't be Micha. He didn't want any woman but Rose. He'd died trying to get back to her.

"Because you want that, too," he said.

Wanted what? A ghost of her own? She'd always found the legend impossibly romantic, but how could he have known that? How could he know anything about her? Besides, she'd sworn off inappropriate men, and what could be more inappropriate than a ghost? She shook her head again, still not willing to admit the truth. But her heart wouldn't play along. It clattered inside her chest. The mere thought of his kiss, his touch, terrified her. This wildness, it was fear, wasn't it?

When his fingertips touched her cheek, she flinched, expecting his flesh to be cold, lifeless. It was anything but that. His skin was smooth and hot, gentle, yet demanding. And while his dark brown eyes were filled with mystery and wonder, there was a sensitivity about them that threatened to disarm her if she looked too deeply.

"These lips are mine," he said, as if stating a universal fact that she was helpless to avoid. In truth, it was just that. She couldn't stop him.

And she didn't want to.

* * * * *

nocturne™

HER BLOOD WAS POISON TO HIM...

MICHELE
HAUF

FROM THE DARK

Michael is a man with a secret. He's a vampire
struggling to fight the darkness of his nature.
It looks like a losing battle—until he meets
Jane, the only woman who can understand his
conflicted nature. And the only woman who can
destroy him—through love.

On sale November 2006.

Save $1.⁰⁰ off

your purchase of any
Silhouette® Nocturne™ novel.

Receive $1.00 off

any Silhouette® Nocturne™ novel.

**Available wherever books are sold, including most
bookstores, supermarkets, drugstores and discount stores.**

Coupon expires December 1, 2006. Redeemable at participating
retail outlets in the U.S. only. Limit one coupon per customer.

5 65373 00076 2   (8100) 0 11265

SNCOUPUS

nocturne™

Save $1.00 off

your purchase of any
Silhouette® Nocturne™ novel.

Receive $1.00 off

any Silhouette® Nocturne™ novel.

**Available wherever books are sold, including most
bookstores, supermarkets, drugstores and discount stores.**

Coupon expires December 1, 2006. Redeemable at participating
retail outlets in Canada only. Limit one coupon per customer.

52607136

SNCOUPCDN

TAKE 'EM FREE!

2 FREE ACTION-PACKED NOVELS PLUS 2 FREE GIFTS!

Strong. Sexy. Suspenseful.

SBOMB06

Christmas comes to

HARLEQUIN ROMANCE

In November 2005, don't miss:

MISTLETOE MARRIAGE
(#3869)

by Jessica Hart

For Sophie Beckwith, this Christmas means facing the ex who dumped her and then married her sister! Only one person can help: her best friend Bram. Bram used to be engaged to Sophie's sister, and now, determined to show the lovebirds that they've moved on, he's come up with a plan: he's proposed to Sophie!

Then in December look out for:

CHRISTMAS GIFT: A FAMILY
(#3873)

by Barbara Hannay

Happy with his life as a wealthy bachelor, Hugh Strickland is stunned to discover he has a daughter. He wants to bring Ivy home—but he's absolutely terrified! Hugh hardly knows Jo Berry, but he pleads with her to help him—surely the ideal solution would be to give each other the perfect Christmas gift: a family....

Available wherever Harlequin books are sold.

nocturne™

USA TODAY bestselling author

MAUREEN CHILD

ETERNALLY

He was a guardian. An immortal fighter of evil,
out to destroy a demon, and she was his next
target. He knew joining with her would make
him strong enough to defeat any demon.
But the cost might be losing the woman
who was his true salvation.

On sale November, wherever books are sold.

BÓMBSHELL™

COMING NEXT MONTH

#113 VAMPAHOLIC—Harper Allen
Darkheart & Crosse

Carefree, cosmo-sipping triplet Kat Crosse hadn't been herself lately. Was she turning into a vampire as her father had before her? Vampire hunter Jack Rawls thought so, but couldn't bring himself to kill this beautiful woman…yet. Instead, Kat teamed up with Jack to stop the forces of darkness before they claimed her as their own.

#114 HIDDEN SANCTUARY—Sharron McClellan
The Madonna Key

Being able to locate the earth's hidden mineral energies had served oil field geologist Tru Palmer well in her career. But when her dowsing gift led her to a set of medieval tiles radiating an unknown force, Tru discovered her own mystical connection to a legacy of powerful women in France—a connection that just might get her killed….

#115 A SERPENT IN TURQUOISE—Peggy Nicholson
The Bone Hunters

When fossil hunter Raine Ashaway teamed up with a renegade Texas archaeologist in search of lost Aztec gold, it was the chance of a lifetime. Myth linked the treasure to the fearsome Feathered Serpent—could this "god" be the undiscovered dinosaur long buzzed about by scientists? Raine was onto a big find—but with dark ritual and a ruthless killer dogging her steps, the bone hunter fast became the hunted.

#116 POSSESSED—Stephanie Doyle

For medium Cassandra Allen, channeling the dead was all in a day's work. But recently, one sinister voice from the beyond had begun to drown out all others. As a series of gruesome murders rocked her town, could Cass focus her powers to exonerate an innocent man—or would the evil spirit thwart her every attempt to find the real killer?